SHADOW CREATURES

ALSO BY CHRIS VICK

Girl. Boy. Sea.
The Last Whale

SHADOW CREATURES

CHRIS VICK

ZEPHYR

An imprint of **Head of Zeus**

This edition first published in the UK in 2024 by Head of Zeus,
part of Bloomsbury Publishing Plc

9 7 5 3 1 2 4 6 8

A catalogue record for this book is available from the British Library.

ISBN (PB): 9781837933167
ISBN (E): 9781837933136

Cover design: David Dean
Typeset by Ed Pickford

Printed and bound in Great Britain by
CPI Group (UK) Ltd, Croydon CR0 4YY

Head of Zeus Ltd
First Floor East
5–8 Hardwick Street
London EC1R 4RG

www.headofzeus.com

SHADOW CREATURES

CHRIS VICK

ZEPHYR

An imprint of **Head of Zeus**

9 7 5 3 1 2 4 6 8

A catalogue record for this book is available from the British Library.

ISBN (PB): 9781837933167
ISBN (E): 9781837933136

Cover design: David Dean
Typeset by Ed Pickford

Printed and bound in Great Britain by
CPI Group (UK) Ltd, Croydon CR0 4YY

Head of Zeus Ltd
First Floor East
5–8 Hardwick Street
London EC1R 4RG

www.headofzeus.com

For my 'mor,' Gro, and in memory of
long-lived Sverra and Rolf.

Also remembering those who lost their lives.

The opposite of courage isn't fear or cowardice, it's conformity.

Attributed to various

A huldra (forest spirit) will keep the fire embers burning till morning, and should be rewarded with a gift.

Nordic folklore

Summer, now

Georgy

Dusk lasts a long time this far north. The sun sets on an oil-calm sea. Behind the house, the forest and hills are dark and silent.

It was the first night of my Norwegian holiday. We sat outside after dinner. Most of the family went in once it got a bit darker, but Grandmother (Bestemor) Tove and Grand-Aunt (Grandtante) Liva settled by the fire pit in armchairs made from driftwood, blankets over laps, sipping lethal aquavit from tiny glasses. Liva lit a saucer of slow-burning herbs, to keep the gnats at bay. My sheep-dog Baxter sprawled on the ground, well fed with leftovers.

They told me I had to go in and do dishes, because, 'You are family, not a guest.' But I didn't fancy that, so distracted them with the story of my encounter with the old woman in the woods.

'You saw Agna?' said Tove. 'She appears every few years, but keeps to herself. A strange bird she is, alone, in her house in the woods, near the ruins of the old village. Only rooks and pine martens for company. How did she look?'

'She wore a long robe. Crow's-nest hair. Huge, scary eyes!'

'Once, before the war, she was a bright young thing, like us,' Tove smiled to herself, 'except *she* had the best clothes from catalogues. Lipstick, when she was no older than fourteen. Unthinkable. She had no father to tell her not to, though, and her mor could not control her. She and Liva grew close in the war. *Our* mor said she was a bad influence on Liva and, well... that is putting it mildly.'

'She was too,' Liva said. 'But in the best way.'

'The old woman? I'm not sure I can imagine her in fancy clothes and make-up. She threw a pinecone at Bax when he barked at her pet crow. She seemed... *wild*.'

'Wild? Yes, she was always that,' said Liva. 'And the Nazis couldn't tame her any more than her mor. Don't be quick to judge her by how she looks, or acts. She has good reason not to like dogs, believe me. Yes, she is somewhat eccentric, but she has been through so much in her life and was – to me, anyway – a hero. Looks deceive, Georgy.'

'So, who was she? Then, I mean.'

Liva and Tove exchanged a glance, and smiled.

'A troublemaker,' said Tove.

'I called her huldra,' said Liva.

2

'What?' I asked.

'Folklore.'

'I *love* folk tales, tell me,' I said, hoping by the time they'd finished someone else would have done the dishes.

'I thought it was the war you wanted to know about?' said Tove. 'You said before supper you have a project. For school?'

'I do, but tell me this folklore tale!'

Tove sighed, looking out to sea.

'Supper is done. The fire is warm. Why not?' said Liva. 'Agna scared us silly with such tales, when we were young. We begged her to stop, then begged for more.' Liva laughed. 'You want to hear? Okay...

'Many years after Adam and Eve were banished from Eden, God came by their hut in the wilderness, to make sure their children were clean and cared for. It was a back-breaking life. Keeping children clean was not always on their minds.

'And the children didn't care. They *liked* rolling in dirt, milling around bushes eating berries till their mouths were stained purple. Chasing each other in the dusk, never hearing, "Time for bed!"

'So, when God looked for scrubbed, doe-eyed dev- otees, Eve hid the naughty, feral children. The kind of children parents despair of, but secretly admire.

'After the business with the snake and the apple, you'd think Eve would know better. God was furious! He

3

CHRIS VICK

found the ferals, and cast them north, to the wilderness of dense trees, tall mountains and cold seas, and named them 'underjordiske'; *undergrounds*, shadow creatures.

'One lives among us now and is called huldra, meaning *covered*, or *secret*. She appears... civilised. But in truth is as tame as a wolf. Looks, as I say, deceive.

'If you discover the huldra's true identity, or cross her... then you are asking for trouble. And no one asked for trouble more than the invaders. They got it – from Agna, yes, and us too. We were all shadow creatures. We nisse and nixies and huldra.'

'Huh!' Tove said. 'A fancy way of putting it. You and your imagination, Liva! The truth is less romantic. We were truants, thieves, smugglers, and,' she took a deep breath, 'perhaps assassins.'

'*Really?*' I said. 'How much do you remember?'

'Oh, Georgy. It is raw and fresh and new, here and here.' Liva pointed at her head then her heart. Her fingers inched up her neck to a leather necklace, which she rubbed, and her eyes drifted to the stars, as though looking for something in the sky.

They told me then, about Agna, the war, and more. They did not stop, until the short night was almost over.

'You see, Georgy,' Liva began. 'This is not something that happened many years ago. It is not even something that happened yesterday. In my soul and dreams, it is always happening... it is happening...

'Now...'

The Invaders

Spring 1940

Liva

I was nine. Short and skinny as a ferret. Everyone said I was young for my age in every way. It was true, though I would never admit it.

The men were home after long months in Antarctica. The whaling had been good and for once all the families had money. There were still patches of snow here and there, the days were cold before the sun came up, but winter was over. Fish were biting, berry bushes sprouting leaves, the bees going crazy. When the wind blew, cherry blossom covered everything. We called it spring snow. There was a lot of it that day. A fresh wind was starting up, roughing the sea, disturbing the trees.

It should have been a joyful time in the village – which is a grand name for our huddle of old pinewood houses and a rotting dock. Anyway, we gathered at Mose and Agna's house. It was fancy compared to our glorified huts. The father was dead, but he had been a fishing boat captain from the far north, and he left Agna and her mor, Mose, money.

We went there when anything important happened, because they had a radio. It was usually for the king's birthday or Christmas carols, that sort of thing. This was different.

There had been a lot of to and fro to Mose's house and a lot of time with the radio for days before. Sometimes a few grown-ups, sometimes many. Afterwards there was much talk and us being told, 'There's nothing to worry about.' No one seemed happy, though, only in that forced way grown-ups have. A mask any child can see through. I hid and listened to whispers. Germans. Quisling. Nazis. I had heard these words before. I had also been told, 'Norway is neutral. We are safe. No soldiers are coming here.'

But I still needed Mor to comfort me in the night, because I had nightmares of trolls, waiting under bridges and in caves to come and get me. Those nights and days were strange.

I asked Agna what was going on. Tove told me nothing, because Pappa told her not to. I thought Agna *would* tell, because she never cared what anybody else did. She was tight-lipped too.

Anyhow, this day all the adults and all the older children went to Mose's, and shut the windows against the wind. We youngsters were told to play on the common where we tied the goats, and were promised waffles, jam and yoghurt if we didn't bother the grown-ups.

A useless bribe. We gathered behind a garden wall next door to Mose's to escape the cold wind, and chose Greta to be our spy.

As if she was stalking a deer, she crept and crawled across Mose's precious lawn – the only lawn in the village – and crouched under the window, with her ear pressed to a hole in the wood, while we waited.

Greta frowned, frozen like a statue with all the concentrating. And we were going crazy, first with curiosity, then boredom, then cold, so I sneaked across the lawn too, determined to know what was making everyone so on edge and secretive.

I peeped through the window. Everyone was gathered around the radio, apart from Agna, who stood looking out of the window, straight at me. My heart boomed, but she didn't *do* anything, as though *I* was glass and she was looking through *me*.

I couldn't hear a thing and Greta put a finger to her lips, so I went back to the others. We stood behind the fence, watching Greta to see if there was any change. After a time, we sat down and no one talked. There was only the silence of the trees and the hills. The wind calmed for a few minutes. It may be too poetic, but it felt that in that moment Norway held its breath.

Then the door opened and Agna ran to us, panting, as if she'd run a race, not across the lawn.

'Germans are coming!'

'*Here?*' I gasped.

'Yes. Now. Today, tomorrow, day after at the latest.'

'*Why?*'

'They are taking *all* of Norway. And you'd better hide anything valuable!' She pointed her finger at me. 'Or they'll take that too.' Agna never added sugar to her words.

I thought of Rabbit, and my christening brooch and necklace with the silver cross. Things which Pappa kept safe, but which were mine only.

'It won't h... h... happen,' Little Lars said. He was breathing fast, on the brink of crying or screaming, and couldn't get his words out. 'The... the... k... k... king will st... stop them.'

'Nu-uh.' Agna folded her arms and said it plain. 'The king fled. He left Oslo and headed north.'

It seemed a strange story Agna told us, but I knew it was real. Agna had our attention. Just like when she told us ghost stories.

'Huge boats up the Oslo fjord, thousands of soldiers!' she said with wide eyes, waving her arms about. 'Those fools weren't expecting a fight so they sailed up without battleships to protect them, only our boys fired the single big gun we have guarding the fjord, and sank their biggest boat and killed hundreds of their best soldiers. A regiment called the SS. So, those that have landed *aren't* in a good mood!'

Then the adults filed out of Mose's, like on Sunday from church and not a smile between them. There were no secrets or hiding things then. Everything Agna told us was true.

Each family marched silently home, including us Eriksens: Mor, Pappa, Haakon, Tove and me. Gathering valuables didn't take long. We hadn't much and only three rooms to rummage through. Mor and Pappa's room, the main living room which was also a kitchen and our bedroom. You see, Haakon was thirteen, Tove twelve and I was only nine, so at night me and Tove had our bedroom and Haakon slept in the living room. The long drop toilet was outside by the store hut. When I think about it now, it wasn't an easy life. We washed in the stream.

Mor and Pappa went through the cupboards and Pappa climbed up in the attic. We had some rings and necklaces, from weddings and christenings over generations. Oh, and some gold and silver coins. We kept them for a 'rainy day'. But even when days were very rainy, nobody sold heirlooms.

I had never seen it all together before. It was put on the floor on a large piece of linen. A troll's hoard.

I kept running outside looking for Germans, but there was only the forest and the hills. Pappa wrapped our treasures up and tied the parcel with string. Then he left without a word. It happened quickly.

We followed Pappa, and Mor did not stop us. I thought he was going back to Mose's, but he went down to the jetty, and by the time we arrived most of the village was there.

Eirik, who was eighteen or nineteen, sat in a rowboat, and one after the other the parents leaned down off the jetty and handed him their boxes or packages like ours. The bottom of the boat was piled with treasure. There was a spade too.

'Where are you going, Eirik?' I said.

'To the islands, to hide what is ours.'

'When will you be back?'

'Soon.'

'Set off now,' Pappa said, 'before the wind gets even worse. This isn't weather for rowing.'

'What about Mose?' Mor said. Minutes seemed like hours, and we waited, stamping our feet, watching the waves get rougher and bigger.

Tove was sent to hurry them up and when she came back with them, we saw why they were last.

Mose and Agna carried a small chest between them. Tove carried a large carpet bag. I imagined them full of gold and the necklaces and earrings they were always wearing. And this was added to the already weighed-down boat.

Pappa nodded to Eirik. He nodded back, then rowed, fast and strong. But it was difficult. The oars creaked in the locks and the blades splashed in the frothing sea. He made slow progress because the boat was heavy. Wind-lashed waves washed over the bow, salt spray whipped our cheeks. It was as if the sea too had woken and was now at war.

No one spoke. Nobody *dared* break the silence.

Eventually, Eirik rounded the headland and we lost sight of him.

Then, we heard a new sound. A lot of tiny *thuds*, like a woodpecker. Faraway, past the lowland hills, from the mountains. I did not know what the sound was. I saw fear on the grown-ups' faces, though. I found out later it was machine-gun fire, but it didn't sound like it does in the movies.

'Home. Now,' Pappa said. I thought he was only speaking to us Eriksens, but everyone went.

Once we were indoors, Pappa told us to stay put and not leave other than to go to the outhouse if we needed a pee. He hugged us all, even Haakon.

'You have to be a man now.'

Haakon nodded.

'Tove, you are the anchor for this family. The calm, sensible one. You must keep these lunatics in order.' He pointed at me and Haakon, and tried to laugh. We tried to laugh with him.

I was last. He held me the longest. So tight, I could barely breathe.

'Pappa, where are you going?' I said.

'I don't know, Litenmus.'

'How long will you be away?'

'I don't know that either. You must be brave now, and not the little mouse any more.'

'I won't be. I'm Liva, not Litenmus. When will you be back?'

He would not say. He could not say. No matter how many times I asked.

Then he grabbed Mor and squeezed her and kissed her hard, on the lips like he did at Christmas after too many aquavits. She was trembling and holding back tears.

Then he left.

We never saw Eirik again.

The Germans arrived next day. With their dogs.

Tove

I was twelve.

We expected them to roar down the dirt road that led to our village in tanks and armoured cars, like we'd seen in the cinema news reels, on rare trips to distant towns. But these Germans – *our* Germans – arrived in the silence of the dawn, by boat. Perhaps it was better that way. To get it over quickly.

The first I knew of it was the relentless barking of a dog, and a thundering hammering at our door. I was stick-straight out of bed, Liva and Haakon too, and Mor in her nightgown, herding us behind her like a mother goose.

'Who is it?' asked Mor.

'Open the door!' The voice spoke Norwegian, but in a bark, like a dog. There was more hammering. The door shook.

'All right, all right!' Mor squeaked. She lifted the latch and there was a storm of uniforms, rifles, thudding boots, helmets and a huge Alsatian. The dog growled in Liva's face, and she hid further behind Mor. I think maybe she peed herself.

There were three soldiers and an officer, who beckoned Haakon outside.

'He's just a boy,' said Mor.

'Ich spreche kein Norwegisch,' the officer replied. A phrase we got to hear a lot. *I speak no Norwegian.* 'Open the door' was, it seemed, the only bit of our language they needed. The man pointed outside, and he and Haakon went. I was terrified, almost fainting, struggling to breathe. If nothing like this happens to you, you cannot know. I could not hide behind Mor's skirts, like Liva, I just stood there, gasping.

The soldiers were not interested in us, though. They looked quickly around our small house, then left, shutting the door behind them. Mor went straight to open it, and to my shame I called out, 'No, Mor!' because I did not want them to take her. She didn't listen. She opened that door and Liva and I followed. We stood on the porch watching our tiny village being gutted of its menfolk.

There were three groups, performing the same routine at each house. A larger group watched. A few others stood apart, facing the woods, their rifles raised.

There was pleading and shouting from mothers and wives. The soldiers ignored them.

The men – boys like Haakon and the old men – were silent. *They* were the ones with rifle barrels in their faces.

In minutes, the boys and old men from twenty or so families were corralled with the goats on the common. They were made to sit on the ground with their hands on their heads. The common was in the middle of the village, though it was a long way from us, down the hill. We could only see the edge of it from our house. But Haakon sat on the outside part where he knew we could see him.

'What now, Mor?' I said. 'What will they do with Haakon?'

'I do not know,' Mor replied. She sounded a little broken, and Liva and I put our arms tight round her waist.

The air itself was thick with the anticipation of violence, of change. In truth, the thing that happened next was nothing much of anything. The dawn invasion that had been rushed and loud, became very still, very quiet. In that silence, we walked slowly, carefully, to the common with the other women and children.

I was fascinated by the soldiers. They were dressed smartly. You see, we lived in a village of whalers and fishermen, whose jumpers had holes and whose Sunday best was hand-me-down suits. The Germans' uniforms were crisp and grey. No mud, no stains, no holes. Many were younger than I'd imagined a soldier could be, more boys than men. It did not strike me till I'd watched them a while, that they were afraid too. Afraid that Pappa and our men might come from the woods and shoot them dead. Their eyes darted here and there, their guns twitching and pointing whenever a woman dared speak up.

The kommandant, though. He was different. Older, maybe late thirties. He strolled around looking at us, *through* us, his cap low, but not low enough to hide his eyes; they were pale blue like a young wolf's. He drank everything in. His face gave nothing away. Other, possibly, than mild interest. A man who has gone on holiday, not sure if he has chosen the right resort.

When he spoke with his men, he was quiet. More than once, he stroked and calmed a dog to stop it barking.

What *were* they going to do now? They could not tell us. We waited. The soldiers smoked. Then two of them came with a pail of water and wooden cups for our men. It had been cold, but now the sun was up, the day heated. Somehow, this small gesture made me feel better, as if the soldiers were men with hearts, not only monsters.

I don't know if the kommandant had ordered it, if they had crossed the language divide some way, but after a time, Mose and Agna came from their house, in their best dresses and coats, Mose carrying a tray of cups, Agna a pot of coffee. Agna wore no make-up as she sometimes might. And even though I was only twelve

I saw how those Germans admired her. The smell of the coffee drifted and they turned to it. Now you must know we did not have any luxuries, but we did have the finest coffee, because the whaling ships stopped in ports in South America where the men bartered for beans.

The kommandant and his lieutenants drank the coffee. I could tell by the tone of their voices they approved.

We waited and waited. The terror in my heart ebbed, like a tide. Nothing had happened to the boys and men, and they had not been taken away. Still, fear became worry, worry became a *slow* dread that gnawed at my insides like hunger. I remember that feeling well, I felt it a few times in those years. And I wondered again: what was to happen now? I only wished that we gave them whatever they wanted and Haakon came home.

The answer came: a sound like a buzzing insect. A motorbike, struggling through the mud and holes of the track from our village of Rullesteinsvik to the road that led to Dallansby.

It took a long time. The motorbike was slow. We soon saw why. A policeman who I recognised, from Dallansby, was riding the motorbike. Attached to it was a side car, and in it, a German officer. It was such an awful day, but in that moment, I struggled not to laugh. I knew that track well. His bum must have been sore as hell and the grimace on his face told me it was. Dallansby in those days was a long journey.

This jack-in-the-box got out. His uniform was black, even smarter if that is possible, and on his lapel two lightning bolts spelled SS. The regiment our boys on the Oslo fjord had sunk and drowned. Not this one, though. On his cap was a shining steel skull and crossbones and I thought, *You may wear a crisp uniform, but you are a pirate. Thank God we hid our treasure.*

He was a Hauptsturmführer, a captain in the SS.

From that day, we understood there were two kinds of invader; black caps and grey caps. The greys were actually sometimes green, and the black caps – the SS – sometimes only had black collars, but these were the two kinds, and these were names we gave them. The black caps were by far the worse.

Anyway, this pirate carried a huge ledger, bound in leather.

He ignored the offer of coffee. He ignored us too, even the soldiers. He spoke with the kommandant only, then the two of them walked off towards Mose's house.

We looked at the policeman, as if he was the oracle.

'What is happening?'

'What are you doing?'

'Are you a traitor?'

This eruption started the dogs barking and got the soldiers alert with their guns once more. I prayed for everyone to shut up.

The policeman put a finger to his lips and silenced our racket like a conductor calming the orchestra.

'You will soon return to your homes,' he told the men, speaking loudly, so all of us could hear. 'We are at war. The Germans have taken Dallansby. They came fast, in armoured cars. Hundreds of them. There was some resistance, but now our army has gone north. Some untrained men have joined them.'

'Were any Norwegians killed?' Eirik's mother, Mrs Bruntland, called from her porch.

'A few.'

My heart beat in my throat.

'Dallansby men,' the policeman said. 'No one from here, as far as I know.'

I thought of Pappa, of Eirik. I crossed myself. And thought of my own silver crucifix, like Liva and Haakon's, hidden among the treasure, and how I would have kissed it if I was wearing it then.

'Any of *them*?' Mrs Bruntland said.

'Yes. Ten or more.'

'Good!'

There were a few nods from the women at this and I hoped the soldiers truly did not understand Norwegian.

Mr Skogvold, who was old and, we knew, losing touch with the world by the day, said, 'I thought we were going to fight the British?'

'That was last month, then we were neutral again, now we are at war with Germany, even though they are already here. It is a mess. They have come by boat, from the air with the parachutes, from the south in trucks and they move north like a tide.'

'We'll stop them,' Mrs Bruntland said.

'I have seen them. We will not.'

'Then the British will come.'

'Some, possibly, but most of their army is in France. And…' He took a breath. 'The Germans have invaded Denmark too.'

There were gasps at this news.

'There is no chance of winning. A lot of Norwegian men are going to die for no reason. Then it will be over. The Germans tell me if your men are still alive, they will go to a camp, then, if they are lucky, they will come home. There is talk of a Norwegian government working with the German Reich.'

'What is a *Ryke*?' Liva whispered.

'The Nazi empire,' I whispered back.

Each sentence was a weight, each word a thrust of the spade digging our graves. All I could think of was Pappa. And our future, a map that had been torn up and thrown on the fire.

The policeman carried on. 'The Germans say if there is no trouble, life will be as normal. Count yourselves lucky. You will rarely see them, out here in this wilderness.'

'Many of our men are whalers,' a woman said. 'Will they go still, each winter, after they return from these camps?'

The policeman shrugged.

'What now, then?' someone asked.

'They have a ledger from the town hall, they want to see who lives here, to make an account. Probably to work out which of your men has gone to fight, possibly for other reasons. Who knows? Each family must bring their documents to the house with the lawn. After that, you can go home.'

'How do you know all this?'

'My superior speaks German and I speak some too. This is what we have been instructed.'

'Well, you do not have to like it!' Mrs Bruntland shouted.

'I do not have a choice. Let's start with the closest house. I'll inform the rest of you when it is your time.'

With that, he turned and walked to Mose's house, too quickly, as though the women might run after him, and the soldiers might not protect him.

'That's it, then,' I said. I walked close to Haakon, as close as I could get.

'Do whatever they say,' I told him. 'Then you can come home. They are going to win.'

'No,' Haakon replied. 'This is not Denmark. We have mountains and forests and islands. We know our country, they don't. We don't have much, but we have that...'

'Schweigen!' a young soldier shouted, raising his rifle.

Haakon stared at him, unblinking, till the soldier met his gaze. They stared at one another a while, till the soldier looked away and made a performance of lighting a cigarette.

We were all sent back home and told to wait. In turn, the families made their way to Mose's house, and when they had done the business with the papers their men were let go. Now, being incomers and having money (and Mose being attractive and with no husband), was already a problem for Agna and Mose. This development did not help matters!

Finally, the policeman came and stood beneath our porch.

'You must bring any papers you have, and don't bother hiding anything, because they ask every family about every other family, who is here and not here and that sort of thing. They already know about your husband.'

Off we went, with Mor carrying the only documents we had, our birth certificates and Pappa's passport, which she wanted to hide, but I made her take.

Mose's front room had been made into an office, with the dining table stripped and the SS man and a lieutenant sitting behind this 'desk'. The ledger was open. The lieutenant also made notes in a tiny book.

Now the SS man *did* want coffee and Agna made it and poured it for him. Everyone seemed more settled, because we knew what was happening and why, and what we had to do. It was better than the confusion and fear of that early morning.

Communication was easier too. It seemed the kommandant and Mose both spoke some English. And what they discussed the policeman relayed to us.

The SS man spoke then, for a good few minutes. I had no idea what he said, but he kept stabbing the ledger with his finger, and pointing at the rapidly filling notebook.

The policeman said, 'There are a lot of missing records. And they can't leave until they have a full account of who lives here.' It seemed there were discrepancies, because the official record of citizens wasn't up to date and not everyone had papers. Pappa was in there, and Mor, and their marriage and the fact that Pappa had a passport, and Haakon and Liva and I. But there was no record of Mose and Agna. They were from the north. There were rumours they might be part-Sami, the nomad folk, who herded reindeer. If that was true, Mose and Agna might not have papers. But the father had been a boat captain, surely, he *would*? It made no sense.

The snooty officials from Dallansby didn't bother much with us villagers, and in any case we had fishers and whalers who came and went depending on work and it was only the families who really lived here all the time who went in these records, and paperwork only got updated every other year or so.

'I have told him he now has a full account of the population,' the policeman said, 'but he is not satisfied. For example, there are no papers for these people.' He nodded at Agna and Mose.

'Well, what does he want us to do about it?' Mor said, smiling, talking quietly and calmly. But I knew that smile; the one when she was impatient.

'I told him the best records are actually in the church, along the coast at Kysten.'

The SS man spoke and again the policeman translated.

'He wants the records. He wants to know how long it will take to fetch them.'

Clearly, the SS had more important things to do; the real business of occupation, whatever that was. Not fiddling around with church records. But I learned something about the invaders that day. They were meticulous accountants. They didn't like discrepancies, or missing numbers.

'Two hours,' Mose said. 'Maybe three.'

'On roads like *that*?' the policeman said, looking dismayed.

'You don't leave town much, do you?' said Mor.

There *was* a road, a way back inland, then out, and there were paths, weaving and clinging to slopes rising from the fjords, or twisting inland like a snake before out again to the far reaches of our coast. Nobody used them much. Why would we? It was easier and quicker by boat. So that's what Mor and Mose told them.

We traipsed to the shore, where three German troop boats lay stranded and leaning in the low tide shallows.

The SS man and the kommandant had a talk.

'He says the soldiers will have to get their feet wet to free the boats. They need someone too, to show them the way.'

And that is when Agna, who had only been a humble coffee servant to this moment, stepped forward. She leaned her head over, and stroked her chin, examining these boats as though she was some kind of expert.

'No. You'll tear the hulls if you take them to sea. You have to wait for the tide to come back. And there are tricky currents and narrow gaps. Rocks below the surface, dragon spines we call them. Those boats are too big and would risk sinking. And the waters are freezing with snow melt.'

Mor and Liva and I stared at each other. What was she saying? The way she described was the route we went in a row or small sailboat with an engine when we went to school. A German boat was bigger but could go south-west till it hit open sea, then go north around the islands to Kysten. A longer journey, but easy and safe.

'A rowboat is the only way,' Agna carried on with her story. 'The church is on an island, you see. Even if you could make it there, you could not land such a big vessel.'

We knew, and probably even the policeman from Dallansby suspected, that this was all goose poop. Mose glared at her daughter. Yes, the church *was* on an island, but it was connected to the mainland by a bridge, and a short path to Kysten where there was a perfectly good harbour.

The policeman translated what the kommandant told him, like a talking puppet.

'He wants to know how you advise we get the records.'

'Haakon is a master seaman,' Agna said. 'He'll take me, I know the pastor at Kysten well and will explain. Oh, and Tove will come with us.'

Agna and Haakon were of an age when it was not done for a boy and girl to head off in a boat together. Anything could happen, so I was chaperone. The Germans and their puppet talked this through, and we were instructed to go. Mor wanted to come too, but they made her stay.

She fetched us a flask of hot milk and some rolls, and we set off in a rowboat in total silence, watched by the soldiers. The only sound was the blades of the oars dipping the water.

I had no idea what Agna was up to, but it was something, and now I was part of it.

Agna navigated and Haakon rowed, though he could have done that journey without once looking behind him.

He rowed steady as always. His face was a heavy cloud, waiting to thunder, and as soon as we were round the mouth of the bay, away from German eyes and ears, the cloud broke.

'What the hell do you think you're doing? Let *them* get the ledger. It's not our problem! And you don't know the pastor. You and your mor are the only family who never go to church.'

'I have my reasons,' said Agna.

'Reasons?' Haakon spat. 'You hope they will remember the favour, is that it?' He pulled an oar from its lock and pushed the end of the blade into Agna's neck.

He pushed so violently, Agna was forced backwards, almost tipping into the water.

'Haaky!' I said. 'Please don't. Let's just get the ledger, so they can make records, then they'll leave.'

'They are the enemy. I should knock her senseless, throw her over, let her drown.'

I knew Haakon's moods. If Agna had tested his temper even a fraction more, or if I had not been there, he would have done it. I'd seen him brawl, I knew what he was like. If Agna had been a boy, it would have been worse, that's for sure.

'All right,' Agna said. She pushed the oar away from her neck. Her words trembled as well as her hands. 'I tell you I have reasons, you'll see.'

In spite of Agna's tales of dragon spines and fierce eddies, the journey passed without event. Of course, we looked for signs of Eirik. There were none.

We landed at the harbour in Kysten. It was quiet and the roads empty. A ghost town, with the sun making clouds of frost from the melting ice. Smoke whispered from the chimneys. Kysten still held its breath.

There was no one around, other than a boy, around Haakon's age, sitting on the harbour wall, fixing a net; cutting bits of it with a hunting knife.

'You seen anyone from Rullesteinsvik? A young man.' I asked.

'No.'

'I know you,' said Haakon. 'You are Kjell, the striker. You scored two goals against us, last summer.'

The boy screwed up his eyes, then clicked his fingers and pointed.

'Haakon. The goalkeeper,' he said.

'Yes,' Haakon replied. 'The Germans have arrived in our village.'

The boy nodded. 'We heard they are in Dallansby. We expect them here today. Or tomorrow. Have you run away?' Kjell made it sound like an accusation.

'No,' Haakon said. 'We have come to borrow your church records. The Germans are making an account of everyone.'

Kjell shrugged. 'Huh! Are you going to fight them or work for them?'

'I will never work for them. You?'

'Fight.'

'What with? That?' Haakon nodded at the knife.

The boy shrugged.

'What are they like?' said Kjell.

'Efficient,' said Agna. 'Cruel if you cross them. That's my guess.'

'Are they like in the news reels?'

'These don't look so brave and some are older and some are younger. Maybe they filmed actors.'

'Any of your men fighting?'

'Of course,' said Haakon. 'Our far.'

I thought again of Pappa and felt both terrible fear and fierce pride.

'Mine too,' said Kjell.

We told him we had better fetch the ledger.

'Well, you return it soon as you can,' said Kjell.

We waited with him while Agna went to the church. She soon came back carrying the huge leatherbound book.

'Pastor wasn't in. I borrowed it. You tell him, Kjell.'

On the way home we looked for any sign of Eirik again. We even called his name.

'Eye- rik! Eye- rik!' we shouted, and the sound was like the call of a wild bird, echoing off rocks and sinking into the woods.

'Do you think he is okay?' I asked.

'I hope so,' said Agna. 'He has everything of value we own.'

This made Haakon spit in the water. 'If he is drowned and dead, it is because he went off too late, it is because the boat was too heavy with all *your* precious gold!'

Agna had nothing to say to this. The rest of the journey passed in silence. Only Agna did a very strange thing. She opened the book and leafed through it. The paper was thin and covered with dense, tiny writing in neat lines and rows and columns.

She tore a corner off, then leaned over the side and dipped it in the icy water. Then she held it up to the cold spring sun and watched as the ink ran off it.

The tiny words became a blue smear.

'What are you doing?' I asked.

'Washing names away.' This explained exactly nothing. She squeezed the paper into a mushy pulp that she rubbed between her fingers before flinging it in the sea. Then she closed the book, but kept a finger between the two halves.

Landing a rowboat on the beach or low tide reef in spring is not easy, if you want your feet to stay dry and warm. But there was the jetty with its wooden ladder. It was for a larger boat; in a rower, if you managed to keep the boat stable a passenger could climb up.

I was first, and there, waiting, was the policeman and two soldiers with their fearsome dog beasts.

They helped me, all the time looking down at Agna and the book. She climbed up, till she was nose to nose with the dog. It sniffed her as dogs do. She looked at it with a sneer, and it growled low. She bared her teeth and hissed at it like a cat. It pulled on its leash and barked, and she held the book like a shield, pushing it at the dog, which took hold of it as though it was a stick or a bone. The book became the rope in a tug of war. The soldier yanked his dog back and the policeman and the soldiers were shouting. When the dog released the book, Agna's hand fell back and the book flew expertly through the air, landing in the water. Just as Agna must have planned it.

'Get the book!' the policeman shouted to Haakon. Oh, the look from Agna to Haakon then, secret and quick! A *tiny* shake of her head, and him blinking in reply.

How he rowed and fished about with the oar! A performance. And a good one, because Haakon, agile as a wolf, native in the water as a seal, was now clumsy and slow.

He fished the book out with an oar, dropped it and tried again and ended up pushing it away, all the time being screamed at by the soldiers. Several pages broke away, drifting like leaves, and clouds of ink blossomed in the water. Agna joined in, leaning over to pretend to reach for the book, but not quite being able to lean far enough for fear of falling in.

Finally, Agna and Haakon swapped, she rowed and he leaned over and he *did* retrieve it. They brought that precious thing to shore.

By now, the kommandant and SS man had arrived and the situation was explained and the damp block of pulp that had once been a ledger was presented as evidence of what had happened. The SS man asked the soldiers a question and they pointed at Agna. The SS man barked something or other at her in German, and the dog strained on its leash till its front legs were off the ground.

Agna inched back and back, each time the dog barked, till she stood on the edge of the jetty. The Germans and the dog made a racket. She stood, eyes closed tight, head down, fists clenched, trembling. Every bit of her shook. But she could go no further, nor could she answer them. She just stood there, a goat kid on a mountain, weathering the storm.

After a time, they stopped shouting, and she dared open her eyes. I saw then, the stone in her soul. No, not stone, more a diamond. The SS man took the ledger, showed it to the kommandant, and made a show of trying to open the mush of pages to read what was in there, making a joke of it. Nobody laughed and the kommandant looked worried. The SS man threw the ledger in the water.

He looked at each of us in turn, as though taking photographs with his mind. He did not need a ledger with our names in it. He knew us then and he had us marked.

He stabbed a finger in the kommandant's face, said something very quietly, then turned on his heel and left with the lackey policeman following. We heard the motorbike start and its straining whine fade into the woods. And I breathed.

The kommandant watched us the entire time, with the same lack of emotion.

Agna spoke. I cannot remember if it was German or English, but she was, I am sure, apologising.

Then, mercifully, the kommandant and soldiers left. We stood on the jetty, blowing out long breaths and smiling. Elated. Thrilled. You would be surprised how fear can turn quickly, between the tick and tock of a clock hand.

We were foolish, of course. We did not know the danger we'd been in. If it had been later on, there would have been punishment. This was the beginning and no one knew the rules, not even them.

When we had gathered ourselves, Haakon said to Agna simply, 'Why?'

'You want them to know everything about us?'

He shook his head and looked at Agna with some wonder.

'It is better if *we* know something about *them*. Now we do.'

'We do?' I said.

'I was there the whole time remember, as they checked their records and made their notes and drank our coffee. I got their names.

'The SS man is Werner.

'The policeman is Hansen.

'The kommandant is Meier.'

'And?' Haakon said. 'What use are their names?'

'Never you mind. If anyone asks, this was an accident, you understand!' Agna said, suddenly harsh, jabbing her finger in our faces.

Haakon nodded.

'You too!' she said to me. I looked at Haakon. He shrugged.

'Okay,' I said.

'Swear it,' Agna said. She spat in her hand and held it out.

We village youngsters did this when something was serious. Haakon and I both spat and shook.

Then Agna brushed herself down and walked, head held high, to her house.

Summer 1940

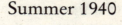

Liva

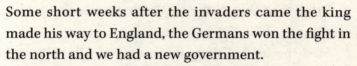

Some short weeks after the invaders came the king made his way to England, the Germans won the fight in the north and we had a new government.

Our war was over. We were amazed it lasted as long as it did. At least we had made it a headache for the Germans, and now they expected trouble and would have to send many soldiers to keep us quiet. And they did. More than one for every ten Norwegians.

We were occupied. The English were soon chased from France with their tail between their legs. The thousand-year Reich had begun and we were part of it.

These are things I understood *after* the war. I knew then only that this new world was for ever. And that I wanted Pappa to come home. What did I know, really? Nothing. I was nine. When you are nine you complain more than anybody about changes, but you get used to them faster too.

The early days, anyhow, were not too bad.

It was summer, and once they had us in their ledger and searched our woods and fjords, we did not see much of the Germans. I cannot say life was the same. It was not so different, though. Not for a child.

The main difference was that our men were not here. The village was used to this, but only in winter. I missed Pappa, that was the worst thing.

We had no word of him, nor Eirik or others. The policeman told us if anyone was killed or captured word would come. We supposed no news was good news.

Other than this, I have two lasting memories of that summer.

First the food. A diet almost only of fish, milk and bread. Milk and wheat we got from the farm. Sometimes an egg or two. We children went carrying pails and bags for grain, and tokens because a lot of food was rationed; business being done with the farmer and a lonely soldier stationed on the farm, who recorded everything. Occasionally, we saw the kommandant and the policeman, that fountain of information, doing business from Mose and Agna's house, but mostly we were left to ourselves. With the milk we made yoghurt and country cheese. There was always a muslin bag hanging over the sink. Fish, milk, bread. Bread, fish, milk. And fishcakes, which were a mix of all three with potato. It was tiresome. But we did not know yet what it is to starve.

No boats went out, because it was banned, so we children fished off the rocks. That was our job.

We all had to muck in, chopping wood, washing clothes in the stream, making or mending garments and making rugs from those too far gone to fix.

I remember all this well. The other thing is Agna and the island, Fjernøy...

I sat on the jetty, swinging my legs over the water. At the north end of the bay Haakon and Tove stood on the rocks, casting lines where the water was deep and the fish big. I was not allowed there because the climb down the rocks was steep and dangerous.

'Go home,' Haakon barked, as if he was a soldier giving orders. I matched him with my fiercest scowl.

'No!'

'Even if you could get down, you would ruin *that*.' He pointed.

I had two dresses. One for church and birthdays and the one I wore that day, which was plain cotton, made from an old sail, with a rose embroidered on its front.

'I'll go and change into trousers.'

'You're not coming.'

'Please, Haaky.'

'Tove, take her home,' said Haakon.

'You take her.'

'I'm a good climber,' I said. 'Like a mountain kid.'

'Go home!' Tove and Haakon said together.

They left me, saying I'd get bored soon enough, and to go back, or find other youngsters to play with. But I just sat there, swinging my legs, planning *exactly* how I'd tell Mor how mean Haakon and Tove were. How they *always* left me out when there was anything serious or fun.

'Boo!' A voice startled me.

Agna stood in front of the store hut. She hid her hair under a cap, wore trousers and a fisher smock, was barefoot and carried a rucksack and a canvas bag, the kind for fishing rods. This strange creature was not the fancy-pants Agna with the make-up and catalogue clothes. She looked like a boy.

'I was tempted to push you in, kid,' Agna smiled. 'What are you up to?'

I pointed to Haakon and Tove.

'Oh, I see.'

Agna went into the hut and came out carrying an oar. She looked around and quickly slid it into the canvas bag, then walked briskly south to the coast path.

'Agna, what are you doing with that oar?'

'Nothing.'

I picked myself up and ran to her side.

'You don't have a boat. Or a license. It's not allowed.'

'Don't tell me what I can and can't do, *Litenmus*!' she said, like that song the other kids teased me with, *liten mus, liten mus.*

'I'm not a little mouse.'

'It's what your mor calls you.'

'Used to call me. I am not one.'

'Yeah, you are. A baby. Small and thin and growly. How old are you now, anyway?' Agna asked, then quickly added, 'Whatever it is, you look younger.'

'IT'S NOT ALLOWED!' I bellowed, stamping on the wooden slats.

This stopped Agna dead. She looked up the coast to where the others fished and back to the houses, then made a play of putting a flat hand over her eyes, and scanning the horizon.

'What are you doing now?' I asked.

'Looking for the Germans who will stop me. Hmm. Nope, can't see any. Not a single one. Have fun, Litenmus.' Agna winked, and walked off down the path.

I waited till she was out of sight, then sat on the jetty again. I looked up the coast and down. Then sprang to my feet and ran after Agna.

I soon found her and followed at a healthy distance. When Agna stopped, dropping her kit on the ground, I hid behind a tree, risking a glance after a few seconds.

Agna veered off the path into the thicket, and emerged dragging a canoe, the canvas and tar-covered wood-frame kind that Pappa was good at making. She took it to the tiny shingle beach, put the rucksack and rod bag inside and pulled out the oar.

There was a broken paddle already in the canoe, bound with string. This, Agna hurled into the thicket.

Then I saw the rifle butt sticking out of the end of the rod bag. I had to put a hand over my mouth so as not to scream.

Agna rolled up her trouser legs and pushed the canoe into the water.

'Hey!' I cried, emerging from behind the tree.

Agna rolled her eyes. 'What now, Litenmus?'

'Hunting is not allowed. Boats are not allowed. Guns,' I paused to take a deep breath, 'are NOT allowed. Where are you going?'

Agna sighed. 'I'm sick of fish, bread and milk. I'm off to get some real food.'

'Where?

'Fjernøy,' said Agna, pushing the canoe into deeper water.

'What kind of food?' I said.

'Honey, cherries. I'll snag a rabbit or bird too.'

My mouth watered. I had to swallow.

'Honey? Cherries?' The village trees had been stripped already. Mor was saving the honey for winter. And I had not tasted good meat since before the Germans came.

'Can I come?'

'No.'

'I won't tell,' I said, crossing my arms. We had a long stare off, before I added, '*If* you take me.'

'You little... What would your mor say?'

'We don't see her breakfast till supper all summer. She gives us lunch.'

'What?'

'Bread and curds.'

'Hmmm.'

'She thinks I'm with Haakon and Tove. She'd *love* some cherries.'

Agna looked out to sea, and back to me a few times, chewing on her cheek.

She shrugged. 'You're not exactly dressed for it in that get up.'

I looked down at my dress. Plain and old enough, but not torn and fixed like my other one.

'I'll be careful.'

'Hmmm. I guess we don't have to be long. S'up to you.'

'I'll bet Eirik buried our heirlooms there. We can look.'

'I already did.'

I knew the way to Fjernøy, Pappa had taken us there often. It was different from other islands, much larger and mostly flat, but with steep shores and cliffs, other than a small, naturally formed bay and rock dock. Inland the woods were dense. In the heart of them were three large clearings where there were beehives, cherry trees, and huts where the men distilled aquavit and smoked meat and fish. In the summer, the villagers would camp there, drink and dance and sing the old songs, and the adults would not bother trying to get us children to sleep.

I sat facing Agna. As she rowed, she sang the story of a boy who loses his heart to a huldra, a girl spirit of the forest. I knew the song well.

The boy visits the huldra in the forest and each time he stays longer. After a time, leaves sprout from his fingers and his skin hardens like a larch tree's bark. One day he does not return. The villagers search for him, but the huldra has turned him into a tree, so he might stay in the forest for ever.

I sang the chorus. I was a good singer, my soft lilt joining with Agna's deeper voice.

> *The tree grew strong and fast.*
> *Strong and fast, strong and fast.*
> *And he was never seen again,*
> *Never seen again.*
> *Never seen again.*
> *Never seen again.*

Our song faded. That was how you sang it. Singing, then whispering, till the final line vanished in the air. Now there was only the gentle splash of the oar in the sea.

We went around this island and that, and rowed through narrow channels, until eventually Fjernøy loomed ahead, rising from the sea like the back of a great whale. The trees were tall and crowded, a dark green coat on the island. The water was that dead calm you only get on summer days, flat and featureless except for rippling rings where fish take tiny flies.

'Is huldra a real thing? Or nisse?' I asked.

Agna smiled. 'Why do you ask?'

I was fairly certain there were no such thing as trolls. They haunted my dreams, but mostly they stayed in the stories Mor read to me from the book of fairy tales. I wasn't too sure about Santa Klaus either. But huldra? Nisse? Those sprites who could either protect you or cause great mischief. They were blamed for mishaps that had no natural explanation. Everyone in the village hung charms to keep them away, and Mor and I made them with shell and human hair and feathers. We left gifts on our porches to keep them sweet.

'Sometimes I have nightmares about the shadow creatures. Trolls and nisse and things. Once some coffee and a knife vanished and Pappa said it was nisse and we should leave a gift. They took it, and after that my nightmares stopped and the knife turned up, but not the coffee.'

'So, they *are* real,' said Agna.

'Pappa said if you stop believing in them, that's when they really get you.'

43

'Maybe he's right.'

'Do you believe in them, Agna?'

'There are more things on earth and in heaven than you know from books or see in your dreams.'

'What?'

'More things than you imagine, than you *can* imagine. That's what the great poets say.'

I thought about this. I couldn't imagine being able to picture more things than Agna already knew about. What kind of things? Of course, if Agna was right, even she couldn't guess what these things might look or sound like. Because they were beyond imagining. And so, I couldn't imagine what she imagined. Everyone said I had an overactive imagination. Maybe I did.

'Er... What? My brain hurts,' I said.

'Never mind. Are they real? I don't know. There could be huldra in the village. Perhaps *I* am a huldra!'

'Are you?' I said in a meek voice.

'You never saw me with no clothes. You cannot know for sure.'

Huldra were known for *seeming* human, but they had a tail of a fox or wolf that they had to hide.

I liked how Agna took these things seriously, not like Haakon or Tove who told me it was silly folk tales one day, then worked at scaring me stiff with those same stories the next.

As we neared Fjernøy, my mouth watered again.

'What will we eat? Tell me again.'

'Whatever I shoot. A rabbit, a bird, or both. It's safe to shoot out here, nobody can hear. I'll cook them on a fire. Mushrooms possibly, it's early for them, but it's rained a bit. There are cherry trees full of plump jewels for a pudding. We can sit in the branches and eat till they make us squit.'

I nodded in fierce agreement and swallowed, so I didn't dribble. As we neared, I saw the small bay, and the exposed seabed. It was low tide. Everyone knew you couldn't get in at low tide. *Everyone.*

'Uh, we may have to wait?' I said, embarrassed by Agna's mistake.

'You think I'm stupid? There's another way.'

'There is?'

Agna turned the boat sharply and rowed up the coast around the back of the island. Which seemed pointless to me, because the cliffs and rocks were tall and steep.

Agna took us in to a tiny shelf of rock. We got out of the boat.

'I'm not going up that!' I said, craning my neck. Just looking at the cliff made me feel sick.

'Ah, but wait!' Agna climbed about a metre up, then shimmied sideways and disappeared behind a boulder. I followed.

Around the rock, was a hidden gully with a trickling waterfall. It was much less steep, there were natural footholds and ledges, even tiny trees, growing impossibly out of crevices, and – best of all – a thin rope hanging all the way down, with knots for hand grabs.

'Go back, pass me the bags. And don't tell about this. Ever. Understand?'

'What if it's a matter of life and death?'

'That's a strange thing to say, but okay, if it's a matter of life and death, but otherwise no. Are you okay with this?'

'I'm good as a mountain kid, everyone says it,' I lied, swallowing my fear, imagining what Haakon would say if he was here.

We climbed up, but halfway my dress caught on a rock and tore. Then Agna led us through the crowded green trees and dark silent glades to the heart of the island, to the clearing with the huts and the open fire pits. At the far end of the clearing were huge oaks and apple and cherry trees, heavy with fruit as Agna promised. Here, the trees stopped the wind. The air was still and warm, sweet and filled with the scent of heather.

The clearing was hidden, wholly surrounded by forest. The trees soaked up sound like snow.

In the distance a bird sang; a sad call I did not know:

Ta – shwoo

Ta – shwoo

Ta – shwoo

Ta – shwoo

Agna mimicked the song. The bird replied. Its song melted slowly in the air, just like ours had earlier.

We gathered sticks and fallen logs, and Agna produced matches and lit the kindling.

'Keep it fed, we'll cook on the embers,' she said, slinging her rifle over her shoulder. 'I'll be back soon. Don't move!'

Dutifully, I fed logs to the fire, only not too many at once as the day was warm and I didn't want to cook myself. Besides, I knew from working the stove at home, it was best to build an ember bed slowly.

The flames were pretty enough, glowing orange and red and red and yellow, and yellow and red. The colours of the late evening. Of ripe cherries.

I was hungry. I looked about the clearing at the trees. Even from my station by the fire, I could see the plump beauties Agna had talked about. What harm could it do to eat a few? To have a bit of pudding before the savoury. I thought of Agna looking for Germans who could have stopped us rowing to the island. Why not? Who could stop *her?* Rules are meant to be broken. That's what Haakon sometimes said. A second later, I heard Agna's gunshot.

'There you are, Germans!' I said. 'You can't even hear that, can you? Ha!'

Making sure there was enough wood on the fire, I went to the cherry tree.

Boy, these cherries were ripe! There were a few on the ground and they looked fresh.

It gave me an idea. I was tall enough to reach a few in the branches, and more if I climbed, because, of course, the best were high and out of reach. With a firm foot on a lower branch, I got a grip on a higher one, then another and shook them with all my might.

'Litenmus, is it? Ha! Watch this!' I shouted to no one. I expected cherries to rain down. But other than a couple, they stayed stubbornly on the branches. I fell back to the ground, thinking, *Never mind, there are plenty here.*

'Heaven.' These sweet red blobs were as not like fish and milk and bread as anything could be. I thought I'd get a wooden tray from the huts and collect some for Mor, but treat myself to a few first.

Later, when my mouth and lips and knees were stained red and my belly was sticking out and tight as a drum, I remembered the fire and ran back to it. I kneeled, feeding twigs into it and blowing to get it going again. Only the twigs didn't land where I threw them and my efforts to blow missed as well. For some reason I laughed and once I'd started, I couldn't stop.

'Mustn't make Agna cross,' I murmured, then laughed some more. Eventually I got the fire going again, and knew Agna would be pleased. All I had to do was sit and wait, and nurse my belly, which was uncomfortable from all the cherries.

And now it wasn't only my tummy that was out of sorts. I felt dizzy.

As I sat there it got worse. And worse. My head felt fuzzy as well as dizzy, as though I was half-asleep, and the fire – which had been a normal and well-behaved fire – began to dance and jump and sway like a rowboat in a squall.

Not liking this one bit, I turned away to look at the trees. They were misbehaving too. An old rowan had grown crooked and looked a bit – no, a lot – as if it had a face and arms. As if it was frozen in panic. Only when I looked again, it seemed not frozen at all, but was swaying, even though there was no breeze. I blinked and rubbed my eyes. For a second it was just a tree again, but as I stared, it changed into a mad creature, waving its many arms. A jötunn! Like in my nightmares. Clawing, reaching hands, the horns of a reindeer. Eyes in the knotted wood, glaring at me.

My breath was coming in gasps, sweat running down my face, but I felt cold, and sidled closer to the heat. Then I grabbed my belly. I wanted to stand, to get away from the sight of the tree, but in a terrible moment, realised I might not be able to stand without falling. I was so dizzy.

'Agna!' I moaned, and was about to shout as loud as I could when the still summer air was cut by a sound I knew too well. A winter sound. And this, from my nightmares too.

A wolf howl.

'Agna!'

There was the wolf howl again. Far away, but not far enough.

'AGNA!' I screamed, holding my aching belly. I tried to stand, I had to find Agna, but instead I leaned forward and was violently sick.

Then I heard gunshot again.

'AGNA! AGNA!' I tumbled to the ground and lay there crying.

Agna ran from the dark of the trees in a blur of action, throwing the gun and a rabbit and a duck to the ground, picking me up by my shoulders, wiping clammy hair off my face.

'You okay, Litenmus?'

'Nooo. I'm dying. Save me, Agna. Wolves and a tree like the song and...'

Agna dodged the next serving of cherries that erupted from my mouth. I sat staring at the ground while she rubbed my back.

Gradually, my breathing slowed. I felt a bit better. And noticed the stains on my dress. And more rips. I must have torn it coming through the trees. And the mud.

'Did you eat cherries off the ground?' said Agna

I moaned. 'Yes.' I looked at Agna, whose expression turned, from concern, to confusion, to relief. She laughed and shook her head.

'I'll fetch you some water.'

'Am I going to be okay?'

'Sure, once you've sobered up. The cherries on the ground ferment. A skinny mouse like you wouldn't need many to get drunk! How many did you eat?'

'Loads,' I groaned.

'You sit there and do nothing. I will skin this rabbit and get the breast from the duck, dig up potatoes Mor planted in spring, cut up the wild mushrooms and we will have a feast. There's a cutting board and plates and jars of dried dill and parsley in the huts. How about that?'

She pointed to some sick in my plaits, loosed my hair and cleaned it with water.

I was thinking it was time to go home, though not looking forward to seeing Mor, or her seeing my dress. But now my stomach was empty and Agna's words were tempting. I watched her fetch the board and plates, a pan, tongs and spit, and arrange them like an expert. The potatoes went in the pan, with water from a clear pool. The rabbit and mushrooms – a yellow kind I didn't know – Agna cut on the board.

'I am never going to drink aquavit or beer,' I said.

'Oh, I've heard *that* before,' said Agna.

'I heard a wolf howl. I saw a spirit in the trees!'

'No, you didn't, Litenmus. You only thought you did. Are you sure you only had fermented cherries? It sounds like you ate reindeer mushrooms. There's some dried in the huts, I thought you'd found them!'

'No, Pappa taught me which to eat and not. The reindeer mushrooms are red and spotted white like a fawn. I would never eat them, they are poisonous.'

'Sure, if you eat a lot. But the Sami magi boil and eat that mushroom. It has to be an exact amount, though, or you die.'

'Why do they do *that*?'

'Allows them to walk with the spirits, it opens doors and paths that will take them into the world of the nisse, a world which is always there and which meets our own at full moon, or on midsummer's eve. Or when lightning strikes the mountain, or when the sky lights flow north like swirling ribbons. Like I say, there's a big jar of it in the huts. It's well hidden, on top of the cupboards, so the youngsters won't find it. I thought maybe you had. You scared me!'

'What? Why is it there? Do we have Sami magi in the village?' I said, thrilled and terrified at the thought of witches living among us.

Agna looked around, as though invisible eyes might be watching, nodded and whispered; 'Yes.'

I gasped. '*Really*?'

Agna rolled her eyes and sniggered. 'No, you idiot. The mushroom is called *fly*-agaric. The cooks put saucers of it out, when they are smoking fish or making jam. It keeps flies and other annoying insects away.'

'I think you *are* a huldra, Agna. To know these things.'

Agna smiled as she cut the mushrooms. 'If you want

good free food, it pays to know all the tricks. Did you never help your mor or far when you came here?'

'No, too busy playing. There was no wolf, no tree spirit?'

'No, Litenmus.'

'I was very afraid.'

Agna stopped her chopping and looked at the fire a while, then to me. 'I tell you what. Have this.' She reached beneath her shirt and pulled out a necklace; carved stone on the end of a leather string, which she took off and handed to me.

'Here. A necklace I did not give to Eirik for safekeeping. This is far more valuable than anything made of gold.'

It was a tablet, with a square, and lines across it.

On examining it closely, I saw its yellowing, soft lustre, and realised it was not stone at all. It was bone, like the handle of Pappa's knife.

'How is it more valuable than gold?'

'It has magic properties. It gives you great bravery when you need it most.'

'What animal is it from?'

'The same as the rune charm speaks of. A wolf.'

'Where did you get it?'

'My far gave it to me.'

I wished then that I had my own necklace. The silver crucifix. But it had gone with the heirlooms Eirik had taken.

'Why are you giving it to me, Agna?'

'You must keep it a secret, and you can hold it whenever you are afraid. It will give you strength. How about that?'

I wasn't sure Agna spoke the truth. But the charm felt somehow good in the palm of my hand. And I was thrilled that Agna had given me this precious thing.

'Thank you, Agna.'

'You are welcome.'

This was treasure and mine, mine alone. I had so few things. I held it and rubbed it and examined the rune closely.

'I won't let you down, Agna. Ever, I promise.'

'What does *that* mean?' she asked, laughing. 'I haven't asked you to do anything.'

'I... I'm not sure. Only that I mean it.'

The afternoon passed. We cooked the rabbit and duck that Agna had hunted and boiled the potatoes she dug up, and the mushrooms she found.

Agna took a flagon of aquavit from the hut and some jars of jam and honey from a place behind the hut where I guessed she had stored them on previous visits. Later we hunted, sneaking behind rocks and trees, till we found more rabbits to shoot. Just like the times I had done it with Pappa.

In the late afternoon we climbed back into the canoe. We had to go down the cliff, then up, then down again, to move all the treasure we'd gathered.

Mor was waiting on the shore, hands on hips. Haakon and Tove sat on rocks behind her, and I knew from their faces I was in trouble. I wondered how they knew the exact spot where Agna had hidden the boat.

At first, Mor did nothing and said nothing. As I clambered from the canoe and went to stand in front of her she was still as a statue.

'We have been looking for you. We worked out who you were with. What have you got to say for yourself?' said Mor.

'Sorry. We meant to come home before.'

'Would you like to explain *this*?' Mor pointed an accusing finger at my cherry-stained, torn dress. 'And this?' My muddy knees. 'And this?' My bird's nest hair.

'I was sick because I was drunk off the cherries on the ground. I didn't do it on purpose, Mor. Am I in trouble?' I gave her my most pitiful smile because sometimes that worked.

Mor looked back at Haakon, who withered and shrank. 'Not as much as your brother who should look after his sister. I cannot have my eye on you the whole time. You will wash and mend your dress yourself, and

Tove will put your hair in plaits and you will not loose them until I say.'

While we talked, Agna emptied the canoe and dragged it up the shore to its hiding place. Then she joined us.

'It's my fault, I let her come and—'

Mor's hand shot up in the air, where it hovered like a snake about to strike. Agna flinched, but did not move. Slowly, Mor lowered her hand.

'I should give you a hiding. You are a reckless child!' Mor stared at Agna, breathing fast, nostrils flaring. Waiting.

'No one bothers with what we do,' said Agna. 'As long as we are home by supper. We look after each other. What do you care?'

Mor pointed to the pile of bag and kit, and the rifle butt sticking out of the rod bag.

'Things are different now. You know that. The Germans don't come often but they *do* come, and what do you think they would make of all this?' She stabbed a finger at Agna's face. 'Be very, *very* careful, my girl. If you must get in trouble, keep my family out of it, do you hear?'

Agna nodded.

I held up a dead rabbit to Mor, who eyed it with suspicion. Then Haakon came and took it off me and we walked home.

Tove

Oh, how I laughed at that after! Liva trying to squirm out of telling her tale with her arms waving about like they always did when she got excitable. I used to say if you tied her hands, she wouldn't be able to talk at all. And what happened next, how could we forget that?

A couple of days later, in the morning, I was trying to teach Liva how to knit a pattern into a jumper, with Liva moaning and not learning a thing. Haakon was outside chopping wood. A normal day. But then Haakon opened the door and let in a panting, huffing Little Lars.

'The v… vi… village … is… s… s… summoned. Common. P… Police… Germans.'

There was no time to ask why before he ran off to the next house.

'All of us, Mor?' I said.

'I suppose,' Mor replied, wiping her hands on her apron. She put the lid on the stewpot and moved it to the edge of the stove, where the skinned rabbit hung on a hook. She shrugged, then told us to put our boots on. I was afraid then, but curious too.

At the edge of the common ground someone had built a great pile of ferns and fallen branches. A bonfire, ready to be lit.

Soldiers stood in a crooked line behind the pyre, some leaning on their rifles, others sitting on logs. They looked bored. The policeman was there too, as he often was, doing their bidding, pen in one hand, clipboard in the other. As each family arrived, he made a mark. On his upper sleeve he wore an armband with insignia I had not seen before; a red cross on a yellow circle, a bit like the German swastika. A Norwegian version.

Once the village assembled, he gave the clipboard to a soldier, then spread his legs wide, placed his hands behind his back, lifted his head high so he could survey the scene from under his too big cap and spoke in a forced way.

'People of Rullesteinsvik. We have reports of trading of contraband, and use of banned items.' He paused, cleared his throat, and looked around us.

My stomach lurched. I fixed my eyes firmly at the ground and tried not to think of boats and guns and oars and rabbits and Agna and Liva's little adventure. I told myself everyone had a store of aquavit and many had jars of honey and jam and other things that they had not got with their ration cards. They had hidden these in the early days. There was no doubt some had hunting rifles too and I hoped they hid them well. A bottle of aquavit might be confiscated. A gun was a different matter.

The policeman coughed.

'You are good people and no threat to the government, but you must understand, almost all food items and alcohol are rationed, and are the property of the government.

'Furthermore, a reminder: citizens are banned from owning proscribed items, including but not limited to, radios, Norwegian flags, guns or rifles of any kind, hunting bows, knives with blades longer than twenty centimetres, boats of any kind unless licensed, oars and other equipment pertaining to travel by boat, unsanctioned published material of any kind…'

'Why is he talking like that?' Haakon whispered. 'Has he swallowed a dictionary?'

The policeman carried on, but I had stopped listening. I scanned the crowd for Agna. She was nowhere to be seen.

Then I looked at Liva, who stood at Mor's side, holding her hand tight, staring at the ground.

'Psst, Liva!' I whispered. 'Stay quiet, it will be okay. If they ask anything, just tell them the truth. Okay?'

Liva looked up for a second at Haakon, who shrugged.

The policeman continued:

'Given the village's record of good behaviour, the kommandant proposes an amnesty. If you bring any goods or items from the list stated, such goods or items will be confiscated or destroyed; but there will be no punishment nor any record made of misdemeanours.

'The amnesty will last until midday. Thereafter, if contraband is found, there will be repercussions, ranging from confiscation to fines, to imprisonment.'

A long, dreadful silence followed.

Some women and older boys and girls shifted uneasily.

Haakon whispered, as loudly as he could get away with, 'Stand fast. Give them nothing, tell them nothing!'

However, several women walked silently to their homes, and returned with knives, bottles of aquavit, even a hunting rifle.

The policeman looked at his pocket watch.

'Five minutes,' he said.

Next the kommandant appeared, walking from Mose's house. Mose and Agna were with him, Agna dressed in Sunday best, her head high, her face blank. A look I'd seen a dozen times at school in Kysten. I imagined Agna speaking to the kommandant, just like she did to Miss Bridget at school: 'Me, miss? No, miss. I don't know anything. It wasn't me. I wasn't even there.'

As soon as the kommandant reached the common, the soldiers stood to attention.

It's nearly midday, I told myself. *But why the bonfire?*

Then I saw more soldiers carrying Agna's boat from the coast path. I looked at Liva. Her face was a mask of misery.

'It'll be okay,' I whispered to her.

The soldiers hurled the boat on the bonfire. Then these soldiers and three others went to the boathouse and came back with oars. Four more soldiers appeared from the north of the bay, from the woods, carrying a rowboat. I did not recognise it.

A soldier lit the bonfire and we watched the boats burn.

And the kommandant, smoking a cigarette, watched us.

The policeman instructed us to remain where we stood as the soldiers went to our houses. I heard doors and windows opening, and much rattling and commotion. I imagined them going through cupboards, searching under beds. I thought of the dead rabbit by the stove, waiting to go in the stew.

'The rabbit, Mor!'

'We'll say Haakon snared it.'

Sure enough, a soldier came back, carrying the rabbit. The kommandant took the rabbit and dangled it in front of Mor. He smiled, seeming amused.

'Well?' the policeman said.

'It is not illegal to eat rabbits,' said Mor.

'Ah, yes, but how did you come by this meat? That is what the kommandant wants to know.'

My heart beat ever faster. They had known about the boat, what else did they know?

Mor opened her mouth to speak again, but the kommandant put a finger to his lips.

He threw his cigarette butt into the fire and leaned over, so his head was level with Liva's. He waited till she looked up at him. Without taking his eyes off her, he spoke and the policeman translated.

'He wants to know how this unfortunate animal met its end.'

Liva looked along the line of villagers to Agna, who was gazing out to sea. The kommandant clicked his fingers in Liva's face, stared at her and pointed to his own eyes. Look. At. Me.

Liva swallowed, her lip trembled.

The kommandant spoke – shockingly – in cold Norwegian:

'Who killed the rabbit? Do not lie. I will know.'

I spoke in my head, *Just tell the truth!*

Liva stepped back, but her eyes did not stray from his.

Slowly, her hand crept to her neck and found, under her shirt, a leather string I'd not seen before. Liva fiddled with this string as she swallowed again and breathed heavily.

Her other hand reached into the air, and with a shaking finger, she pointed at Haakon.

'He caught it in a snare.'

The kommandant looked at Liva a while, then smiled, stood up straight, put a hand on her head and ruffled her hair. He said something to his men and they laughed.

'Enjoy your stew,' he said to Mor. He left us then and went to the shore, standing with the policeman, pointing to the islands, asking questions and nodding. The soldiers dispersed.

I looked at Agna; her jaw set, her eyes unblinking, watching the Germans. And then at the fire, where the burning tar of her boat churned out acrid smoke.

'No more trips to Fjernøy, then,' I said. Agna turned to me, and I shrank from her wolf-eyed fierceness.

'I will make another.'

News

Winter, 1941/42

Tove

The only information about the war we had was from the Germans. They told us the British were losing. The Russians too.

In the school yard in Kysten there was a lot of talk.

'I h... heard there was a radio broadcast and the British say they will fight on the beaches, and in the streets, if they are... invaded,' said Little Lars.

'*When* they are invaded,' an older boy said, 'then they too will lose. This is not a nightmare we will wake from, Little Lars, and then the men come home, the Germans leave, the king returns. This is life now. This is our future. Get used to it!' The boy pushed Lars sharply in the shoulder. His friends laughed.

Mor worked on the farm all summer but after harvest the farmer didn't need help. And Pappa's money from his last season at sea ran out.

We lived on rations. Bread, cheese, sometimes tea, packets of fat. Sometimes pork, or even eggs. Fish we caught, berries and mushrooms we picked. Herrings we pickled.

We barely saw the Germans. Now and then they would appear, to check if we were planning a revolution.

Months passed. Snow arrived, covering everything in white silence. Each day was a mirror of the one before.

There was no reason for hope.

But hope does not listen to reason.

On a bitter evening Mor laid out bowls of milky fish soup sprinkled with dried dill, a plate of cottage cheese, a mound of stale bread.

'Tak,' we said in turn, as Mor ladled it out.

Mor said grace, thanking God for what we had.

'Not much to be thankful for, is it?' said Haakon.

Mor glared but didn't reply.

'You know,' he said, through a mouthful of bread, 'they are even going to ration potatoes and vegetables.'

'We had better stock up while we can,' Mor replied with a forced smile.

'You cannot buy what does not exist, with money you do not have, Mor.'

Liva leaned over her bowl examining her soup intently. 'Smells good, Mor!'

I sighed. 'Please don't argue.' *Not again*.

If Haakon pushed it, we all knew someone would say – eventually, 'You are not the man of the house!'

Haakon didn't push it. He waited, until we had finished eating, before clapping his hands together. 'Who wants pudding?'

Our jaws opened wide. Our eyes popped. He might as well have offered us champagne.

'What?' said Liva.

He went out to the woodshed and returned with a parcel wrapped in brown baker's paper. He placed it on the table and carefully unwrapped it. Inside was a heap of broken pastries. The bigger bits lay on a bed of crumbs, currants and shards of icing.

Mor, Liva and I stared in disbelief.

'Where did you get *this*?' said Mor.

'This is only a taste. We are eating better from now on,' he said.

'*Haakon?*' Mor narrowed her eyes.

'I got a job with the baker in Dallansby. I am to go to the farm with the order from the police. The farmer checks with the soldier stationed there and the police deliver the ration of grain to the baker and he mills and bakes. I take fresh bakes to the garrison, then I bring and distribute the loaves here. Twice a week at least. I get paid, and I can get more bread for us. And this?' He pointed at the pastries. 'Sometimes Mr Elstad makes pastries for the soldiers, with ingredients sent from Germany. This is leftovers and broken bits. A perk. *And* I can trade it for tinned goods.' He sat back, folding his arms, basking in our shock.

'It's wonderful, Haakon,' I said. 'But you would… er…' I paused, I didn't know how to say it. 'You would be working with… *them*?'

'We need to eat. Pappa is not here; someone has to provide.'

'A lot of boys would take work like that,' Mor said quietly. 'Why you?'

'Dunno.' He shrugged, popping a piece of icing in his mouth. 'Maybe because I live here. It saves on delivery time, and I'm fast. I think the baker heard about my orienteering. I am the nixie, remember?'

Haakon had the nickname of the forest creature.

'Yes, and the nixie will always find his way home,' said Liva, who knew such things from all the folk tales she read at school.

'Is it a problem?' said Haakon.

Nobody asked any more questions. We ate the pastries.

And Haakon was right. He was strong and fast. Our skis and sleds had not been taken from us. Sleds tall enough to push, like huskies pull. Sleds you can load with logs, or hay. Or bread! We had no dogs, only our legs. Haakon loved his sled. He loved his job. I think he loved time away from us too.

Word came just before Christmas.

For weeks the air had had a vicious bite. The sky was white, the ground patched with dangerous ice. 'Too cold to snow,' everybody said. We had logs stored like all families, but this run of 'too cold to snow' had lasted longer than anyone could remember, and the ceramic stove had an endless hunger for fuel.

'When is Haakon coming home?' Liva asked, on a brutal late afternoon when wind whittled the cold ever sharper. We were making paper chains with paper and glue. This year the paper was brown bakers' paper, not red and green. But we had brought in red berries and holly and Mor had brought down the elf dolls from the attic.

We had spent weeks making presents too. I had painted a wooden plate for Mor and knitted a hat for Haakon. Liva was trying her own plate painting. But she didn't have the skill, or the patience.

'Shall I light the candles?' Liva said. We had brought in a tree, of course, but we used fewer candles and only lit them when Haakon arrived home.

'Will he bring more logs?' said Liva.

'Don't worry, he will be home for supper, I am sure,' Mor said. 'He has had a busy day; he will be hungry.'

Liva licked her lips. I knew she was hoping Haakon might bring a treat. 'Well, he's late.'

'The tracks are difficult, journeys take longer,' I said. 'He'll be home soon.'

Night arrived and Haakon did not. The moon shone through the clouds and lit the snow. Still, Mor told us Haakon would be okay.

Then it was supper time and Haakon had not appeared. I knew from her face that a knot of worry grew inside Mor's heart.

There was a tiny knock at the door and behind the door stood Little Lars.

'Come in, lad,' said Mor. No one left a door open in such weather.

'Message from H… Haakon. He is doing his rounds, and w… will be home s… soon.'

Mor let out a sigh. 'You see, Liva? No need to worry. Tove, a biscuit for the messenger.'

I fetched a biscuit from the tin Haakon had brought home the week before. Lars munched and crunched it on the spot, before saying, 'Tak, Mrs Erikson,' and leaving.

Mor smiled, rubbing her chin. 'I have a feeling Lars might deliver a lot more messages in coming weeks.'

Haakon had no sugary treats, but a sled loaded with larch logs.

'You see, Mor. Money made from biscuits and cake, gets as many cut logs as we want.'

'You are late today,' Mor said, fishing for information, watching Haakon stack logs by the stove. 'I got worried.'

'Ice. The track is fast in some places, tricky in others, and bread is precious cargo.'

'Why haven't you taken off your coat? I know you are cold but you cannot forget manners, my lad.'

'You'll see.'

'See what?'

'I am not the only person to visit Dallansby today, or maybe we had a secret visitor from somewhere else.'

As though it was planned, there came a soft, but insistent knocking at the door.

'Back so soon?' said Mor.

'C… come quickly,' said Little Lars 'The common. Dress w… warm.' He vanished, without waiting for a biscuit.

'It is dark and freezing,' Mor said. 'Whatever it is can wait.'

'No,' said Haakon. 'It can't. Get your coats.'

A great bonfire lit the common with sparking, roaring flames. The shadows of villagers danced on the trees and rocks. Some warmed their hands or dragged branches and deadfall from the woods to feed the flames. Others gathered, huddled over sheets of paper, trying to read by the light of the fire.

'What's going on?' asked Mor.

'News,' someone replied.

'What?'

People jostled, straining to read.

'Milorg,' another voice said.

'What is Milorg?'

'We are. Us! Norway!'

Mose and Agna arrived last. Mose grabbed a sheet and switched on a powerful torch. The bustling ceased; the crowd fell silent. Agna held the sheet while Mose shone the torch on the paper, and Agna read in a voice as clear as church bells.

'*Greetings to my people...*' she began. There was a great gasp. Only one man would start a message like this.

'The king!' people shouted.

The sheet was a kind of newspaper. And there *was* a message from the king, telling us the fortunes of himself, the prime minister and their cabinet in London. There was news too of the Milorg, the military organisation.

There were actions, mostly in the north, but in the south too. The Milorg hiding in forests and mountains, even in towns. Blowing up train lines and supplies, stealing from the Germans, gathering intelligence. Workers' resistance, sabotage. The list went on.

Our fighters will vanish as quickly as they appear. They live among you now, like nisse and huldra in the old tales, disguised, or hidden in the shadows. You will not know who they are, you will not know them by their names, but by their deeds.

At the bottom of the news sheet was a message from the prime minister in exile, urging the people:

Join if you can. Resist how you can. Do not assist the invaders in any way. If you speak German, hide it, if they try to speak Norwegian, pretend you do not understand.

Make noise, protest at the smallest things. Every soldier they send to keep us quiet, is one less fighting the British. And they have sent hundreds of thousands.

Stay loyal. Fight. Disrupt.

In the name of the king, God and Norway. We will make their occupation difficult and finally impossible.

The day will come when we are free. Until that day, the invaders will pay and the cost must be high.

Smaller items on the back of the sheet told stories of brave individuals, a woman who smuggled food to men in labour camps, a team who helped people into Sweden.

When Agna finished reading, we demanded she start again. Haakon looked at the faces basking in the words, as much as the warmth of the fire.

A bottle of aquavit arrived, with many tiny glasses.

Then Sofie, who was fourteen and our finest singer, began,

> 'We love this country
> as it rises forth,
> rugged, weathered, over the water,
> with the thousands of homes, —
> love, love it and think
> of our father and mother
> and the saga-night that lays
> dreams upon our earth.'

One after another we joined in. Only some could not sing at all, because the words stuck in their throats and tears ran down their cheeks.

'Is Pappa with the Milorg?' Liva asked.

'I hope so,' Mor said, with a sniffle.

It began to snow, fat, heavy flakes falling from the dark. But the fire was raging now and the snow did nothing to dampen it.

More aquavit was drunk. More songs were sung. Carols, in full voice.

The children who lived north of the common challenged those who lived south to a snowball fight. Even Haakon and some of the adults joined in.

We returned home with jumpers and coats crusted with snow and damp underneath where we had been wrestled to the ground and snowballs had been forced down our tops by the enemy.

We changed into dry clothes, then huddled round the stove and fed Haakon's fresh supply of logs into it. Mor produced the sheet from her pocket.

'I was the last to read it, nobody asked for it back. Nobody seems to know how it got here either.'

'I guess someone knows, but cannot say,' said Haakon.

As if it was a story from the fairy tale book, we sat, rapt, as Mor read the words again, start to finish.

'Milorg. A secret army! Shadow creatures,' Liva said. 'Imagine. They are fighting in the north.'

'Well, they are not only in the north, are they?' said Mor.

It was true. Somebody had printed this paper, somebody had delivered it. We looked at each other, and wondered. How had this paper arrived in the village? Who had brought it?

With a last, longing look at the sheet, Mor crumpled it into a ball and fed it to the flames.

'Mor!' I said. 'What are you doing?'

'It is wonderful to see. But it is dangerous to keep such a thing. The last thing the invaders want is for us to know this.'

'Mor is right,' Haakon said. 'We have read the words. Nothing will be forgotten.'

Liva

Mor had her suspicions. Haakon could spin a yarn. He was clever. Whoever he delivered the news sheet to waited a day or more. Then it appeared, often while Haakon was away, on a doorstep or under a mat. As though nisse had left it.

She wanted to believe him or maybe she did not wish to stop the food that was no doubt payment for his service.

Then other news came, and with that she knew for sure.

Tove and I lay in Mor's bed. She said she needed the living room to herself to lay out embroidery, and that we would only be in her way.

I dozed, listening to the crackle of the fire, Tove's sing-song voice reading from the book of fairy tales.

Mor waited for Haakon. He was late, it was long after dark, but by now this was not unusual.

Eventually he came in from the cold, with a bag of loaves. The aroma was mouth-watering. Tove and I came running as if a bell had rung.

Haakon opened his mouth to shout, but Mor put a finger to her lips and shook her head.

'I have to speak with Haakon,' she said, then shut the door tight on us. I heard the front door open then close. Of course, we came out of the room then sneaked to the window, and peeped out. We could see their backs and could just hear their whispered words.

'Mor, I've been working, I need to wash and get warm, else I'll catch a chill,' he said. Words she would usually speak.

'Son,' she said, in a shaking voice. 'You have to stop. I know what you are doing and why, but there will be other ways to get reports to the village.'

'Mor,' he said quietly. 'When you see what I have brought, you will change your mind.'

She shook her head gently.

'A man came from Kysten today,' Mor said. 'He walked the coast path. There was a boy there, Kjell, I think.'

'Yes, I know him. Good footballer. You said *was*. There *was* a boy there?'

Mor nodded. 'He was trading black market goods. He was betrayed by someone from his own village. They fined his family, put him in a cell for a night, roughed him up a bit...'

'Then it is not the end of the world, Mor.'

'That's not all. A day or two later, he was involved in guiding a boat to shore and carrying guns from this boat. The Germans were tipped off and...' Mor gripped Haakon's hand tight and fast, as though she would never let go.

'And?' asked Haakon.

'The black caps took him to Dallansby. They say he might be executed.'

Haakon swallowed. 'Bastards!'

'Your far is doing god knows what, and we make ends meet. We are doing our bit and...' She too swallowed and took a deep breath. 'They killed one of the men this Kjell was with. They said he was running away, but the man from Kysten said they had surrendered.'

'Mor, this is exactly why I must do my duty. I am almost a man. You really don't want me delivering news sheets or bread? You will see.' He tried to tear himself away, to go inside to show her what was in the bag. But Mor wouldn't let him go.

'You are a boy. Do you remember when Liva was with Agna with the boat, and they knew somehow about the boat afterwards? This is not a game. Someone in the village may find out about you, they may betray you. You, Agna and others... you are only children.'

'Only?'

'No amount of food is worth it, Haakon. You do not have to do this. I am begging you!'

'We all have to do something.'

'I am your mor and you will listen. If you carry on, yes, we will eat well, yes, we will find out sooner what we would eventually learn anyway. But what if they find you? Prison, a labour camp, worse? And what happens to us if they catch you? Think of that. You have responsibilities.'

'*If*, Mor. Come, see what I have brought.'

'I am not hungry.'

'It is not food.'

They came in, and Mor glared at us, but didn't tell us off. We watched Haakon take a loaf from the brown paper bag. He placed it on the table, then found a knife and opened the loaf from the underside. Inside was a small package, wrapped in baking paper. Inside that was the news sheet, and inside that, a small envelope, that had already been opened.

Mor took a step forward, then another. She pulled out the letter and read it. She grabbed hold of the back of a chair, as though to stop herself falling, and began to cry.

'Mor! What is the matter?' Tove cried out.

'Nothing my love, nothing.' Mor smiled, through her sobs. 'It is something wonderful.'

'It's from Pappa,' Haakon told them. 'He is alive. He is safe. In England.'

I did not hear much after that. The details, I took in later, when Mor read Pappa's note again, which she did, a dozen times. In that moment, I only took in Haakon's words.

He is alive. He is safe.

Mor asked Haakon if we could write a letter to him, and Haakon said no. There was to be no more correspondence. This was a once-only wonder.

She did not ask Haakon too much about his business from that day on, unless it was away from our eager ears. And if she did, it did not stop him.

Mor told us she burned the letter. None of us saw her do it and none of us believed her.

I remember one day. Haakon was away, and Tove was at school in Kysten with some of the others (we only went on some days). I was at home with a cold, and Mor was off to have tea with Mrs Bruntland, leaving me with a great pile of sums and reading, because when we did not go to school that is what we had to do.

I went to the outhouse for a pee and there were tracks from Mor's boots in the snow. They did not make a trail to the village, they led to the woods and the steep hill behind our house, where the trees grew close together and the ground was uneven. Another set of tracks came back, then joined the path to the village. Mor had not bothered to cover her footprints. Why would she? We never went there, nor did anyone else. It was snowing and soon her tracks would be covered. I fetched my coat and mittens.

I trudged through the pines, glancing over my shoulder every few seconds. The snow fell quick and heavy, a curtain of large light crystals, laying a blanket Pappa always called the 'magic silence'. The deeper in the woods I went, the louder the magic silence grew till the wind could not be heard at all, and there was only the crunch of my boots and the soft sound of my breath. It was tough going. I should have worn snow shoes, with wide mesh underneath that keeps you above the snow, but in my normal boots I sank too easily. I was careful to place my feet in Mor's tracks, it was easier to walk that way and it meant I wouldn't leave any marks of my own.

I struggled on, navigating the uneven hidden ground. Those tracks made questions that needed answers. Why had Mor gone into the woods? Why had she not said?

The answer lay in the hollow of the old tree where her tracks stopped. Inside was a tin can and inside that was the letter.

I took off my mittens.

Oh, to hold the paper Pappa had held! Just for a few seconds, before cold numbed my fingers.

The first part Mor had read to us many times. He *was* in England; he *had* told Mor to kiss us for him. He *had* written how much he missed us and prayed for when we would be together. He had not mentioned our names and he had only signed it, P.

But there was more.

You must burn this letter. It took a lot of effort for me to ensure it could reach you, I endanger you by writing it, but how can I not? I want you to know I am safe, and working with our government in England.

The Milorg run a network of news and letters. Information about the Germans comes through the network to us. We in turn supply the Milorg and aid them. This much the enemy know, but you may not. More I cannot say.

Now, my darling, you might well believe that our little village is a place away from the war. But the Milorg work under the Germans' noses and use the forest and steep valleys and mazes of islands. The war can be anywhere. Keep away from the islands and hills. Keep the children safe. Watch for patrol boats...

After I'd read it, I folded the letter and put the tin back exactly – I hoped – as I'd found it.

'Better be home quick,' I said to myself.

There was no path back, only the tracks I had followed and which – now I thought about it – *anyone* could follow.

'Careless, Mor!' I said to the cold air. But the tracks were being covered by the snow, and that was good. It was later in the afternoon; the dark was coming.

I made my way back, trying not to imagine soldiers in the shadows beneath the trees. Or wolves. Or trolls.

I took a mitten off and found my pendant, the gift from Agna. I rubbed it, to get rid of the fear of monsters. And then the worry that Mor might be home, waiting for me.

She wasn't. I walked all around the yard, kicking and messing the snow as much as I could, to make sure no one would see *anyone's* tracks. As I scuffed the snow, I chatted with myself:

'I must warn Agna about the patrol boats! Then, 'Hmm, no need. Nobody would go to the islands in this weather, even if it was allowed. You'd have to be crazy.' I paused, catching my breath. 'But... Agna *is* crazy!'

I planned to tell Agna about patrol boats as soon as possible, but did not see her next day, or for a while after that. There were terrible storms and in the weeks that followed the coast was tortured by high winds, towering waves and fierce snows. The old folks said Njord, the god of the wind and of hunting, had brought the storms. The days were short.

I told myself Agna could not be up to any island mischief in *this* weather. The storms left as quickly as they arrived, and I walked to the common early one morning and saw Agna heading to the harbour and south along the coast path. Over her shoulder she carried the tell-tale fishing rod bag.

Agna wore snow shoes. I am not sure she needed them on the path. She was wearing them to make sure she would not leave tracks. Or maybe because she needed them on the island.

I followed.

Agna walked past where she had hidden the old boat, and a long way south before veering into the woods. As before, I found a tree to hide behind, and sneaked looks.

Agna did not appear. Minutes passed, and still no Agna. But on the headland a way south, what was that? A boulder covered by snow? A large ball of snow like a snowman's body? It had moved though. I saw a flash of something black.

There! It moved again. Perhaps a bird, or some other animal.

I was looking so intently I almost missed Agna paddling her homemade canoe round the headland. I had missed seeing her get it into the water. There had to be another inlet out of sight.

I must warn her about patrol boats, I thought. I was going to run along the coast down to the shore, but something kept me rooted. What *was* that thing on the headland? It was still now, but it *had* moved, I was certain. As I watched, it began to take shape. I blinked. Was I imagining things? Could that be a pair of binoculars? A hand?

It was not a rock. There *was* a figure, all in white. And another. A glint off binoculars as they swung round and looked directly at Agna.

I ran a few steps, put my hands either side of my mouth to shout, to warn her.

Suddenly, a gloved hand covered my jaw before I could scream. An arm wrapped around my chest like a tentacle squeezing.

A whisper, hot breath in my ear, the stink of cigarettes. 'Stilles kind sein!'

The hands held me fast. I watched in dumb terror as Agna rowed the canoe towards the islands until all trace of her – oblivious to what was happening – vanished.

Only then did the hand leave my mouth, the arm unwind. These hands spun me round and I looked up, panting, into the face of the soldier. He wore a uniform that was entirely white.

'Halt,' he said, as if I was running. I was glued to the spot. I scrabbled for my necklace, but my mittens made me clumsy.

Two men came down the path from the village then. Germans, dressed in the same white camouflage uniforms. As they got closer, I recognised the kommandant.

'Hallo, girl, what are you do?' he said in broken Norwegian, his accent thick.

'N... N... Nothing.' I could barely speak, barely breathe.

'Where is your friend go?'

I sucked in breath, tried to say, *I don't know.* But to my horror, I couldn't speak at all.

The soldier took his rifle off his shoulder. I started to cry.

He pointed it at me, prodding my shoulder with the barrel.

'Sprich, Mädchen!'

I closed my eyes, covered my face with my mittens and gave myself up to sobbing and bawling and howling.

'Sprich, Mädchen!'

'Sie ist nur ein kind!' the kommandant barked, and I did not know if it was to me, or the soldier. Then in a gentler voice, 'Do not afraid. Nobody hurt you.'

I heard the crunch of boots on snow, and after silent seconds dared to open my eyes. The kommandant was still there, but the soldier was walking off towards the headland, waving and shouting at the soldiers there. In the distance, I heard the ugly grunt of a boat's engine.

The boat came around the headland and, to my surprise, turned for Rullesteinsvik rather than after Agna.

The kommandant squatted so he was the same height as me.

'You know what friend do?'

I shook my head.

'Your friend. Milorg?'

I shook my head vigorously.

'You know where go?'

No, again. *I don't know anything*, I wanted to say, but only thought, *Please let me go*.

'What is your name?'

'L... L... Liva.'

'Home here, yes?' He pointed up the path to the village. I nodded.

'Ah, yes. Girl with rabbit. Come.' He walked briskly and didn't bother looking back to see if I was following.

I looked to sea, but Agna was nowhere to be seen.

Mor was fetched, and she too was questioned, holding me, still sobbing, to her side.

'Who is boy in boat?' said the kommandant.

'Girl. Her name is Agna,' said Mor.

The kommandant raised an eyebrow.

'Milorg?'

'No. She is probably hunting.'

'Where?'

Mor pointed west.

'Come.'

The soldiers took Mor and me to the large grey metal boat, and we boarded and sat there with the kommandant and his men.

As we left, we saw a crowd gathering on the shore.

We found the island. I led them there; Mor gave me no choice. And we found Agna's canoe. The soldiers took delight in destroying it. First, they cut the tarred canvas with knives, then they smashed the frame with their rifle butts and threw the bits into the water. Two of them went inland, searching for Agna and quickly returned with her. She'd heard the engine too late to escape and she knew there was no point in hiding. How else would she get home?

I thought that would be the end of it, that we would return and Agna would face whatever punishment was coming. But the soldiers who searched for Agna spoke, and the kommandant listened.

He went inland himself. Of course, he was looking for evidence of Milorg. He found none. But he did find our huts and from that day the island – and Agna – belonged to him, and we knew the words in Pappa's letter were true.

The war can be anywhere.

I followed the bobbing, weaving light of Agna's torch through the trees to the clearing, a space away from grown-ups where we children sat on logs around the fire pit, making toast on sticks, telling blood-curdling tales.

'Agna, Agna!' I panted, falling into the clearing.

'Litenmus. Following me *again*?'

Agna picked up the fir branches that covered the pit and began sweeping the snow away. I collected twigs to make a nest, so the fire would catch, even as the ground ice melted. There was plenty of light from moon and snow to see what to do.

'They *made* us take them to the island, Agna.'

'I know. It's not your fault.'

'They didn't arrest you?'

'No.'

This baffled and silenced me. I wasn't sure what to ask next.

Agna lit the kindling, and we sat opposite each other, and soon had flames to warm our hands.

'How did they find me?' said Agna.

I told my story with wild gestures, spotting the lookouts, trying to warn her, struggling with the soldier.

'I wish I'd *bitten* his hand!' I said. 'Then I could have shouted to you, but I only thought of it after.'

'You were brave.'

'Did they take your gun?'

'Of course.'

'But... But...'

Agna sighed. 'You want to know how come I'm not in jail. You want me to spell it out?'

'Well... yes,' I said, not wanting to look stupid, but feeling confused.

'The kommandant does business from our house, he drinks our coffee. He's been visiting a while now and not always with good reason. I think he likes Mor. Throwing me in jail wouldn't exactly get him in her good books. Letting me off does. There!'

'He's soft on her? Hasn't he got his own wife?'

'Yes, in Germany. A kid too. They might even come out here, it's happening with some of the officers. Right now, he's here alone. And we have no papers and are waiting for some. If he sent me to Dallansby, life could get difficult quickly. That's what he said in his pathetic Norwegian. Now we must work for him.'

'Was he angry about the island?'

'No. He's relieved it is not a Milorg base, and pleased he found it before it became one. He actually thanked me. He said it will be perfect.'

'What for?'

'The camp he's been told to set up.'

I imagined soldiers there, sitting round a fire in the summer dusk, eating cherries, drinking aquavit.

'It's *our* camp, they can't use it.'

'They can do whatever they like. Anyway, it's not the kind of camp you're thinking of. He is a kommandant. He has orders to find locations for labour camps for prisoners. That's why we don't often see him. Now he has found a location, here.'

'For captured Milorg?'

'Anyone they don't like. They have a long list, believe me. They are going to be teaching all about the Reich in school apparently, then we will see who is on that list. You don't like it? You'll go to a camp too. Some holiday that will be! I've heard about such places. From before I came to Rullesteinsvik.'

'What things?'

Agna turned, opened her mouth to speak, then sighed and shook her head.

'Not saying. You're too young.'

'Tell. There's only us here.'

'This isn't a folk tale, you fool,' Agna barked.

I was taken aback. Tears filled my eyes. For a time, the only sound was me sniffling and the crackle of the fire.

'Sorry, Litenmus. Don't mean to scare you. You shouldn't even be talking to me, your mor wouldn't like it.'

'Why *did* you come out here? Is *he* in your house now?'

'No. I came here to do something.'

I looked around, into the dark trees. Then at Agna, and the ground around her. She hadn't brought a rod bag, or anything I could see.

'What?'

'You mustn't tell anyone.'

'I didn't tell the kommandant about the boat, did I? When we went in summer. And he was like this in front of me, before the whole village.' I held my hand in front of her nose and made a defiant face. 'And I tried to warn you when they caught you. You can trust me.'

Agna looked up to the moonlit sky, then reached inside her coat and pulled out a piece of folded paper.

'Is that a secret message?' I said. 'From the Milorg?'

'No. How would I get such a thing? It is... it's...'

'What? Tell.'

'Well, in truth, now I am here, I feel foolish, but I have to do *something*.'

'Tell me. This *is* the place for it.'

The clearing. The place for folk tales, for jokes, for ghost stories. For truth or dare. For spitting and shaking and swearing oaths.

Agna chewed her cheek, examining me with screwed up eyes. 'Hmmm… well…'

She leaned forward. The light of flames danced across her face.

'Do you believe in spirits, Litenmus?'

'Ghosts?'

'Ghosts are mostly harmless. I mean the kind that walk the earth, unseen, but are all the time in the shadows. Beings which can do harm or good.'

'Undergrounds? Shadow creatures, like huldra and nisse?'

'The darker kind. The truly invisible kind.'

I nodded and was about to say, 'Sure,' but paused, remembering this was a place where you told the truth if you weren't telling a story. 'Honestly? I don't know if I believe in them.'

'Well, I think they are just as likely as a god in his heaven. My bestemor, when she was alive, she *did* believe. She talked with them all the time. She was guided by them.'

I listened intently. Agna and Mose *never* talked about their past. It was a door that shut quick when you tried to pry it open.

'She told me magic is a thing *everybody* can do. Not like with religion and priests. You have to take it seriously, though. You have to mean what you wish for. She used to go in the woods at night and 'lift up her soul', whatever that means, and ask the spirits what path she should follow. She said answers always came, not always the ones she wanted or expected. She said you have to be careful with magic, because you cannot always control it. You have to be prepared for that too.'

'Is that...' I swallowed, 'Um... *true?*'

'On my mor's life. And I have come here to do some. Our secret?'

I spat in my palm and held it out.

Agna spat in her hand. We looked deep into each other's souls, and shook.

'Now,' Agna said. 'My mor doesn't have the gift, but when my bestemor died, she said I might.'

'I'll bet you do.'

Agna shrugged. She leaned closer to the fire, then lifted her head to the sky, as though searching the moonlit blue. The flames cast shadows on her face. When she spoke, it was no more than a whisper.

'I summon you, spirits of the earth, of the sky. Use me as your vessel and bring damnation on these men for the wrong they have done.' Then Agna read from the paper which she held in her trembling hands.

'The SS man whose name is Werner.

'The policeman whose name is Hansen.

'The kommandant whose name is Meier.

'I curse them. For all they have done, for all that they are.'

She reached into her coat and drew out an old bone-handled knife, with its blade wrapped in leather. She took the leather off and cut her thumb. She yelped, having cut too deep, then let the blood drip on to the paper. Sucking her thumb where she had cut it, she used her other hand to cast the paper into the embers. The blood sizzled and smoked, filling the air with an iron tang.

Only then did Agna look at me.

'Can you stop it now, please?' I whispered. 'I'm scared.'

'You asked. Anyway, it is done.'

'What will happen to them?'

'I don't know. But I tell you, I am going to take revenge and the spirits might help.'

I wanted to stand, to run. But I had no torch, and even with the light of the moon, I did not want to walk home by myself.

A soft wind whistled through the clearing. Sparks flew. A cloud covered the moon, plunging the clearing into shadow.

The fire cast a dancing shape of Agna across the trees. For a second, no more, the shadow looked to me like a giant crow. Then the cloud passed.

'Agna, look!' I pointed to the sky.

A lick of yellow light flickered over us, as though the sky was on fire, glowing, pulsing.

'The skylight. The northern lamps!'

Vast waves of emerald green emerged from nowhere and swam above our heads.

'Northern lights,' Agna said. 'It's been a long time.'

And it had. An age since we had sat and told stories of where this miracle came from. The road to the dead. Or maidens dancing in Asgard. Or the spirits of the sky.

A river of lavender purple, sun yellow and sunset red spread across the night.

We craned our necks till they hurt and for a time forgot about war and curses.

The lights ended as quickly as they had begun.

'It can't be a coincidence,' I said. 'You have done magic. Do you think everyone else saw them?' I asked, already relishing the idea of telling Haakon and Tove what I'd seen, though not what I thought had made it happen.

'I think I had better go home now,' I said.

'Go, then. Off you trot.'

The light in the sky had been beautiful, but now the shadows beneath the trees seemed darker than before.

'Will you take me? Please?'

'Sure, Litenmus.'

The Camp

Spring 1942

Tove

I was fourteen. Liva was eleven.

The winter snow melted, and spring was a promise. But of what?

The Germans waited till the thaw was over. Then they came, in their caterpillar tracked vehicles, felling trees to widen the track, filling holes with sand and rocks.

After that, trucks arrived, loaded with metal sheets, posts and huge rolls of barbed wire.

All of it was shipped across the water in metal boats that crowded the bay.

The quiet of our home was utterly broken. Instead of birdsong, we had the groans of engines. The meadows where wildflowers grew were churned into mud.

And now there was not only the kommandant and a few soldiers. There were dozens of them, running to and fro and driving their machines through our village. Some of them black caps. The SS.

Liva watched them whenever she could, hiding in the trees. She told me about Agna's curse. I knew nothing could stop these monsters, though, grinding, crunching, roaring through our lives.

Still, they had not properly built the camp. As it turned out, they needed more than German hands to build it. I was afraid for Haakon. For other boys. For all of us. Who knew what they might make us do?

But they did not need us. Not for that.

I was feeding the goats on the common on a cold misty morning when a column of prisoners arrived. Fifty or more, trudging silently through the mud.

My god! They were rough. I wondered what hell they had they been through. They wore heavy coats, ill-fitting hats and too-big boots, uniforms with insignia I did not recognise, stained with dirt and – I looked closely – some with blood. One man had a bandage around his head, another an arm in a homemade sling. Another prisoner, a boy too young to hold a gun, smiled at me. He had raven black hair, and narrow, sea-green eyes. A nice brown face.

I smiled, and waved, to be polite, and because I felt sorry for him.

Many were skinny, as though shrunk by the fighting; they seemed more clothes than men. They were not the ghosts they later became, but even now had the look, the same as a starved, injured wolf we once found in the woods that Pappa had to shoot. The boy was different from the others, though. He looked, in a word, healthy.

They filed through Rullesteinsvik, with their heads bowed. I was surprised to see them carrying axes, iron fell wedges and sledge hammers. Tools for forestry, but surely weapons too. How was it allowed?

Yet here they were, and with only a few guards carrying machine guns slung over their shoulders as casual as you might carry a picnic bag.

The Germans took the prisoners to the boats.

Suddenly, a soldier called out, 'Hi, junges Mädchen!' and pointed at me. I looked about, hoping he might be speaking to someone else, but there was only me and the goats. He smiled and mimed sipping (they did a lot of that) and made a slurping sound. 'Kaffee!'

My heart beat so fast, because they never talked to us children. I nodded, dropped my bucket and legged it to Mose's house, where she and Agna were hanging curds in muslin.

'There are p... prisoners,' I gasped. 'Lots. On the shore. The guards want coffee.'

'Anyone we know?' Mose said, washing her hands.

'I don't think they are Norwegian soldiers.'

'How can you be sure?' said Agna.

'Er, uniforms. One of them looked maybe Sami,' I said, thinking of the boy. 'A couple of others too. Northern people. Lots had dark hair.'

I waited while they brewed coffee, because no way was I going back out there. When it was ready, I followed behind Agna. We reached the shore and found most of the village there, watching. Agna and Mose set to doing what they often had to: pouring coffee.

The prisoners stood, or sat on crates, or on the jetty with their legs hanging over. Some smoked pipes. I got a better look at them. Some, yes, like the boy, had eyes like the Sami people; others had wide, rugged faces, or skin darker than any Norwegian I'd ever met. Were they from our country, or another, or many? They did not speak. They only stared at the steaming cups of coffee.

I remember another thing from that day. Agna was pouring and she looked up and she and the green-eyed boy saw each other. She almost dropped the coffee pot. The soldier whose coffee she poured shouted at her. Her legs seemed to buckle, she took a step back, then steadied herself, all the time looking at the boy not the soldier. She opened her mouth to speak, then didn't. She looked away and made herself busy with her pouring duty. And her cheeks were red as cherries. She did not look up again. The boy kept looking at her, though. If I had not known better, I would have thought they recognised each other. Yet they had never met.

It is rare. But I knew what I saw. They had fallen for each other.

We did not see the prisoners for months after that day. Soldiers came and went in the boats. The Russians (as we learned the prisoners were), we never saw. We knew only that they were on the island, building the camp.

When a westerly breeze blew, we heard the trees toppling. Like thunder. On clear days, we saw smoke from fires.

I lay awake at night and thought of that boy and his smile for Agna. I imagined him and his friends in a hut they had built and hoped they were warm and had enough to eat.

Once Liva asked Mor, 'Why don't they fight? Why do they not escape? They have axes.'

'Because,' Mor said, 'if some escaped, the black caps would not be nice to those left behind.'

That was the end of that conversation. Liva always asked questions, but did not want to know more of what this might mean. We knew. Haakon found out from the policeman and told me. If one escaped, they would shoot ten. Who would want that weight on their soul?

The kommandant gave Agna and Mose work preparing rations for prisoners and soldiers on Fjernøy.

They were go-betweens, sandwiched between an older, grim-faced soldier called Hans on one side, and farmers, butchers, bakers and fishermen on the other. Agna had learned enough German to understand what was needed, and how much. Each item was counted, weighed and portioned, when it left, and when it arrived at its destination: bags of flour, sacks of vegetables, chunks of butchered meat. Hans was responsible for the counting and weighing, paperwork, van driving and leaning against walls, smoking. Mose and Agna for the lifting and carrying. Would the Reich's larder never be full?

Occasionally, Agna told me, she and Hans were alone. She declined the cigarettes he offered, even though they were more valuable than coins in your pocket when it came to trade. Everyone knew that.

The business with Hans was never friendly, she told me, in spite of his efforts, but it was polite. Relations with villagers were more difficult. Agna knew she and Mose were accepted, but had never been well liked. Now there were the goings-on with the kommandant. And she, Agna, had led the invaders to *their* island, which had led to this work given to them by the occupier. This work opened a tap that had been dripping for a long time.

First, it was how the villagers addressed them. 'Good morning,' or, 'Good afternoon.' Only ever in response, not with their names.

Then even this stopped. Some folk crossed to the other side of the track to avoid Agna. Others glared.

Nobody was outright rude. Everyone had heard about the woman in Kysten; the girlfriend of a German. Someone called her a Quisling whore in the street and spat at her. Their house had been raided in the night. Three times.

Life went on. Then, in winter, the list of food to find and prepare grew much bigger. In a couple of weeks it doubled, then tripled. Hans and his van were replaced by three soldiers and a truck. They worked just as hard as Agna and her mor.

No one saw the new prisoners arrive. It was assumed they came to Fjernøy on a ship from the north.

Mose and Agna were re-assigned to work on the island. They and a whole gaggle of girls and women from the village were to be ferried to the camp every day with the supplies. This was major news. 'Orders of the government.' We knew that meant anyone refusing would be arrested.

Agna told me all about it. I was curious. She didn't want me to approve, only to understand. And I did. Reports about the island came from the other women and girls too. Everyone wanted to know what was happening there. Some information came that way, but I too eventually worked there, so remember.

The soldiers and prisoners had been busy. Trees had been turned into sentry towers and posts, linked by rows and rows of barbed wire. Behind the wire, the forest had been cleared, leaving a stubble of white wood stumps all the way to a two-metre-high wall of logs, each with its end sharpened to a point. Beyond that, where no Norwegians went, were the tops of huts and trees that had been spared the axe.

The old sheds where we once made jam and smoked fish were now part of an 'administration block' with new kitchens, tin roofs and annexes built with fresh planks that reeked of sap and tar.

Was this Fjernøy? Agna said she tried to remember where the cherry trees and the fire pit had been and found she couldn't. *That* Fjernøy seemed like a dream.

On the first day a Norwegian policeman greeted them outside this administration block, talking in warm tones with a silk smile and with a note, so they would not forget what they had been told.

'Each day a column of prisoners is taken out of the camp to fell trees. Some timber is processed here, some bundled and floated off the island. When this island has been cleared, they will clear others and bring the logs here. Your task is preparing and cooking food and the cleaning of soldiers' quarters and the administration block. You take your orders from Norwegian officers of the administration. Most of you will rarely come into contact with prisoners. Speaking with them is verboten. You will receive wages in the form of ration coupons the amount of which is discretionary.'

'Any questions?' he asked them, waiting barely a second. 'Good!'

'Only ones I don't think you will answer, 'Agna replied, under her breath.

'What was that?'

'Nothing,' Mose said loudly, then in a whisper, 'Be quiet, Agna!'

Agna bit her lip. She was quiet. She told me this was another world, where different creatures lived by different rules. Best to learn them.

As they waited for orders, Agna heard axes in the distance, *thud, thud, thud*, in a heartbeat rhythm. Then a terrible creaking and crashing as a tree fell.

It was two days later she saw the boy for a second time. Not long before lunch she had gone to the latrine hut and sat a while, appreciating the silence and rest. The quiet was disturbed by barked orders and the shuffling of feet, and when she came out, there he was, with a handful of other prisoners, an axe hanging over his shoulder. His hair had been shorn, he was thinner, but his smile and those green eyes were the same.

The prisoners set to ripping up the ground with shovels and pickaxes. A new latrine pit, no doubt. The boy stood, waiting his turn. His smile turned into a grin. Agna didn't know what to do, she half-smiled, then looked at the ground and wondered if he'd seen her smile at all.

A Russian called after her as she walked back to the kitchens. There was laughter. She told herself not to turn, but her body disobeyed. The prisoners laughed even louder. But not the boy.

Now she knew she must go, before her tongue lashed out. The boy said something. The Russian's grin vanished. The others laughed afresh. The Russian went to push the boy in his chest, but the boy swerved and laughed himself.

Agna looked at him. He looked at her. Quickly, Agna walked away, but not so fast that it would look like she was rushing.

Next time Agna saw him was in the kitchens. Part of the hut had rows of benches for cooking meals for soldiers, the other part for preparing prisoners' food.

Agna was in the crew turning groceries into German meals. They were given recipes for sausages, cabbage, meatloaf, potatoes. Various breads to bake. It wasn't fine food, but it was luxury compared to the prisoners' meals, which Mose and some other women prepared.

First, they baked huge loaves, then mixed a stew made with scraps from the German food tables; potato skins, bones, strips of cut-off fat. The amounts were small, so the stew was swelled with more potatoes, oats and water before being boiled to get the most out of the bones. When it was done it was collected by prisoners, along with the loaves.

Agna had just sliced a mountain of onions, stopping every few seconds to wipe tears from her cheeks, and was about to start on a plate of sausages, when a mighty clattering rang through the air. A prisoner had dropped a huge pot. Muddy potatoes scattered. The soldier and policeman on duty shouted at the poor man as he scrambled about picking up the spuds.

'Is their food so awful it makes you cry?' said a voice right by her. There was the boy, walking down the aisle towards the drama. He turned, hands held up, with a look of mock surprise, then threw himself into helping his fellow prisoner.

When the pot was full again, they carried it away.

'Get back to work,' the policeman shouted.

That was impossible. Agna's knife, and the two sausages she had been about to cut, had vanished.

Several questions raced through her mind, she told me later that same day.

How could she quickly cover this crime and find another task?

How had the boy hidden what he had stolen?

Had he and the other prisoner planned this? It seemed a lot of trouble, for sausages.

And how had he spoken Norwegian with no accent?

She saw him almost every day after that. Sometimes taking a case of papers from the policeman and couriering it to the main camp, sometimes carrying piping, a stove door or other equipment, and occasionally in the kitchens; always saluting the uniforms and quick with orders. He often appeared when there was some minor trouble, but at other times vanished as soon as the shouting began. He could stand out, smiling, chest puffed, proud. Other times he would stand with hunched shoulders, part of the huddle, or scuttle along the wall, like a lost squirrel. When the guards were distracted, or off to the latrine, she would catch a glimpse of him. He could be bright in the sunlight, or part of the shadows.

She never *saw* him take anything. But when things went missing, she knew. She gave him a nickname. Nisse.

She saw all this. He rarely seemed to notice her. Yet as they stood on the dock waiting to return home, Mose told Agna, 'You have an admirer.'

'Do I? Who?' she said, dreading that Mor would say one of the uniforms.

'Green eyes.'

'Oh,' said Agna. The smallest word, spoken with as little interest as she could muster.

'Don't pretend. I'm your mother, I've seen you. You can't make friends with them. It's verboten.'

'Forbidden, Mor. *Verboten* is a German word.'

They travelled home in silence. Words sat in Agna's stomach like bad mussels. Words about Mor's chats with the kommandant, words like 'coffee' and 'small cakes.' She forced the words to stay where they were. Unspoken, difficult to digest.

The late autumn of impenetrable mists and ice-needle rain passed. Soon it was winter, with long nights and the earth buried by snow.

One time, after the women had boarded the morning boat to Fjernøy, a squall blew up, the dark air was viciously sharpened by the north wind, the boat heaved through freezing, lashing waves.

Agna worked hard that day, simply to keep warm. When she had to go to the latrine hut, she struggled out of the door, bowing her head against the wind and snow to make the few metres to the hut.

When she came out, there he was, hugging himself, stamping his feet on the ground.

Agna looked at the sentry posts. The helmets of the guards were visible above the walls of the machine gun nests, where the guards huddled on the floor, escaping the wind. She and the boy were alone.

'You speak Norwegian?' she said.

He nodded.

'You have a coat,' she said. 'Why aren't you wearing it? And *how* do you speak Norwegian?' She almost had to shout to make herself heard.

'I am Finnar people. Sami. We crossed the border into Russia, fleeing, then I got conscripted.'

'Finnar? Sami? Not Russian? Why are you talking to me? It could earn you a beating.'

'What?' he said, cupping a hand behind his ear. He moved closer, grabbed her by the lapel and pulled her around the corner in the pocket where the hut met the wall, out of the worst of the wind.

'I said, why are you talking with me?'

He shrugged. 'I like you.'

'You don't know me. I don't know you.'

'Then talk with me and you will know me. I like you.'

'I'm practically the only girl you ever see. Of course you do.'

'You might be the *last* girl I ever see. Anyway, I do know you. A bit. I know you didn't tell.'

She knew this – whatever *this* was – had to be quick. Each second was a coin spent. For a precious moment he looked into her eyes, and she into his.

'Help us,' he said.

'You seem to be doing okay.'

'I'm fine. Others are starving. In there.' He pointed to the main camp.

'You are their workers, why would they starve you?'

'Really? You ask this? Can you bring cigarettes? I can trade with the police for food. Some of the grey caps too. I think the kommandant even allows it. Not the SS, though, and we see them more and more. I can pay you.'

'With what?'

'A kiss?' he said, grinning. Agna stepped back, in case this boy tried to pay her. He laughed. 'Don't worry. We have coins. Some silver.'

'That's crazy, I don't believe you.'

'It's true, I swear.'

'So, buy food with it.'

'Are you that naïve? They'd take it all. We need cigarettes or goods. Can you join the crew who make our food?'

'Ah, *now* I see why you say you like me.' Agna folded her arms and told me she gave him her best shrew eyes.

He looked up at the sentry post.

'I have to go. I'm getting cold. Please help us. Look, take this. A thank you.'

He reached inside his shirt and took out a small figurine: a model of a creature carved from wood.

'I can't.'

'Take it. I have no use for it.'

'Why did you make it?'

'Can you get a letter to the Milorg?'

'I don't know any Milorg.'

'You don't understand. Please!' His smile vanished in the chill air. She saw how he was shaking. Here, now, in a second, was a different boy. 'Please. Pl... please... the cold, it works so fast,' he mumbled, through chattering teeth, his shoulders trembling. 'Please. I have to go...' He held out the figurine.

'I can't.'

He grabbed her lapel again. 'I'm b, b, b... egg... ing you.'

They looked into each other's eyes again. Agna felt the walls around her heart fall.

'Are they *really* starving?'

He nodded. 'Without more food, some will die.'

'Okay,' she sighed. 'I'll try.'

'Thank... you.' He took her hand, placed the figurine in it and closed her fingers around it.

'I will… go… back… first. Wait a minute before… f… f… f… ollow.' He brushed at his arms and shoulders, to rid himself of the evidence of snow. 'Look… Okay?' he said.

'Not quite.' She reached out and skimmed snowflakes off his head. There was that smile again. Then he was off and through the door.

Agna waited. She brushed the tears from her cheek, before they froze.

She told me what happened next that evening. She showed me her bandaged hands. She'd been cutting onions and more tears came, like the last time she'd spoken with the boy, and a storm of voices in her head, she said. All of which were her own.

Is he always this much trouble?

I can't help. I don't know any Milorg.

I said I would try. A promise.

I'm in enough trouble. Are there camps like this where they put girls?

You know men are starving? They will die. He had said it. So matter of fact.

They wouldn't starve their workers. It wouldn't make any sense.

This is my fault. I brought the soldiers here. Everybody knows that.

He likes me.

You are one of the only girls he ever sees.

He is Finnar. The northern folk. Like Pappa.

She tried to recall her last memory of her pappa: her fourth birthday. Pappa leaning down, kissing the top of her head, giving her a toy horse he had fashioned from a piece of driftwood. She had hoped for a dog. 'There wasn't a dog in the wood,' he'd told her. 'You see, the wood tells you what's inside, what spirit needs to be released.'

Now like the cherry trees and fire pit, she could not exactly remember his face, could not pin it down.

As soon as she was by herself, she looked at the figurine the boy had made, and thought of what he had said and—

'Ow!' She returned from her thoughts to the icy kitchen. In her left hand was the knife. Her right hand was white and trembling. A stripe lay across the back of her fingers. Where had that come from?

A dark cherry river trickled over her hand, dripping on the floor.

'I didn't…' The world went dark.

Agna woke in an office she had never been in, sitting in a large desk chair. Her right hand was a bundle of white bandage. Her mor was there and a policeman. Agna's nose filled with the aroma of coffee.

'Drink this,' her mor said. Their own coffee was long gone. Sometimes the kommandant brought some. Mostly they drank pretend coffee made from roasted dandelion roots.

This black gold was not dandelion root.

'What happened in there?' the policeman asked. 'Are you trying to get out of work?'

She shook her head.

'This will take time to heal. One-handed cooks are no good. We'll have to replace you.'

'My hand is okay.' She made her best baby-cow eyes and spoke exactly as she thought a girl who had just fainted should.

'Can I swap with a girl on the prisoner tables? I want to work with my mor. And that work is simpler.'

'Okay, you can count potatoes and stir soup. First you lose a knife, now this. You clearly cannot be trusted with a blade!'

'No.' Agna tried not to smile. 'I can't.'

Liva

I clambered down the steep rocks, on the headland, where the fishing was good, but I had always been forbidden to go. I was older then, almost twelve, and – I thought – a good climber.

I crunched through the banks of snowdrift, careful to place my feet where Agna's boots had been so as not to get caught in an unseen hole. Huffing and panting I reached the shelf of rock, where Agna sat with her rod, next to her bag and a wooden bucket. She stared intently at the orange cork float, bobbing in the pine green deep.

'What are you doing, Agna?'

'Oh, hi, Litenmus. I'm doing my homework.'

'You don't even go to school any more. You're fishing.'

'Well, if it's obvious, why did you ask?'

I shrugged. 'Only making conversation. Is your hand healing?' Agna wore a mitten on her right hand and held the rod in her left.

'I'm fishing, aren't I?' Agna nodded at the bucket.

I peeped inside. 'Oh, you've got a fat beauty there! Just one so far.'

'I'm only keeping the biggest. I need two.'

'What for?'

Agna opened her mouth, paused, then swallowed whatever she had been going to say.

'Um... well... to feed a nisse, who is *very* hungry.'

'I think they prefer chocolates or waffles. You have to hang them from the porch cover so the nisse can get it, but creatures can't.'

'Our chocolate supplies ran out. This nisse will have to do with fish.'

'You need fish? Your mor is friends with the kommandant. You have enough.'

'I told you, it's for a nisse.'

'I'm almost twelve now, don't think I believe in nisse.'

'Well, Litenmus, I am sixteen and I do, so there.'

I sat by Agna, and together we watched the orange cork on the line, bobbing in the calm.

'Thought you weren't allowed down here?' said Agna.

'I'm good at climbing now.'

'Don't let anyone see you talking to *me*. Wouldn't want you to catch whatever it is I've got.'

'I know you are not a traitor.'

'Not a Quisling to be avoided?'

'No. Lots of women go and more would if they could. We all need to eat. Who is the fish really for?'

'I told you, a nisse.'

I sighed. Agna was clearly going to keep this game going.

'How do you know the nisse is hungry?'

'He's too thin.'

'You've *seen* a nisse! What did he look like?'

'Thin. Rather handsome, though. Sea-green eyes.'

'Oh.' I wasn't at all sure why Agna was talking this way. But then, she'd always been unpredictable. 'What will the nisse pay you?'

'He already has. But not with his first offer...' Agna smiled and snorted, sweeping her hair off her face. It was that mischievous smile she always had at school. I had not seen it a long time.

'Not *yet* anyway.' Agna laughed and rubbed her cheek.

'I am not sure I believe this story, Agna.'

'Actually, he *did* pay me. Look.' Agna reached inside her coat and handed me the wooden wolf.

Its eye was a knot in the wood. Its fur, engraved lines along the grain. It had a large open jaw, even tiny fangs. Each line, each cut, had been strengthened by black markings.

'You know how that is done?' Agna said.

'Yes. Pappa does it. You leave a wire or point of a knife in the fire, and burn lines into the wood. He says the Sami from across the north, where they herd reindeer, make the best. Like this.'

I held the wolf, and looked at it, and wondered at its lithe shape and details of its hair and eyes and ears. I hoped Agna might give it to me, just as she gave me the pendant. But she waited patiently till I handed it back.

Suddenly, the cork vanished and Agna yanked the rod. She reeled the fish in easily, and got me to hold the rod while she lifted the fish. Its scales glistened in the light, its mouth gaped and gawped. Its eyes stared.

It was a nice fish. Agna gently took the hook from its cheek and, with her good hand, held it under its stomach, then she leaned down and held it in the water, till it found its strength and swam away.

'Go, silver treasure,' she said. I was surprised how tender she was. Almost loving.

No sooner had Agna thrown the line again than the cork vanished.

This one was a struggle. A fish so big, I had to help again, holding the rod up while Agna reeled in.

We fought till the fish – almost as long my arm – was on land. It flapped and gaped and bounced, threatening to find its way back to the water by sheer force. Agna took a large stone and lifted it high. I looked away, as I always did when Pappa or Haakon caught a fish. But I heard the *thud* and the next, and could not bear to look till it was done. The fish didn't move, or gawp now. Blood ran into the snow and sweat ran down Agna's forehead.

'I'm glad I'm a human not a fish,' I said, then regretted it, because it was a stupid thing to say. Agna didn't laugh.

'It's horrible. I know. We must eat, though. This is kinder. They suffer if you let them suffocate.'

I knew this was true. I also knew I could not do that myself, no more than I could kill a deer, even though I loved to chew on their meat.

'I think the world needs Agnas,' I told her.

'You are very wise, Litenmus,' Agna said with a wink, as she placed the fish in the bucket. 'I have two now, we can go.'

'I hope your nisse is grateful.'

Tove

For weeks we looked at Mose and Agna with envy. They had tobacco, schnapps and chocolate as well as more basic things. Everyone assumed it came from the kommandant, of course, not some secret trade. These things in turn they bartered for whatever they needed: cut logs, a good pot, some plates and cutlery. Anything Mose wanted.

The Germans recruited even more workers, and many were happy to help on Fjernøy. Some women still refused. For a while, at least. It was a question of being practical, or a patriot, you see. Some wanted nothing from the Germans or those that did business with them. They believed the Moses and Agnas of this world were worse than the Germans, who at least were doing their duty for their country.

It came down to getting used to things, to living with how the world was now. Hope of the British saving us was a candle Hitler had blown out. The

Russians were fighting, but losing chunks of their homeland every day and who knows how many of their people. Millions. No one much believed in hope or rebellion, though the news sheets Haakon delivered were full of it as well as – sometimes – bad news. The German air force, the Luftwaffe, had bombed villages in the north, for what reason, or with what excuse, we did not know. The British had done it too, even when their target was in a town. Many ordinary people died, caught between overgrown schoolboys slogging it out.

So, which were we, patriots or collaborators? Pappa was away, we did not know if we would ever see him again. Money was not easy to come by. But Haakon had his bakery delivery and we had his wages. So, when Mose came round, saying work was on offer, Haakon sent her on her way. The second time Mor told Haakon to go inside. Then it was she who said no to Mose. The third time, Mose told Mor the food she and Agna prepared on the island was not for German soldiers, only for the prisoners. And that Russia was in the war, and we should do for them as we would do for our own. On the basis of this, it was not a bad thing to accept the offer of work. Mor said to us after that Mose was having her cake and eating it.

However, Mor had a big heart and saw an opportunity. What else could she do? There was only so much collecting and drying mushrooms, only so much fishing and smoking you can do to plump up the rations. And only so many books you could read. She said yes.

She worked some shifts. It was in January or February, Mor became sick with what we thought, at first, was flu. We needed the provisions her work provided, so Mor told Haakon to help Mose and Agna. There was no shouting or arguing, only folded arms, a tight jaw and a shake of the head. And that was that. Haakon refused.

The policeman came round and said if Mor could not work, she would lose her job, because they would offer it to someone else. He said Liva and I could do Mor's work between us. Mor said Liva was too young, but the policeman said there were a few of her age on the island already. 'I can make it a directive, if I need to. We need workers. Orders of the government.' We had no choice.

That is how Liva and I came to be in the patrol boat heading for Fjernøy with Agna. The soldier Hans piloted the boat, a half-smoked cigarette usually hanging out of his mouth. We sat on iron benches with Agna and Mose and others, or on the boxes and parcels and sacks. Some of the sacks had potato peelings and cut off bits and scraps of fat and I thought they must have pigs on the island. Pigs and goats are a good way to turn things people don't want to eat into meat, milk and cheese.

But Agna told us the way of things.

'We make a stew and reduce it. The bones give up their marrow, the vegetables flavour and onions and herbs infuse.'

'What's infuse?' said Liva.

'Steep, soak, boil the flavour out. Then voilà. Un stew!'

'What's vwa-llah?'

'Never mind.'

'Voilà!' Hans repeated.

'Before, what they had was disgusting, but we have made it better and we bring extra. With a little help, yes, Hans?'

Hans turned from the wheel. 'Ja, es ist gut! Cigaretten, Agna.' Agna took from her coat a cigarette and a lighter. She lit the cigarette, coughed – which made Hans laugh – and handed it to him.

Liva and I did not know what to say or do. Was Agna friends with this soldier?

Before we landed, something else strange happened. From a bucket, Agna took two huge fish that were connected by a string and hooks in their gills. She pulled the string around her neck and hid the hanging fish in the folds of her coat. Then she gave Hans a coin.

We landed and were met by a soldier with a clipboard. Hans took the clipboard and looked up and down it and at the goods being delivered. I could tell by how he spoke that he was assuring the other soldier all was in order.

We worked to put the goods on a cart that was waiting there, and we pushed the squeaking cart through near virgin snow to the gate of the camp. Why they didn't use a sled was beyond me.

We had not been to Fjernøy for a long time. Liva cried, though she tried to hide it.

We did not see prisoners. Apart from the boy with short raven hair and green eyes. The one Agna told me about and who I recognised from the day the prisoners arrived in the village. He helped Agna unload the goods and take them to the benches and stoves in the kitchens.

I looked at the boy, and he saw me, but averted his eyes.

'Agna, Agna,' I whispered, pulling at her coat. 'Why does he not say hello?'

'It is not allowed,' she whispered back.

Most of the goods went to the tables where the soldiers' food was prepared. There it was checked again by another soldier.

The sacks of peel and bones and scraps went to the tables where we worked and into a vat, which the boy filled with water from buckets. On the last trip with the bucket, Agna – like lightning – took her necklace of two fish and dropped it in the bucket. She handed the bucket to the boy, then – with a quick glance round – reached inside her coat and produced a packet, maybe of tobacco, and a small bag, possibly some kind of grain. She dropped these in the bucket and the boy left with it.

All this happened under the noses of the soldiers. I could not understand why they did not wait, because once everything was underway, the soldiers left, and we were supervised by two Norwegian policemen and everything was much more relaxed.

The boy appeared again. Only this time, he did not keep his eyes down, but talked to Agna in Norwegian. I saw what Agna had told me with my own eyes. The look that passed between them that first day had been the seed of something that had grown and flowered. They disappeared at one point, and I went out to the latrine hut and there they were, arms wrapped around each other, kissing and lost to the world. A stolen moment.

'Fools!' I said. 'What if you get caught?' Agna only laughed and they carried on. I looked at the sentry towers, but the soldiers faced the other way. I felt, I admit it, a bit jealous. And afraid for Agna.

In the huts, the boy came and went, quick as mercury, taking orders from the policemen, always saluting them.

At the end of the working day, when we were scrubbing the tables, he took from his pocket, of all things, a toy dog, made of wood and wire. He looked to make sure Liva saw.

He put it on the table.

Each part of the dog was a piece of wood. The parts were joined with wire and some screws. It was not a fine piece of toy making. It was rough, not sanded or painted, but the pieces were well put together.

The boy pushed the dog from behind with his finger, and – a miracle! – it walked.

We were enchanted. Liva went to the table and pushed the dog herself, to make sure it was not a trick. Sure enough, when she pushed, it walked. The boy held his hands up and took two steps back. Was it now Liva's? Could she take it?

'Liva,' I said, 'we have been taught not to take kindness from strangers. All the folk tale stories with that in end badly.'

Liva ignored me, she looked at Agna, who looked at the policeman, who looked at the door to check if any Germans were about to walk in. He glanced at Liva and saw, I think, hope in her face. He nodded, and carefully she picked up the toy.

Agna said something to the policeman, I cannot recall what, and he took a pack of cigarettes from his pocket and offered them to the boy.

Agna watched the doorway that the boy left through for a long time.

'What is his name?' I asked.

'I don't know their names,' said the policeman.

'Then how do you know them? What do you call them?'

'They have numbers stitched here.' He pointed to his chest. 'His friends call him Trickster.'

When our work was done and the food taken away, the tables and floors scrubbed, we walked through the snow, carrying empty boxes and sacks to the cart. I looked behind to make sure Liva was out of earshot.

'Is that all the food they get?' I asked Agna.

'I think so,' Agna said. 'And there are a lot of mouths to feed.'

'I see why you are helping. But it's a dangerous game to play.'

'They are looking for items that go missing, not for anything extra. As long as they can put ticks on their lists, they don't worry. It turns out, in war, almost everyone can be bribed! Who knew?'

'Don't be too clever, Agna. It's a big risk. And why would they work them hard but not feed them well? Would you make a horse pull a plough and starve it at the same time?'

'Tove. These are men, not workhorses.'

'Yes, I'm sorry, but… it doesn't make any sense, does it?'

'No.'

'Can we get them some more food?' said Liva. She was there, a quiet shadow behind us. I should have known better.

'Difficult, Litenmus,' said Agna. 'There is only so much I can do.'

'Then maybe just for the trickster boy?' said Liva.

'Oh, I see,' I said. 'You like him too, because he made a toy you are too old to play with anyway.'

'Oh, it's not *me* that is sweet on this nisse.' Liva tried not to snigger.

Agna huffed. 'What I can get hold of is not much. Not enough, he says. In any case this is why he made the dog. It's a kind of thank you. A sort of payment.'

'Haakon can get more food!' said Liva.

I gave her a look then, so stern. To shut her up. But Agna saw. The cat was out of the bag. And no way to put it back. She opened her mouth, I think to ask us how – exactly – Haakon might get food, but closed it, nodded and smiled.

'The news sheets. I did think it might be Haakon. *He* is Milorg.'

No one said anything after that.

I had been correct. Liva was too old to play with the toy. After all, it only did one thing. You pushed it and it walked.

All the same, she did play with it, at home. She kept pushing it, watching it. Each leg was in two parts, which moved like a real dog's. But how?

Were there cogs inside, secret wires she could not see?

She wanted to take it apart to see but then it would be broken and the magic would not work.

Liva

We sat on logs around the fire in the clearing. Haakon, Tove, Agna and me. Our house was small. A wonderful home, with the furniture Pappa had made and the few books we had, and we made our own games or sewed or knitted. We never stopped making things and trading with them. Yet even a home can feel too small a place. We went to the clearing often.

Agna told Haakon about the camp and the boy who had given me the wooden dog. About the food for the prisoners. Tove sat in silence, her arms folded and a frown on her face.

'What has this to do with me, or with the Milorg?' said Haakon.

'I thought you might be able to help?' said Agna.

'I told her no, already,' said Tove 'A hundred times.'

Haakon looked at each of us in turn. Tove shrugged. I shut my mouth and eyes, waiting for a storm to erupt. But it didn't. Haakon only sat warming his hands. When he spoke, it was in a quiet voice.

'Who else knows about me?' He looked at Agna. 'Don't look away. Who else?'

'No one. There are rumours. People guess. They guess all sorts of things about all sorts of people. It's like a game. Nobody wants to endanger anything. Or anyone. Do you not see? Most do not *want* to know. Not really. Knowing is dangerous.'

'Who. Else?'

'I honestly don't know. I only know *I* have not told anyone.'

'What about your mor?'

'Of course not. She takes coffee with the kommandant.'

'Do you know what will happen if I am discovered?'

I put my hands over my ears. 'Please, Haakon. Don't.'

Haakon gently pulled my hands from my ears.

'Little sister. This isn't a fairy story where you are excited to hear it, then cover your ears when we get to the bits that scare you. You should go home.'

I shook my head fiercely. Then Haakon stood over Agna.

He took off his glove, spat in his hand and held it out.

'Swear,' he said. 'You will tell no one.'

Agna looked up at him a time before speaking. 'Do I *need* to, Haakon?'

Haakon sighed. He shook his head, wiped his hand on his trousers and sat back down.

I wondered why Haakon was not angry. He seemed sad and somehow this was worse.

'Now, why did you drag me here? To tell me you are smuggling food? I will let my superiors know.'

'We can work together,' Agna said. This surprised Haakon. He almost laughed.

'*I* don't get to decide who works for the Milorg, or what they do. I don't even know who *I* work for higher up, only my contact. It works that way or not at all. That is that.' He stood. 'Don't be late back, girls.'

I expected Agna to plead then, to make Haakon listen. But she shrugged.

'Please yourself. See you later. Probably best you don't overhear our plans.'

He turned. 'Plans? You don't have any plans. Understand?'

'If you like. Bye.'

Haakon strode back to the fire, pointing his finger in Agna's face.

'Whatever you are thinking, my sisters are *not* involved. Understand *that*?'

'See, Agna?' said Tove. 'I told you he would say this. Now you hear it.' Tove got to her feet. 'Come on, Liva.'

But I stayed put and shook my head.

'Liva?' said Haakon. 'You want to join the Milorg?'

'I want to help. I want *you* to help.'

'Come home.'

'Nu-uh!'

Everyone was a statue. We waited, to see what Haakon would do. He looked at the sky and rolled his eyes.

'Okay, I will listen.' He sat down again, rubbing his hands. 'I am all ears, Agna. But, Liva, go home.'

'Nope.' I folded my arms.

'NOW!'

I sniffled and sat stubbornly but Haakon knew all he had to do was wait. Eventually I marched off. 'I *hate* you, Haaky!'

I waited a while before I crept back through the shadows, making myself part of the dark and silence. There was no wind, and their low voices travelled.

Agna told Haakon about the food, how it was prepared, how she smuggled rations into the sacks, how she bribed Hans and the police.

'If you can get more food, I can get it in. Easy. Please help.'

Haakon *had* listened, more intently than he ever had listened to Miss Bridget at school, nodding here and there, grimacing in parts, smiling when Agna told him how easy it was to bribe Hans.

'Well?' said Agna. 'What do you think?'

'I listened. I said I would. Here is what I think. You are crazy. The Milorg won't risk this, they have other work to do.'

'True!' Tove agreed.

'Haakon, Tove. They work them dawn to after dusk. The prisoners are going to starve to death.'

'They wouldn't do that,' said Haakon. 'They are not stupid. They need them to work.'

'Everyone says that. But you don't know them. The SS. They are different. You should come, see for yourself.'

'I can't. Look, I will make sure my superior is aware, but we can be sure the Milorg probably already know what is happening. You are not the only girls at the camp. That's all I can do.'

'Then... nothing will change.'

Haakon sighed. 'Are any of them Norwegian?'

'One, called Sergei, is Sami, Or maybe half-Sami. A couple of others too. I think the others are Russians.'

'Then there is nothing I or anyone can do. Be home soon, Tove.'

Haakon left Tove and Agna in silence. Eventually, Tove stood.

'I told you, Agna. And now you know.'

Lessons

Winter 1943

Tove

We were a small village. Knocks at the door came with friendly voices.

'It's me,' whoever it was would say. 'I've come to borrow your axe, coffee…' Some such thing.

We knew each person by how they knocked. A knock we didn't know meant only one thing…

I was knitting with Mor. I can't remember where Liva was. I opened the door, just enough to stick my head out to see the kommandant and a grey cap standing on the porch. Oddly, the soldier wasn't carrying a rifle.

'Yes?' I said, wondering, *Is this about Haakon? Thank god he is not here.*

'I speak your mother,' the kommandant said.

'She is not well.'

'It's okay, sweetheart.' Mor pushed me gently aside, wrapping her coat tight around herself to cover her nightdress.

'You shouldn't be up,' I said, holding her hand.

'I'm okay,' said Mor. But her hand was cold and her skin too pale. When she spoke, she wheezed.

The kommandant took off his cap. He waited. No one moved or said anything. He looked about and pointed at an old crate by the wood store, which the soldier fetched for him to sit on.

'As you will not invite, this my office.'

'You should not come close anyway,' I said. 'Mor is not well.'

'Please, you get chair for her sit.'

'There is no need,' said Mor.

'I will be quick. Why is your girl not to school? She is camp work, and young.'

'You mean Liva? We need the money. Besides, school is in Kysten. It is a long walk, or a boat ride. In the snow the children only go if one of your Norwegian police friends takes them on a boat. We can't take them as we did before.' Mor held her chin high, speaking in as unfriendly a voice as I've ever heard.

'Before? Ah, before we came?'

'Yes, I... *hacch.*' Mor coughed. She tried and failed to stop herself coughing more and had to bury her face in the folds of her coat.

'Mor. Enough, you must rest.' I looked at the kommandant with pleading eyes. 'She must.'

'Hmm, how much time she has this flu?'

'Not long,' said Mor. 'Tove, go inside.'

'You see doctor?' he asked.

'It is only a cold. Tove, inside.'

'She won't go,' I blurted. 'She says she can't be ill.' I put a hand over my mouth, to stop more words. Then whispered, 'Sorry, Mor.'

'I can look,' said the kommandant.

Another silence followed, in which Mor and I glared at each other, at the kommandant then back at each other.

'What?' said Mor. 'Did you... say?'

'I can look. Er... understand sickness.'

I gasped. Mor reached to the lapels of her coat and pulled them ever tighter around her neck.

'You. Are. Not. A doctor,' she exclaimed.

A wry smile crept across the kommandant's face.

'I was. Before army.'

Mor coughed again and squeezed my hand tight.

'No! Thank you. And why are you asking about my other daughter and school?'

'Because now she must go. Girl, put your mother bed. I will come here back soon. It is an order.'

The kommandant said something in German to the soldier, who nodded and saluted. Then the kommandant left, leaving Mor and me with the soldier, who sat on the crate, smiling.

Not knowing quite what to do, we went inside, stoked the fire and sat by the stove in gloomy silence.

When the kommandant returned he ordered the soldier to stay outside. He opened the front door himself, put his leather case down, removed his cap, boots and jacket, and put on glasses I had never seen him wear before. From the bag he took a stethoscope and a thermometer.

He took Mor's temperature then used the stethoscope on her chest and back. He put a hand to Mor's forehead, and asked her questions about how difficult she found it to breathe, to walk, if she thought she could run if she had to, what she ate, how much liquid she drank and many other questions.

When he was done, he put his jacket and cap back on.

'I cannot penicillin, it is for soldiers but I will, ahh! German is *verschreiben*.'

'Prescribe?' I offered.

'Yes. I will prescribe Sulfonamide. Your brother is work in Dallansby, I think. He will collect. She must soup drink, rest. Here…' He took from his bag a bottle of aspirin and gave it to me.

'Now, the other girl.'

'My sister?'

'Yes, this is business today. She will to school on boat. Two days each week. This is the least. She will still work camp also.'

Mor, who had not spoken, other than curt answers to his question, said, 'Why do *you* care if she goes to school?'

'*Mor!*' I whispered.

The kommandant smiled as he opened the door. 'I do not. It is orders from Berlin and from your Quisling in Oslo. We tell all families.'

Liva

All us pupils arrived at the dock and dutifully filed on to the boat. The youngest was seven, the oldest thirteen.

'How is Miss Bridget?' I asked Henrik, because I had not seen her for a few weeks. 'What are you – *we* – learning?'

'The usual,' said Henrik.

I asked more questions, but didn't get answers. Everyone was quiet, the mood on the boat was cold and damp as the morning air.

'What's *up* with you all?' I said. Miss Bridget always worked us, but unless there was a test set and we were cramming, the boat ride was a time for comparing lunches, discussing homework and making plans to get one over on the Kysten children in some way.

'Nothing's up,' said Henrik. He made a play of wiping his nose, and with his finger secretly pointed at the policeman piloting the boat.

'Oh. Well, how is Miss Bridget?' I said, more quietly.

'She is well.' Henrik glared at me, so I zipped my mouth and turned my face to the sea to watch the inlets, cliffs and waves. This was pleasant, because I had not been anywhere or seen anything other than the village and the camp on Fjernøy for a while, and in Kysten there were other children from the village and from the farms and hills too.: Enemies in snowball fights, rivals in football, skiing or orienteering. Sources of knowledge.

As soon as we landed and were out of earshot of the policeman I started on Henrik.

'What's going on?'

'It's all changing. You'll see. Be careful what you say and not only in front of the grown-ups.'

We filed into the schoolhouse, an ancient building of dark pine, with a dusty classroom of wooden desks, a blackboard, huge open fire and two cupboards, one of which had a piece of driftwood hanging from a nail on its door, painted with the word: *Library*.

We busied ourselves taking off coats and satchels, and collecting pencils and paper. Miss Bridget stood by the blackboard with another woman I did not know. Both had their hair in blonde buns and wore beautifully knitted cardigans and long skirts. They could have been sisters. This new woman was smiling and nodding and saying, 'Good morning.' Miss Bridget, who was usually cheerful as spring sun and chirpy as a blackbird (that was her nickname), stared at the floor, with her hands clasped in front of her.

'Miss Bridget!' I called.

'Liva!' She walked fast down the aisle between the rows of desks, put her arms around me and squeezed tight. I froze in shock. I had never seen Miss Bridget hug *anyone*.

She stepped back and said, 'It's so *good* to see you. I swear you've grown.'

'I've been working, I'm pleased to see you too, Miss Bridget. Who is that wo—' But Miss Bridget walked quickly back to the front of the class. She was acting strangely. And so was everyone else.

We took our places in silence. I sat at the back like always, near the library.

There was no, 'Hush now, for goodness' sake!' No, 'Settle down!' No, 'Quiet, please!' No, 'If you work there will be a story from the library.'

Instead, 'Good morning, children. It's lovely to see you, especially those I have not seen for some time. I am very pleased you are resuming your education.'

It was Tove who had given Miss Bridget her nickname, the blackbird. Now, her voice was dull and grey.

'This is Miss Hildur, she is a new teacher.'

We had heard rumours from other places, of 'new teachers'. There had even been a teachers' strike the year before. None of that had happened here, in our backwater.

'Good morning, children,' said Miss Hildur.

'Goooood... moooorning, Miss Hildur,' we replied, in a flat, slow chorus.

'Oh, surely we can do better than that?' said Miss Hildur. 'Good *morning*, children.'

'Good *morning*,' we chanted.

'That is better. Now, Miss Bridget has something to tell you.'

Miss Bridget lifted her head and smiled.

'That is correct, first we must make Miss Hildur welcome. She has come all the way from Oslo, *just* to teach you. You are lucky, because now you have two teachers. Miss Hildur will be your main teacher, and I will visit once a week, to teach maths and geography and... yes, Lars.'

Little Lars had his hand in the air. 'Wh... what will y... y... you do the rest of the time?'

'I am giving private tuition in Dallansby. Now, does anyone have any questions?' The two women scanned the room, looking for hands.

'Surely you must have some questions?' said Miss Hildur. 'Where is this insatiable curiosity Miss Bridget has told me so much about?'

No one raised a hand for a long time, but eventually Hannah did, as she always did, with her sparkling eyes and front-row keenness.

'Yes, Hannah,' said Miss Bridget.

'What is it like in Oslo, Miss Hildur?'

'Hannah!' said Miss Bridget. 'That is not school business.'

'That's okay, Miss Bridget,' said Miss Hildur. 'The city is thriving. Imports of all kinds of goods, chocolate from France, cheese from Holland...'

As Hannah and the new teacher chatted, I took the opportunity to slip a sheet of paper on to my lap, scribble on it, and pass it to Henrik.

Why is she leaving us?

Henrik shrugged.

'Now,' said Miss Hildur. 'We will begin today with history. You, at the back... yes, you two, what are your names?'

'Liva and Henrik, Miss Hildur,' said Henrik.

'Well, Liva and Henrik, in the cupboard you will find a crate of new books. Please give a copy to each student.'

'We don't need to share, miss?' said Henrik.

'No.'

We rose from our desks and went to the cupboard.

'No!' Miss Hildur shouted. 'Not that cupboard, the other one.'

'Oh, that's not a cupboard, Miss,' I explained. 'That's the library.'

'Actually, I do mean that one.'

I opened the door. Most of the books that once filled the shelves were gone. A few remained on the two top shelves. The floor was filled with boxes.

I looked at Henrik for some explanation, some reaction, but he just glared at me, before lifting a box, opening it and handing out books.

'Liva,' said Miss Hildur. 'Please help Henrik.'

There were many copies of the book. More than enough for the school. These books smelled fresh, their spines were uncreased, their covers (showing a map of Europe) were not faded by sun and age.

I did what I was asked to. And thought better of asking where all the story books had gone. But as Miss Hildur read the first page, I thought of nothing else.

Facts and dates were written on the blackboard, passages from the book read aloud, in turn by the keener students. Miss Bridget sat and watched Miss Hildur teach. And I watched Miss Bridget and thought she looked sad. Afterwards I couldn't remember a single thing we had been taught. My mind burned with questions I dared not ask.

At the end of the lesson, Miss Bridget said goodbye, telling us she would be back in a few days to do some maths. There were some playful groans at this.

'Oh, come on, children,' Miss Bridget said, forcing a smile. 'You know the trade. If I hear you have been good, I will read a story, I promise.'

But from what book? I thought.

There were some cheers at this. I watched Miss Bridget leave. She looked directly at me and smiled.

The next lesson was grammar, which I hated as much as I loved stories.

At the end, before she let us go outside, Miss Hildur said, 'Thank you, children, for your warm welcome and for being so well-behaved. Later there will be a story.

You are all good Norwegian children. Heil.' Miss Hildur raised her arm in the same way the soldiers did to greet their senior officers.

I felt a twist of strange, cold sickness in my stomach. The school room swam in front of my eyes. I could not understand what I saw. But some of the children, like mechanical puppets, raised their arms, mirroring Miss Hildur's salute.

Miss Hildur stood stock still, a gentle smile on her lips, as she looked around. She didn't speak, only stood there, with her arm stuck in the air. Time froze.

'Lars,' Miss Hildur said. Little Lars raised his arm. So did all the others, till there was only me and Henrik left.

'*Do it!*' Henrik whispered in the lowest possible whisper. I shrugged, and as though my arm had a will of its own, it raised in the air.

'Good,' Miss Hildur said. 'You can go and play now.'

I stood, ready to make for the door, but Miss Hildur said; 'Liva, please stay.' The others left, without looking at me.

Miss Hildur walked down the aisle and I seized up tight, not knowing what to expect. She walked past me to the cupboard that was once the library, returned and sat on Henrik's chair. She put a book on my desk. I knew it well, though it was a new edition, not the battered copy with the pages falling out that I was used to. It was *Grimm's Fairy Tales.*

'Liva,' Miss Hildur said softly. 'Are you okay? I know how much you love Miss Bridget and this is a big change. She is the only teacher you have ever had. But she is not going anywhere. She has told me so much about you. You are a promising student. She tells me you have a *wild* imagination.' Miss Hildur's eyes flared. Her mouth contorted into a mischievous grin. 'She tells me that you are strong-willed and clever. These are wonderful qualities. We are in difficult times, but these times will not last. And when we come out of this, we will be more powerful. Norway is going to be a very important country in the future, more than Britain, more than France. We will need young women like you.

'As I say, I know this is all new. But you will adapt. I know too how much you love stories. Nothing is going to change in that regard. You know this book, don't you? Isn't it your favourite?'

I only looked at Miss Hildur and felt unsure what to say. Or do.

'Well, isn't it?' said Miss Hildur.

'Yes.' That wasn't true. I did love it. But my favourite was the book of Nordic tales. I nodded. I forced a smile.

'Good. Why don't you choose which we get to read before home time?'

'Okay,' I said, trying to work out what to say that would get me away from Miss Hildur as fast as possible.

'Briar Rose, the sleeping beauty,' I said.

'Oh, my favourite too. Good, now go outside and… what is that you are playing with?'

I was holding my wolf pendant and rubbing it. I hadn't noticed I was doing it.

'Oh, nothing,' I said. I got up, and at the door, as Miss Hildur walked to the front of the class, took my satchel and my coat.

In the yard I headed straight for Henrik.

'I *told* you,' he said. 'Play along. If you don't, you'll get in trouble. There are snitches.' He looked at the other children; two boys wrestling in the snow, some girls playing chase. Others, in a group, talking.

'Sure. I think I can guess who. Do you know where Miss Bridget lives?'

'No, why?'

I marched up to two Kysten sisters, whose father had once paid Pappa to fix his boat. 'Do you know where Miss Bridget lives?'

'In a cottage on the hill road.' The girl pointed to the bottom of a steep dirt road that snaked up the large hill overlooking Kysten.

'Thanks.'

'Where are you going?' Henrik called as I walked out of the gate. 'Class starts soon.'

I turned, but kept going.

'Better get to it, then. Tell her I had to rush home. Tell her I got a young woman's stomach ache. And be *really* embarrassed about it,' I said, raising my arm to the air. 'Heil, Miss Hildur!'

'Hallo, Liva,' said Miss Bridget. 'Shouldn't you be at school?'

I shrugged.

'Can I come in?' I said.

'You better had.'

Miss Bridget fed larch logs into the stove, and I sat beside it, warming my hands while Miss Bridget prepared a pot of tea.

'A treat,' I said.

'I got it from the mother of a pupil in Dallansby. There is a market for Norwegians learning German. Which is ironic, because most of those that do speak it pretend they don't. It makes life that bit tougher for the Nazis.' She sighed as she spooned tea into the pot. 'And there is a market for Germans learning Norwegian.'

'You teach the Germans!'

'No.' Miss Bridget smiled. 'Not yet anyway. I hide that I speak German from *them*. Even Miss Hildur doesn't know I speak it. Milk in your tea? Honey? I've got some stored, don't tell anyone,' she said with a wink.

'Loads of both, please. It was Miss Hildur I wanted to talk about. I'm not going to her stupid lessons.'

Miss Bridget paused, holding a spoon of honey, letting it drip into the cup. She spoke slowly and calmly, all the time watching the spoon.

'Now listen to me, and carefully, because this is the most important thing I will ever teach you, Liva. You will return to school after this cup of tea and you will do everything Miss Hildur asks. You will learn and you will do well. You are clever and I want you to have the best education.'

'Then *why* won't *you* teach us?' The words sounded harsher than I meant them to.

Miss Bridget put the pot to the side of the stove, to let the tea brew. She pulled up another chair and sat opposite me.

'I don't need to ask myself if I can trust you, Liva, and that's rarer these days than it should be. So, I am going to be honest. I will teach maths and geography. However, I don't like the rest of what they want me to teach. Their nonsense. That is why. We've escaped their curriculum so far, but now their fingers reach everywhere.'

'But you're happy for me to learn this "nonsense"?' I said, folding my arms.

'No. Anything but. Look, it's complicated, Liva. If you don't go back to school you'll get in to a lot of trouble.'

'Henrik is covering for me. I'm not going back.'

'Liva, I don't mean today. You must go at least twice a week, like they say. Do this, for me. Please.'

'Why? If you don't like what they teach, why would you want me to learn it?' Miss Bridget knew I was a cat after fish bones when I wanted an answer.

She poured the tea and we each had a cup.

'You are smart enough to see past it. Not everyone is.'

'Are you sure? I work in their camp. When I leave school if I want a good job, I'll have to join them. So, what is the point of my education? Because I never will join them.'

'Bide your time, young lady. Don't put yourself in danger unless it really matters. Unless you have no choice.'

'Oh, so there is a time for that?'

'I know you, Liva. I know your family too.'

This was an odd thing for Miss Bridget to say. She looked at me in a way that was difficult to read. As if she was a bit amused. As if she knew something. Did she know about Haakon? Of course, I could not ask.

'Look.' Miss Bridget went to another room, and came back with my true favourite book, the Nordic folk tales. She opened the book and for a second I thought she was going to read a story. Inside, like a bookmark, was a brown sheet of paper, which she handed to me. It was a news sheet. The kind Haakon delivered. It was addressed: *To the teachers of Norway*. I read it. It was about the strike.

'It's from last year,' Miss Bridget said. 'But like I said, it didn't affect us here. Not then.'

'What is a strike exactly?' I said.

'The Milorg requested we refuse to teach their ways in subjects such as history. Then if they got heavy-handed, teachers were supposed to refuse to teach altogether. If one person does it, they can deal with them. If many do, it's more of a burden. So, there may be another strike.

There will be a time to resist. Maybe even for you children too. But you must bide your time. Don't stick out, Liva, don't be an Agna. Yes, I heard about her. She plays with danger as if it's a toy. For now, be a shadow creature, like in the books. Be hidden. Above all, be safe. When you are grown up, if you want to rebel, rebel all you want. But now you are still a child.'

'No, I'm not. What if it's too late by then? It's not only grown-ups resisting. It's some of us youngsters.' I burned with wanting to tell her about Agna and Sergei, the Russian boy, and Haakon too. I wondered what Miss Bridget might tell me in return.

'There'll come a time, Liva, we'll have cake as well as tea, and then we will have a good old gossip about what went on in the war. In the meantime, be a shadow creature.'

I took the book from Miss Bridget. I ran my fingers over its cracked cover, its worn, once golden lettering, that was now only a fine trace of yellow dust. I ran my fingers over the ruffle of pages where the leaf edges met. I sniffed it, the dry dusty smell.

'You used to call this *the door to other worlds*, Miss Bridget. Is this now banned?'

'Verboten? Yes.'

'Did you rescue it?'

'Yes.'

'What about the other books from the library?'

'Gone.'

'Where?'

'They took them to Dallansby, with similar books from other schools. They have a list.'

'What do they do with them?'

'Burn them.'

I gripped the book tight, as though invisible hands might tear it from me and hurl it into the flames of the stove.

Then, carefully, I opened its pages. It fell open on my favourite story: the Ash lad who fooled the troll. It was as if the book itself remembered me.

I felt sick and cold. Angry.

'They can't,' I said. But as soon as I did, I thought, *Of course, they can.*

'Why, Miss Bridget? They are *just* stories?'

'Stories are the most dangerous thing of all. More than guns and bombs. Look at that one you opened. A small boy defeats an evil troll. They don't want anyone getting ideas. It's not only about stories, it's who wrote them. It has stories from the Sami people, from gypsies. There's a Yiddish tale or two in there too. Jewish. You know what they think about Jews.'

'Could you be arrested even for having it?'

'As crazy as it sounds, yes.'

'There has been too much, Miss Bridget. Pappa, the invasion, the camp. They have everything they could want, why do they want this?' I held the book, looking at it as if it was an alien thing; something I had never seen before.

'I said, stories are dangerous. They don't only want our land, Liva, they want our dreams.'

'They are not having mine. Can I take it?'

'What?'

I held the book tight to my chest. 'Please?'

'Absolutely not!'

'You said there is a time to say no to authority. I'm taking it. I am a shadow creature,' I said. 'I'll hide this. It's safer with me than a trouble-making teacher.'

'Hmm... Well...'

'Everyone can do something, Miss Bridget. This is *my* something. Anyhow, I'd best get back to school.'

'You are going?' she said, her voice rising with hope.

'Yes, I... No, I cannot lie. I am not.' I went to the door, popped the book in my satchel and put my coat on.

'Liva.'

'Yes, Miss Bridget.'

'Be careful.'

'You too. You are brave.'

'Not really. Whoever delivered that news sheet, *he* is brave. Um... assuming it is a *he*, of course.' Miss Bridget smiled. I opened my mouth, then shut it and smiled back.

I wondered if I would come back to Miss Bridget's cottage. Or was the cake and tea and gossip a dream that the Nazis had already taken?

'Miss Bridget, do you think we will ever beat them? We are not the Ash lad, they are not the troll. They are more than us, they have more and better weapons. They mean business.'

Miss Bridget nodded. 'You really must go, but let me tell you a quick story, Liva.

'Norway, Liva, is a small country. But very proud.

'When the world decided on an international sports competition called the Olympics, we sent a team. We did not do well, of course. But we tried. Then, in the 1920s some bright spark made a different competition, an Olympics only for the winter sports. Norway did very well.

'Now, some short time ago, before this mess began, my father was tasked with finding the Olympic champions of tomorrow. A team of orienteers you will know well, called the Young Wolves. They are excellent map readers and skiers, and can cross the most hostile terrain, in the harshest weather, in the quickest time.

'My father held a contest for the boys in this region. The best, and those who believed they were the best, came forward. The most experienced, the smartest, the fittest, the strongest, the bravest.

'These would-be Wolves set off at intervals, each with a map and a compass, a rucksack and skis. You know how it works, they reach checkpoints, are given new coordinates and set off again.

'On this particular day there was some discussion about the weather. It wasn't only cold, the heavy snow made visibility difficult, the wind bit through your clothes and into the bones. It was almost called off, but my father said as long as they had stewards, and not only at the checkpoints, they should run the race.

'Two of the best, who you might think would win, did so.

'My father still had three places to fill for his training team. The next to complete the course and make the set time was in the team. Everyone cheered when my father confirmed it.

'But the next boy crossing the line asked why he was not congratulated. My father said, "Because I have not decided on the other places yet."

'"I came next!" the boy shouted. He complained to *his* father, who took it up with *my* father.

'"Very well," my father said, after they had argued a while. "I have decided, he is not in the team."

'"What! What happened?" the boy's father complained.

'"Something he and you did not expect. And look how he reacted. Such a character does not make for a good Wolf."

'The boy who came next was very fit and very experienced. In the end, he did not make the team either. My father said he was good, but his result was based simply on the amount of practice and training he had, and it did not mean much, because his father had made him do these things from a young age. It was experience and expectation that put him in the top five, not talent.

'The other boys came in. Some very late. Once they lost the track or got too slow, some believed they would for sure not make the team. They carried on, so they would not look bad. Others quit. The weather was getting worse.

'There was a boy who was only just old enough to enter. He failed to make the minimum time for consideration. He turned up at each checkpoint. The people there patted him on the back, and said he had done well, but he was the last and had nothing to prove. He should stop there. But the boy said no.

'Eventually he crossed the line.

'"I would have done much better," he panted. "I got badly lost. Twice." He was exhausted. To find his way back on track, he had clawed through frozen mud and climbed rocks. His trousers were torn, his knees bloody. His face so dirty, it was easy to see where the tears had run.

'Worst of all, his rucksack had cut into his shoulders with all the sweat. They had to peel his clothes off his back.

'My father asked the boy, "Why did you carry on, when you knew you had lost?"

'The boy shrugged. He was too young to know himself.

'He made the team, much to the annoyance of boys who were fitter, more experienced, better with a map and compass and had better placings. He had other qualities.'

'Is that the end of the story?' I asked.

'Yes.'

I thought on this. 'And is this how *we* might win, Miss Bridget? Is that the point of your story?'

'No, Liva, I do not know how we might win. Or if. I only know for sure how we might lose. When we were invaded, the king declared war. He knew we were going to lose. That the Nazis would occupy Norway. Everyone did. But we fought anyway.'

I did not return to Miss Hildur's classroom.

I thought of the book in my satchel, and felt a thrill, knowing I was carrying contraband; a book full of mischievous nisse, cunning wolves and enchanting huldra. Stories of tyrant kings and pretty, spoiled princesses. Ravens and wolves who could talk and make magic, trolls who were powerful bullies. And sprites and simple peasant folk who survived the most awful trials. Sometimes by doing terrible things. Liars, thieves, even murderers.

When I got home, Haakon was outside, chopping larch logs. These were good because you did not need to season the wood before you burned them.

'How was school?' he asked.

'They've got a Nazi teacher.'

'Oh. Here too, then?'

'Yes. I'm not going back.'

'Ha! Let's see what Mor says about that. You have to go, if they say. You don't have to listen to the teachers, though. I didn't, and that was before they were Nazis!' he said, swinging his axe, splitting a huge log.

'I went and saw Miss Bridget at her house. She's giving private lessons now.'

'The blackbird? How much did she charge you?' Haakon joked.

'Nothing. Anyway, she didn't give me a lesson, she told me a story. Talking of stories...' I took the book from my satchel. 'We have to keep this safe; can we do that?'

'Sure.' Haakon shrugged, as if it was nothing. 'I remember those stories. Same ones, again and again.'

'This was a good one. I hadn't heard it before. Not this version, anyway.'

'What was it about?'

'You.'

Night

Late winter 1943

Tove

Agna and Haakon sat on logs in the clearing, holding bread on sticks, turning it to toast on the embers.

Liva and I had been running an errand but stopped when we saw the two of them walk along the path into the woods.

My first thought was to call out. But I knew that no matter the reason they were skulking into the woods together, they would say it was not our business.

Well, I told myself, *I'll* make *it my business.* So, we followed carefully, before leaving the path and arcing into the shadow of deep woven branches on the hill that overlooked the clearing. Why did we do this? Liva was just inquisitive, and I didn't want Haakon getting in trouble. And Agna *was* trouble.

Even though it was the clearing and even though it was dark, they spoke in low voices. We crouched, close as we dared and cupped hands behind our ears.

'Do you miss your far?' Agna said. 'Have you heard from him?'

'Of course. Do you miss yours?' Haakon said, answering only the first question.

'Yes. Though I don't remember him much.'

They were sitting beside each other, their coats not quite touching. When Haakon looked at her, she looked at the fire, and when she looked at him, he did the same, as though they were shy. Was this romance? This thought was immediately followed with another: *what about Sergei?* Loyalties pulled at my heart like trolls heaving ropes in a tug of war. Intrigue sparked in my head like fireworks. I took another – oh, so careful – step, forward, gently lowering my foot, to be sure not to snap any twigs.

'Can your man help?' Agna said. 'If we need him?'

'For what?'

'I'm not exactly sure yet, answer the question.'

Haakon shrugged. 'I've sent messages and reports up the line. I never get a reply. From what I hear, the Milorg are clear they are not a post service. Why the questions?'

'There's activity, in the night. Your house isn't near the dock so you wouldn't hear. A truck comes at dusk and parks. In the morning, it's gone. It's happened a few times. The other night I heard a boat's chugging engine. I think it stopped, out at sea. But fifteen minutes or so later the truck engine started up. There have been lorries and trucks in the night before, but rarely; now there is a pattern. The truck arriving, the boat, then the truck. It happened twice last week.'

'It's worth checking. Could be something or nothing. What's it to do with the Milorg?'

'I have a feeling, Haakon. A terrible feeling.' She looked at him and did not look away when he returned the gaze.

'What do you think it is?'

'I don't want to say. I just think the Milorg should know. It's so quiet, whatever it is. There's none of the usual shouting, and all in the dead and dark of night. It's not nothing. I feel it in my bones. Someone should look. It's difficult for me, because…'

'The kommandant and your mor?'

'He… he stays sometimes.' Agna's head sank to her chest.

'You're burning your toast!' Haakon took Agna's stick off her and blew on the bread. 'Look, I'll sneak out late, set up a lookout in the woods. Then report whatever I see up the line.'

'I didn't want to ask… you. But…. I can do an earlier shift, you know, if *he*'s not around. You'll freeze to death after a couple of hours if you're not moving, no matter what you are wearing, so we'll have to do it between us.'

Haakon nodded.

'Like I say, we can take shifts, two hours each.'

'Me too,' Liva said.

Haakon stood and fell, staggering back over the log into the snow. Agna shrieked.

Liva walked into the clearing. With me following, and angry at her.

'You imp,' Agna cursed and shook her fist. 'You scared us to death.'

'I can, though.'

'No way!' Haakon and Agna said together.

'You'll get yourselves killed,' I said.

'You going to help us, Tove?'

'No!'

They all stared at me. I started to walk away. They didn't say anything, that was the worst thing. The silence itself was an accusation.

'Come home, Liva.'

'No.'

'You are all insane. And stupid. And pointless and… and…'

'Will you help us?' said Haakon.

I sighed. 'I will help you not get caught. No more than that.'

It took a day to gather and hide supplies and clothes without our mors noticing. The day after that, Haakon and Agna made a hideout with branches and logs in the woods above the rocks looking down on the small bay, careful only to work when there were no boats or soldiers about.

Haakon took the first shift next night. Agna tried to stay awake, waiting for the front doot to close, so she would know the kommandant had left. But the night wore on and she couldn't keep her eyes open.

She told us later that she rose, dressed quietly and picked up the supplies she had hidden in the broom cupboard. She was grateful the kommandant had been this evening, because there was a third-empty bottle of some dark spirit on the kitchen table, and she could hear her mor snoring. Only, when she reached the door, she saw his boots still on the mat. She almost vomited, and wished she *would*, right into his bloody boots. Answering Mor's questions as to why she was out was one thing. Answering his would be quite another.

A blanket of cloud hid the moon. There wasn't a whisper of sound, or anything moving. Only the short bursting clouds of her breath. Agna met me as we'd planned. I had sandwiches and a flask of coffee, and we stayed in the shadows, like pine cats, and made our way to the lookout.

'Okay?' Agna whispered to the jumble of clothes. Only Haakon's eyes were visible below his woollen bobble hat, above the scarf over his mouth and nose. He nodded.

I took the top off the flask and poured. 'Careful, it's—'

Haakon had his hands around the cup in a second, blowing then slurping with trembling lips and shaking hands.

'Not all of it, Haakon! Agna will need it!' I whispered fiercely.

Haakon rose to come home with me, but then we heard the boat, in the depths of the dark, and we crouched and looked.

As Agna had said, the engines cut to their lowest. The clouds shifted and the boat loomed like a sea monster. The engine died; the boat floated into dock.

'Let's go! Let's go!' My heart was almost bursting through my chest.

'No!' said Haakon. 'They won't see us if we stay here.'

The driver of the truck got out and opened the back of the truck.

The passengers of the boat disembarked. Silhouettes of men wearing – we eventually saw – ragged striped tunics. These were the prisoners, bowed and stumbling. Half a dozen of them. And standing, watching them, the caps and coats of soldiers. Stiff, mechanical puppets.

Two of the prisoners carried a long sack that sagged in the middle to the truck.

'What are they…?' Even before Agna finished her question, I knew. We all did.

'Jesus,' said Haakon, and crossed himself. Not knowing what else to do, so did I. And Agna too.

Nineteen sacks were loaded on to the truck.

That was enough. Possibly they had no more space to bury them on the island, perhaps the ground was too cold. Whatever the reason, it persuaded Haakon.

He talked to the baker and the baker talked to the Milorg and it was decided.

More food would be smuggled into the camp, and coins smuggled out.

The true nature of this business was not in the trade of coins for food but, let's be frank, for life. Because that is what Sergei and his friends were buying. Their own lives. The chance to live another day, not to be one of those in sacks, delivered by boat in the night. No, the real trade was not the gold and food.

The Milorg asked Haakon to make a promise. And he knew they would ask more of him than smuggling food and delivering news sheets in loaves.

And he made that promise without hesitation.

Then the trade begun in earnest. Larger bribes, boxes of food.

Oh, how clever we thought ourselves! Little elves and fairy folk, hidden creatures performing our magic tricks. Weaving illusions only some soldiers and police saw. And those who did see were handsomely paid.

Supplies for the barracks came in heavy wooden crates, each nailed down, each with a stamp of an eagle holding a wreath, containing a swastika. Mostly the crates were broken up and used for firewood, but some were returned to be used again.

The Milorg took some and made others and filled them with food. Oats, potatoes, dried fish, even fresh fish, though only the freshest so there was no smell. The Milorg supplied the Russians with their beloved vodka and tobacco, which as you know was not only prized but was in itself a currency. Honey, sugar, cakes. All kinds of things. And a steady supply of coins came out. A miracle! Where did the money come from?

The legal system of goods in and out was run by a pyramid, first by Norwegian workers, above them police, then the grey and green caps, and finally the black caps, the SS. The accounting was done by them. They had lists, they were meticulous. But they were looking for boxes and goods going missing; it never occurred to them that there would be too much going in.

Hans and others among the green and grey caps, and many police, were happy to turn a blind eye. As long as they got paid.

In this way, food found its way into the camp, under rag cloths, in a small vat inside a larger one that was supposedly empty, creating a false bottom. In wheelbarrows loaded with logs. Sometimes in bags hurled over fences. Sometimes buried in the woods, and dug up later by work crews. Rat runs they called them. Finding new ways was all part of the game. But, oh, it sounds like I was involved. In truth, I only learned the details later. I worked some days and so did Liva. She went to school very, very rarely. We had the excuse that Mor was ill, so she had to be at home or working.

The prisoners for their part, made objects as thank yous. Small wooden toys, carvings of trolls or nymphs fashioned from driftwood roots. Boxes with scenes carved on them. Flutes and whistles.

The Germans allowed these gifts, thinking the making of them made the prisoners less restless. And the fools saw the Norwegians give them a little extra bread, or some potatoes brought from the mainland as payment. It was only a decoy, of course, part of the trick. The real goods were smuggled in the rat runs, and the real thanks were the coins of gold and silver hidden in the toys.

This trade went on for a long time. More than a year.

Of course, it did not prevent all deaths, but it saved many men.

Then we learned something important about the deal...

Liva

Me and Agna sat in the clearing.

Agna took the boxes or toys straight to Haakon, who took them to the Milorg. Often, the gifts were handed to me or the others first, so it did not arouse suspicion. When it was my turn, there was no way I was giving anything up before seeing what it was. This time it was a less fine work that held the treasure; a small chest, about half the size of a shoe box. On its lid was a scene of a cottage by a river, with mountains in the background. The cottage had a big round window, and a tall chimney. The mountains rose into the sky, on the far side of a great forest. *A Russian scene*, I thought. Perhaps the home of whoever made it. It seemed a shame to break it up, but after much examination I reckoned it was the only way in. There were joins, but no small nails to pry apart.

It was heavy too. Too heavy for the wood it was made from. I shook it, but of course it did not rattle.

I fetched a stone and reluctantly smashed the side of the box, hoping at least to save the lid.

It worked. The walls of the box fell apart, and Agna and I could clearly see the straw packing sandwiched between the false floor and the real one. Agna took her knife, wedged it between the two sheets of wood and opened it like a clam. Inside was something wrapped in paper nestling in the straw.

I opened it. As though it was Christmas.

I held a necklace made of silver. A heavy crucifix hung from the chain.

'Gosh!' Agna said. 'Do you think it's real? The cross, I mean, do you think it's silver?'

I just stared at the crucifix, and did not speak.

'Are you okay?' Agna asked. 'You look like you've seen a ghost. I said, do you think it is real?'

'Yes,' I said in a hoarse whisper. 'It is real.'

'How can you tell?'

'Because it is mine, Agna. This is my christening necklace.'

'Oh. The coins, the silver. It's ours! It's what Eirik hid.'

'Yes.' My hand shook with the effort of holding the necklace. Agna guided my hand to my lap, where she gently wrapped my fingers around the crucifix.

'This is a dreadful secret. It must stop, it...' But Agna faltered. 'No, no, of course it can't. If the trade stops, men will die.'

'Then we should tell the village,' I said. 'These are their heirlooms being traded and...' Now it was me who faltered. Agna said aloud what I had already worked out.

'We cannot. Many would want their valuables, of course. And it only needs one villager to tell the SS, who would be too delighted to find it, and to punish Sergei and others. Including us.'

'Oh.' I stared at the crucifix. The only valuable thing I'd ever owned. I wanted to hold it and never let go. I shed a tear then.

'You must keep it,' Agna said. 'It is yours, after all.'

I shook my head. 'How can I? How would that be fair? And you are right, Agna, we can't tell anyone. Well, maybe one person.'

'Eirik's mor? Can we trust her?'

'Yes, I think so. She hates the Germans. We must take that risk anyway. This tells nothing of him exactly, but it tells us something, doesn't it?'

Tove

Did we suspect before? No. Though once we found out it made sense. Agna was furious!

Agna dealt with Sergei; I saw the whole thing.

He took her by the hand and pulled her away from the table where she was chopping potatoes, and quickly out of the door.

I followed, knowing what storm was coming.

Arriving at their favourite hidden spot, he spun her round like a dance partner, bowed, leaned forward, eyes closed, puckering his lips.

It was a practised move. He reeled from the slap Agna gave him, eyeing her in disbelief.

'What was that for?' he said, rubbing his cheek, barely recognising the girl scowling at him, hands on hips.

'You found it, didn't you?' Agna spat the words.

'What?'

'Don't play innocent. The money, the treasure. You found it here, on the island.'

Sergei nodded, his cheek reddening with shame and pain.

'It's ours! Most of the village live in cabins that are not much more than huts, this is all they have! Some of these heirlooms are *hundreds* of years old. One of our boys hid it before the war. You knew that, because I told you! I've been so naïve, believing you carried gold and silver with you. The Nazis would have got it off you. You lied to me! And you hid it well, for a time. Now the coins are running out, aren't they, so you are using the jewellery as well.'

'Some we smelted down. But yes.'

'Why didn't you tell me, Sergei?' He looked to me, as though *I* was his accuser. In truth I pitied him.

'Because we need it.' Now his whisper was as fierce as hers. He lifted his jumper, showing his stomach and chest. His skin was bluey white, the lower ribs showed, reminding me of the skeleton of a whale we once found on the shore. To make his point more clearly, he reached under Agna's coat and pinched the fat on her hip. Then he took her hand and put it to his cold, scant flesh.

'Do you understand?' he said. 'I have it better than most. I am not going to die. Not yet, anyway.' The feel of her hand on his skin, of his on hers, perhaps softened her.

'You didn't have the right. And you didn't *trust* me.' Agna's voice wobbled. It looked to me as though all manner of thoughts and feelings were rushing through her head. She pulled away and ran back to the huts.

'Do *you* understand?' he said to me.

I had seen those bags in the night. Now I had seen how a man looked, not long before his body gave in, before he too, disappeared into the endless dark.

'Yes,' I said.

I knew what was at stake. Why Sergei did what he did. And Agna and Haakon too.

I was afraid, though. The two of them were in waters deeper than they imagined.

The details of what happened next, I found out much later.

Aktion

Winter 1944/45

Tove

I was sixteen, Liva thirteen. And Haakon, almost a man…

The instructions were delivered to Haakon at the bakery by a short thin man, with dark leathered skin and fierce blue eyes. He greeted Haakon as 'comrade'. This meant he was communist as well as Milorg.

The baker left the two of them to talk in the back room and kept lookout in the shop. Haakon and the man talked in low voices, so they'd hear the door if it opened and would know to be silent.

The man placed a rucksack on the workbench, where Haakon usually kneaded dough, and took from it a series of items: a small storm lamp, a bottle of kerosene, a lighter, a box of matches, a folded ordnance map, a compass and a watch.

'You shouldn't need the lamp or lighter, they are for back-up. You are to ski and trek north-east, deep into the hills. Should be easy for you, I hear you are an orienteering champion. They call you a nixie, a wood sprite, don't they?'

'I'm the best. Fast through valleys, forests and up mountains. Sometimes I climb rather than trek to get ahead. I strip down and wade through streams or rivers to cut distance, even in winter. I can deliver news sheets anywhere you like. That's what I'm doing... isn't it?' Haakon said, scanning the lamp and other objects. 'Am I travelling at night?'

'I heard about the news sheets. And your involvement in smuggling food to comrades in the camp as well.' The man nodded, regarding Haakon with something like admiration. 'Oh, yes, you think we do it only for the money? Many Milorg will not risk helping those in the camps. But for us they are brothers.'

'Us? Communists? How did you know about me—' Haakon stopped himself asking. There was no point.

The man took another map from his pocket and spread it on the table and tapped a finger on a marked red cross.

'Your map doesn't have this. It is your destination. This precisely. You need to remember the coordinates. Can you find it?'

'Sure. I've been hunting up there. That's near the old lumber mill and oil refinery. There's a single road in, a rail track too.'

'We know. From the south. You head north,' the man said, tracing a line across the map. 'Then come in from the west. This point is a couple of hundred metres from the mill, on an escarpment looking over the valley. Can you reach it? I mean, without leaving tracks they could follow.'

'In the snow, difficult. There are ways, though. Streams I can follow, bare rock to walk over or climb... am I going to... set the refinery alight?' Haakon coughed, to clear the high pitch suddenly affecting his voice.

'No. You won't go too near it. The woods around it are crawling with fascists. You won't go near them either. If you spot any, or they spot you, get the hell out.'

'Why?'

'Why what?'

'Why am I...Am I lighting a fire?'

The man smiled in way that chilled Haakon to the bone. Haakon nodded, afraid to speak, fearing his lips and words might tremble. And regretting how boastful he'd been. He breathed deeply.

'It's not a mill any more... is it?'

'No.'

'What, then? A camp?'

'No. But something important. The Germans have been making good use of the railway at night. Few traitors are involved. There's tons of equipment going in and a lot of soldiers. We have our ideas, but don't ask, because I can't tell you.'

'So, what do I do?' Haakon swallowed.

'Reach the spot. Make a bonfire. Set it alight at exactly nine p.m.'

'Is that all?' said Haakon, praying it would be.

'Yes. Your kit stays here for now, till I take you in two days' time. Tell your family you need to stay overnight to help the baker with an order for the fascists.'

'What do I do after I light this fire?'

The man grabbed Haakon by the shoulder and leaned in.

'You run, comrade.'

Two days later, in the afternoon, the man drove them in the baker's delivery van to a remote farmhouse high in the hills.

Haakon travelled through the night and into the light of the next day, mostly skiing, but also climbing and walking. He was careful to take an erratic route, and never to be too exposed; to walk around the open banks of virgin snow. Other than an eagle, hares and some deer, he saw no one and nothing. For him, it was like before the war. As if the war didn't exist.

When he rested, it was in the thickest part of the forest, or under rocks by the many streams he crossed. He never stopped long enough for the cold to settle in him. He never travelled fast enough to break a sweat that could turn to a chill.

He reached the hill at seven the following evening and made his way up through the trees and over banks of rock, climbing, but all the time looking at the slopes, planning his ski route back.

There was the edge. He dumped his kit, lay down and crawled. He knew the Germans were in the valley. Other than a few perimeter lights, the mill was dark and silent. He watched for a long time, but didn't see a single soldier. He chose an exposed shelf of rock backed by trees, so he wouldn't make a silhouette, and made a pyre of twigs, dry moss and fallen branches. It was a clumsy, air-filled pile, but it would burn, fast and fierce.

When this was done, he sat among the trees and from time to time, lit a match inside the dark of the rucksack, to check the time.

And waited. And waited.

At one minute to nine precisely he poured the kerosene on to the pyre, counting whispered numbers through chattering teeth, 'Twenty-three thousand, twenty-four thousand, twenty-five thousand.'

Then, 'Sixty.'

Even with gloves his hands were so cold it took a few attempts to light a match and throw it.

The fire erupted. He put the rucksack on his back, his feet in the ski bindings, the poles in his hands and took a final look over his shoulder.

Three more fires blazed in the night. North, south, and directly opposite, east. Points of a square with the mill in its centre.

Then the valley flooded with lights, wailing sirens and the *ack-ack-ack* of crackling gunfire.

Thunk, thunk. The tops of trees shuddered and shook as bullets hit. A shower of snow fell over him.

Svish, svish, thunk, thunk. Two bullets raced past his head into the woods behind. He was away, racing, panting, slaloming through the dark trees, all memory of his planned route forgotten; round this tree then another, in a blur.

When he reached the bottom of the hill, he started with his poles, pushing and skiing faster than he ever had, grunting with every thrust. Faster, faster. As if he would never stop.

Liva and I sat on logs in the clearing. Mrs Stovold was with Mor and we had this time to get out of the house, to speak freely. Neither of us said it, but we were relieved. The house had a heavy atmosphere and not a minute passed without one or both of us beside Mor, with her wrapped in her blanket, wheezing by the fire or lying in bed sipping hot water.

I stabbed at the embers with a stick, wishing it was Haakon I was poking.

'*He's* made her ill. She's sick already. Now she is sick with worry.'

'Do you think he will be home tonight?' said Liva.

'Who knows? That nonsense about the baker. Not even Mor believed *that*. He's up to something. And he's a bad liar.'

'It must be a secret. He *can't* tell us.'

'D'you know why, sister? Because they don't tell him. He's just their puppet.'

'Don't speak like that. You are not being you, Tove. It's because you are worried for Mor. The police, the Quislings, *they* are the puppets. Someday you'll think Haaky is a hero.'

I pointed the smoking end of my stick at Liva. 'A live hero or a dead hero?'

'Don't say that.'

'You've heard him talk. He thinks he's one of them now. And he's so angry!'

'He's only a delivery boy. They wouldn't make him do anything really dangerous.'

'Liva, it's *all* dangerous. Boys playing war. The thing is… Liva… *Liva*? Why are you looking up at the sky? Are you even listening?'

'Can't you hear that?'

'What?'

Liva stood, craning her neck.

To my ears there was no sound, other than birdsong. Nothing unusual in that, except…

'Wait, yes. The birds. They're going crazy.'

The air sang with whistles, chirrups and caws.

'That's a chorus for a summer dawn not a winter night,' I said. 'And there are not so many birds now. They've flown south. Why are these making this racket? They… Oh, wait, there must be sea eagles near. These are warning songs.'

Liva cocked her head, turning south-west, looking at the stars in the moonless night.

'Not birds. That's not it.'

'What, then?'

'A rumbling, like thunder. You really don't hear?'

I threw my stick in the fire. 'No. Maybe it *is* thunder.'

'Thunder comes after lightning. This is a continuous sound.'

'It's your imagination. Like when you think the wind is howling *actual* words, and—'

'Tove. Listen!'

I closed my eyes. The birds were still disturbed, chattering and calling alarms. There was no thunder.

'It's like trolls grumbling in their caves,' said Liva.

'Well, it's trolls then!'

'It's in the sky. From the west... the south.' Liva turned, and looked, though there was nothing to see but darkness and silhouettes of the treetops.

'O... Yes. I know that sound,' I said, suddenly aware of it. I knew it from news reels and films. 'It is an airplane.'

We looked at each other in wonder. We knew of bombing raids further north, but we had never heard or seen a plane.

The rumble drowned the birdsong and shook the air. Snow fell from the topmost branches. The embers in the fire hissed. The sky sounds became deafening.

'Not one plane,' I shouted. 'Many!'

We pressed our mittens tight over our ears. We vanished into shadow as a low flying bomber filled the gap where the sky had been.

A second plane passed over, then a third.

Liva took a hand away from her ear and shook it in the air.

'Bastards!' she shouted.

They were headed north, where the Milorg were very active and the Germans had bombed villages.

Liva shouted something, her lips moving, but her words were sucked into the dark thunder in the shadow of the planes. Huge dark crosses in the sky, flying so, so low, engulfing us.

She shouted or mouthed the same thing again, but I could not hear. Then she came to me, and pulled my mittened hand. I felt her breath in my ear.

'They're *not* German. I saw, on the underside of the wings: a red, blue and white target.

The planes went on their way, till they were hidden against the forests on the mountain.

'Why are they flying so low?' said Liva.

'I don't know. Come on, we will see better from Seal Rock.'

We raced back to the village and up the huge boulder that flanked the north of the village.

Almost everyone was there, looking north, as though waiting for the aurora to appear.

'Where are they headed?' people asked. 'What will they do?'

'Ah, they'll be going a long way. Through the valleys.'

'We won't see them again.'

'So, the Brits are finally coming to help, are they? Better late than never.'

'It's freezing out here, best get back to bed.'

But no one moved.

'They're turning, getting louder again!' said Liva.

Brilliance lit the sky. Flashes that erupted from the earth, followed by exploding booms.

One.

Two.

Three and four.

Then the horizon filled with a chorus of explosions. The valleys turned into day. The light of a thousand fires.

We stood, open mouthed, wide-eyed and silent until the planes returned. As the bombers passed over, people shouted and cheered, whooped and clapped. But not Liva or me.

'Do you think this is anything to do with Haaky?' Liva said, putting her arm around my waist.

'I pray not.' I put my arm around her shoulder, pulled her tight and kissed the top of her head.

We watched and listened, till the drone had almost vanished and we could see no trace of the bombers.

In the far distance we could make out a whirr of engines, and *tac-tacs* of gunfire in the dark.

'The bombers are under attack,' said Liva.

'I hope they get home safe,' I said.

'Tove...' Liva looked up at me. 'What does this mean?'

'How should I know? More trouble, probably.'

'Yes, but...'

'What?'

'When they passed over... I never heard anything like that, I never saw it either. I never felt so small. I was afraid. Then I saw... well, that plane, it was us, wasn't it, not them?'

'Us? It was the British.'

'Yes, but it's not just them any more, is it? It's the Russians. It's the Americans. It's the Milorg. It's Haakon. It's Agna, you and me. You want to know what I think? I think they're going to lose, Tove. One day, they're going to lose.'

'I wish I had your hope, little sister. Even if you are right, what will happen before then?'

'I don't know.'

'Whatever it is, I'm afraid of it. A cornered, injured wolf is the most dangerous, no? Come on, let's go home to Mor.'

Liva

Tove was right. We did not know what was coming.

Many German soldiers died in that bombing, and some Norwegians. Probably Russian prisoners too, though it was never confirmed. And many thought of the Milorg as murderers. What did that make Haakon?

A whirlpool was forming in the sea of this war. I was dragged in before I knew what was happening. Much I remember, and the rest from what Agna told me later...

The first sign of trouble was the policeman standing on the common in the late afternoon sunlight, declaring, 'Tomorrow will be a longer shift, you won't return home till late. You are also not required to report for duty on the dock until afternoon.'

Agna wasn't suspicious. This had happened before. A special meal they had prepared for some date on the Nazi calendar. She didn't even bother walking to our house to tell us.

The second sign was the stack of crates on the dock the following morning. Each was half a metre wide and stamped on every side with a red eagle holding a swastika in its talons. There were so many crates Agna wondered how the workers would also fit in the boat. She said later, she was relieved too that – today, at least – she had no contraband on her larger than a pack of cigarettes.

She gave the pack to Hans.

'Good, I have no more,' he said. But he didn't open the pack and smoke as he normally did.

'What is boxes?' Agna asked in her rough German. She spoke some and understood more.

'From Berlin,' said Hans.

'Why?'

Hans shook a fat finger in the air then pointed at the crates; the sign language Agna was used to. *No questions, get to work.*

He organised the women and girls in a line, lifting and passing crates. Agna was tasked with stacking them in the boat.

Almost all the workers were there, but not Tove and me.

When all the crates were loaded, they boarded. There were so many crates, Agna had piled them on the seats, so it was standing room only, like being on a tram in a city on the way to the cinema. Once Hans herded them on, he loosened the dock lines tethering the boat.

'Hans. Why?' Agna tried again. 'What is?'

'Food for guests.'

'What is word *guests*?'

'Visitors.'

'Sorry, Hans. No understand.'

'Soldiers. Many are coming to the camp.'

'Soldiers? Why?'

'SS,' he said.

Those two small letters. Two boots in the gut, two cold injections in the heart. Women whispered. Was the SS's business on the island? Or was it a stop-off on the way to some mission? If so, Agna thought, they would arrive at the village in silence. Like the day of the invasion.

She had to get off, to go tell. Who? Yes, Haakon. The Milorg.

But Hans was already pushing the boat from the dock.

I saw the boat leaving as I walked from our house.

'Wait for me!' I shouted and ran, till I stood puffing and huffing on the dock. 'Mor is so ill, Tove had to stay.'

'Steig ins boot,' Hans said, beckoning me to jump and grab hold of his hand.

'Go home,' Agna gabbled. 'There's no room and—'

'What? Yes, there is,' I said. But still, I didn't jump.

Hans shrugged, turned and started the engine.

'Listen, Liva,' Agna said, as calmly as she could. 'Tell your br—' The roar of the boat drowned her words, and then – oh, into the heart of the whirlpool – I leaped, landing between two women, who steadied me with helping hands.

'Good jump, no?' I shouted. 'Could have gone in if I wasn't so nimble. What were you saying, Agna?'

'Nothing.'

The boat coursed through the calm sea.

Why was everyone looking so worried? Why all these boxes? I examined one. And saw the letters.

SS

I felt sick. Then ice chill. Then a sort of numbness, as though I was made of stone, not flesh.

Fear. In my heart. In others' silence, in their faces.

Between leaving the previous day and arriving in the morning, the workbenches had been rearranged. As though nisse had done it. Perfect rows, with knives, pots, bowls and chopping boards set out.

On a table nearest the door to the yard, leading to the soldiers' quarters, were stacks of plates and rows of tiny glasses. The kind for aquavit.

I counted the glasses in one row, then the number of rows. Ten times fifteen.

One hundred and fifty in all. The sight of those glasses made me weak with worry.

Agna and I were assigned to the bread-making table. We were to make the mix and knead the dough, to set the loaves to rest and rise before baking.

A short, older woman waddled up to us, struggling

with a sack of flour. I helped her land it on the table like a large fish, then got back to kneading.

'SS,' the woman said. 'Cannot be good, eh?'

'No,' I replied. 'The poor prisoners. Agna, do you think your nisse will be okay?'

'Who is nisse?' the woman asked.

'A friend,' said Agna.

'Ah, *your* friend,' the woman said, smiling and nodding. 'The trickster. I am sure he'll be fine. It's *our* men we should worry about.'

I stopped kneading. 'What do you mean?'

'Why do you think they are keeping us here late tonight?'

'I did not know they were.'

'They didn't tell you? Yes, we must stay late. And they go to the mainland in the night. I hear they have a list of troublemakers to arrest. Someone has squealed. Any Milorg are for it. They are keeping us here so we don't warn anyone they are coming.'

We watched the woman walk off, and I turned to Agna with wide eyes and a trembling jaw.

'Haaky!' I whispered.

'Keep working,' Agna said, watching the guards. 'They don't like it when we stop and chat. And keep your voice down.'

'Why didn't you say?'

'Because I didn't know, of course!'

I returned to kneading, but my hands trembled and we carried on whispering, in short, desperate spurts.

'He. Is. Involved. What if they have his name? There have been arrests. They know Pappa is fighting. They might suspect Haaky.'

'No one cares about a news sheet delivery boy. They are after the men who smuggle guns from Shetland and blow up trainlines. Haakon will be fine.'

'They are after *anyone* who is against them, Agna. You can be arrested even for *reading* the news sheet.'

Agna didn't say anything more. She knew I spoke the truth.

'We can steal a boat,' I said.

'Don't be crazy.'

'Bribe them, then. To use their radio.'

'Litenmus. Seriously!'

'But...' My voice faltered. I wiped sniffles and tears away with my sleeve. 'We have to do *something*.'

'You!' The German soldier barked as he walked towards us. We stepped back from the workbench and stood to attention, hands by our side, heads bowed.

'Herkommen.' He beckoned Agna, and when she stepped forward, put a 'halt' hand up to me. He pointed to the far corner of the kitchen, by the door that led to the yard. It was a place only those on cleaning duty ever went. With dread, I saw that of the twenty or so older girls and women, they had selected the prettiest.

Agna looked around and about, searching, absurdly, for Sergei. He was not there, and nor were any Norwegian police.

I watched Agna vanish through the door, as though it was the gateway to the underworld. I wondered if I would ever see her again.

I was alone. Helpless without her.

Why had she ever brought me to the island that summer day? Why had she been such a rebel? She was nothing but trouble, and that trouble had led to this.

Then I remembered something she had told me that day, about the old times before the war. And what the villagers stored. And I had an idea...

Hans waited in the yard and when he saw Agna's fear, he laughed.

'Keine sorge, sie wollen nur dass du ihnen das Abendessen servierst. Nichts mehr.'

Agna didn't know every word, but she understood enough.

'It's okay,' she said to the others. 'They want us for waitresses. That's all.'

The door to the soldiers' quarters opened, and out came a man dressed in the raven black, spotless jacket and riding trousers of a senior SS officer.

She knew him, from that first day. The officer who had wanted a record of her name, but who did not get it. Werner.

He was tall, stiff-backed with piercing eyes. Hans threw his cigarette to the ground, stubbed it out with his boot, threw his hand to the sky, and shouted, 'Heil Hitler.'

'Heil Hitler.' Werner saluted, but with less enthusiasm. If he recognised Agna, she said later that he gave no sign of it. He perused the girls coldly as if they were statues in a museum. Then turned on his heel and walked back to the door.

'Herkommen, bitte,' he said.

The girls followed and entered a dining hall with rows of benches and tables covered with white linen cloths.

Someone had laid the tables – cups and plates and glasses – as uniform and neat as though that same someone had measured the place of each polished knife and gleaming glass to the millimetre.

The girls stood and waited. A policeman arrived. He told them others would deliver the plates of food. Their job was to pour wine and aquavit, refill bread baskets and keep the fire fed. He would be present throughout and they had nothing to fear.

'Now, where are your clothes?' he said. 'Do you have the dresses you were told to bring.'

'We were not told this,' Agna said.

He sighed and shook his head.

Then they waited.

Minutes passed like hours.

Agna didn't hear any boats arrive and nor did we in the kitchens, where I was working on my plan. She didn't see any guards, or soldiers or prisoners. Everything was quiet.

The SS arrived at the hall at dusk, filing in in pairs, chatting and joking.

They were so young compared with other soldiers. Blonder, fitter, and – yes – Agna had to admit it – some good-looking. One of the other 'waitresses', Brigit, a dark-haired beauty, smiled and casually flicked a curl behind her ear. Agna stared at Brigit unblinking, till she noticed. Then kept on staring at her, and staring, till Brigit turned red and focused on the ground.

The SS soldiers sat, and the girls served them bread rolls and poured wine, which they tucked into with gusto.

Agna knew soldiers, their bawdy comments, leering looks and guffaws. But these SS were different. They were polite, they thanked her for everything, they gave the girls space when they needed to lean in to refill a glass.

They were more than boys, but many of them not yet men. Some, with their horn-rimmed, round glasses looked more like librarians than soldiers. How, she thought, could these man-boys be killers? How?

Werner and the senior officers sat at a top table, overseeing the whole corps.

As the evening progressed the men drank. And this, Agna thought, was promising. Possibly the rumours of them going to the mainland were just that. Surely, they could not drink, then go to what was called an 'Aktion'. Could they?

The evening passed. It was gone ten when the girls were ordered to pour a shot of schnapps for each soldier. Then Werner stood, arms behind his back.

He gave a speech. Agna did not understand all of it. The boys sat rapt, unblinking, almost not breathing, as their leader explained their duty. Sometimes they paused to clap or laugh, or shout, 'Ja!' in fervent approval.

Werner finished his short speech with a curt 'Heil Hitler', and they downed their schnapps then clapped and clapped and stamped their feet, till the hall was filled with their voices, and stood raising their hands to the ceiling in salute, roaring:

'*Sieg heil.*

Sieg heil.

Sieg heil.'

Row by row they left, quickly, almost running, in total order. *Like ants*, Agna thought. Out they went till there was no one left but the policeman and Werner, who doffed his cap and said, 'Thank you for dinner and your service, girls,' in Norwegian, before leaving them in an empty hall, with tables littered with dirty plates.

Agna grabbed a half-empty glass of wine and drank it.

She prayed Haakon and no one else from Rullesteinsvik was on their list. She prayed, guiltily, that they were headed for Kysten. As did I.

The other girls started clearing plates, but Agna ran back to the kitchen huts.

The remains of the meal we had stacked in a corner, next to the table where we were now making porridge. There were empty cans, hessian sacks, crates that would go for firewood. Drained bottles. And a huge empty jar, the sort we Norwegians use; the discoloured, uneven-glass type. The kind for keeping jams, or aquavit. Or dried mushrooms. Even poisonous ones.

Agna saw it immediately.

'Liva?' she said. 'The jar. Please tell me...'

'I found it. On top of the shelves in the old huts they didn't knock down. You told me, remember, that day we took the canoe here. It was so high, I had to climb. It was still there! And it won't kill them, it will only make them ill.'

Agna picked up the jar and held it to the light. It was totally empty.

'Litenmus. What have you done?'

I had used it all. Every bit of the dried fly agaric powder.

I found my pendant and rubbed it.

Tove

It was reported later that some soldiers were 'seasick' on the journey to the mainland, even though the water was calm.

When the boats landed, the sickness continued. Men fell in the shallows and tripped on the rocks.

A woman, cowering in her house, heard an officer shouting, 'Are you drunk?'

Some villagers dared to peep between the cracks of quickly drawn curtains.

As men fanned out, pointing their guns into the dark, more keeled over and vomited, some stumbled and fell. Others screamed, firing their guns into the dark woods. Some panicked. Men hid behind rocks, or ran to the cover of a small house, firing more of their weapons into the woods and hills.

But they were not under attack. There were no spits of fire in the dark nor gunfire other than their own.

'Cease fire,' Werner shouted. 'Cease fire!'

A soldier later told Hans he swore he'd seen Milorg moving through the trees, ready to ambush them.

Another said he saw a pack of wolves.

Others did not dare report to Werner what they had seen, but told Hans.

Trolls, imps, ghosts.

Soldiers danced dizzy in the darkness, falling, shouting, hiding, firing furiously, without aim or purpose.

Those that had names of families and houses to target got lost. Some ran and ran, till they were away from the noise and chaos, and crouched, whimpering under porches, or holding tight to pine trees in the dense forest, as if they were boys again and the trees were their mothers' legs.

Mor, Haakon and I rose from our beds; Haakon peered through a crack in the barely opened doorway. The night was alive with screams, shouts and *rat-tat-tat*.

Gunfire arced in the night like fireworks. I watched through the living room window, as the fire and shouts grew closer.

'You have to go, Haakon,' Mor said. 'In case they are making arrests. You can come back when it's safe.'

'I know,' he said. Mor opened the stove door, to give some light from the dying embers. 'Though if they have my name, it will never be safe. I have to leave for who knows how long.'

Haakon dragged a chair under the attic hatch, and was on it, and had the hatch open and lifted himself up in seconds, fast and athletic as an acrobat.

A full rucksack landed on the floor, quickly followed by a coil of rope, skis and poles, then Haakon. All of it already prepared.

'Back window, bring the rest!' he said, picking up the rucksack.

We followed him into Mor and Pappa's room with the skis, sticks and rope. He opened the window and climbed out.

'Where will you go?' I gasped, struggling to breathe, looking back to the living room, to the door they would come through. Just like the day of the invasion.

Another burst of gunfire cracked through the night. It was close.

'The road's not safe, and, if they are here, they will be in Dallansby next, or Kysten. There are places in the mountains for this situation, it's all prepared and planned. I'll meet anyone else who escapes there.'

Haakon leaned through the open window and Mor and I grabbed him and kissed him and held him tight.

'You'll come back, tomorrow, the day after?' said Mor.

'No, Mor. Hug Liva for me,' he said, prying himself away.

'Wait!' I whispered. I went to the main room and came back immediately with Liva's book of fairy tales, that we had hidden behind a cupboard.

'If they come, they'll take it. It's verboten. Keep it safe for Liva.'

'I will.'

'For all of us.'

He reached in his pocket and handed over two silver coins.

'Take this, and give it to Liva or Agna, it was meant for the Milorg to buy food for the camp. Make sure they use it wisely.'

'I love you, my boy,' Mor sobbed. 'I love you.'

'Hey, Mor. I am a nixie, remember? And what does a nixie always do?'

'Re… return home.' She reached to hold him once more.

But Haakon stepped back, placed the book in the rucksack, picked up his skis, poles and rope and tramped into the night.

Mor fell to the floor, holding her hands over her face, weeping, letting out an agonising cry. I kneeled beside her and prised her hands away, to look into her eyes, just visible in the light of the window.

'Haakon never came home tonight, understand?'

No matter how tightly I gripped Mor's hands, no matter how I whispered this same thing again and again, it was as if Mor did not hear. She cried and cried, and but for me holding her would have lain on the floor. Broken.

'It's too much. Too much. My husband is gone. I am worried sick waiting for Liva, now this. What else will they take from me? What will become of us?'

'Mor, listen. Get to bed; if they come, we say Haakon did not come home tonight. Understand?'

Mor only wept more. I shook her violently.

'Understand?!'

Mor nodded weakly.

We went to bed and waited for the wolf at the door howling, 'Let me in,' for the rifle butt smashing the door down. For the bark of dogs.

But no soldiers came, and after a few minutes, the gunfire and shouting stopped, leaving a tense silence.

We waited and waited, holding each other in the dark, till around twenty minutes had passed. Mor rose, went to the front window and peered out. Then she put on jumpers, a coat, hat and boots and went and stood on the porch, waiting. And she would not come in and go to bed, no matter what I did or said.

An hour? More?

Nothing moved, there was no sound, until we heard the familiar chug of boat engines, and we ran and ran and ran, meeting Liva at the dock. I grabbed her and held her, till she struggled to breathe.

'Have soldiers been here?' she whispered in my ear, so the Germans could not hear.

'Yes.'

'Haakon?'

'He escaped. He is safe.'

Mor hugged us both, as if we were one being, not three; a huddle of coats, cold cheeks and tears.

Agna tapped Mor on the shoulder.

To Agna's great surprise, Mor reached out and hugged her too.

Liva

Agna was taken from her home at dawn the following day and I did not see her or talk to her for a long, long time after that. When I did, she told me the memories were burned in her mind, like the cut, charred lines in the wooden toys the prisoners made...

There was no chorus of stamping boots, no barking dogs, only a knock at the door and the kommandant shouting for Agna and Mose to wake.

Mose opened the door, squinting in the morning light, hugging her coat tight against the cold. The kommandant removed his cap. Agna came to the door and saw straight away how worried he was. Some twenty metres away an armoured car was parked on the track, its driver leaning casually on the bonnet, holding his face to the rising sun.

'What is it?' Mose croaked.

'Agna,' the kommandant replied. 'She must come with me.' He turned and walked to the car without another word.

The engine was loud and the road bumpy. The journey passed in silence, other than a brief exchange:

'Why?' Agna said.

'I do not know,' the kommandant told her.

Before long Agna was delivered to Dallansby town hall. It was exactly as she remembered it from before the war: a square formal block of smooth stone, with fancy balconies and tall doors. Three huge banners decorated its edifice. A red cloth emblazoned with a black swastika hanging down the centre of the building, flanked by two smaller ones.

The kommandant led her down a corridor, past open doors and offices where secretaries typed, to an office. Inside Werner and a junior SS soldier waited in leather chairs, behind a huge oak desk. Agna glanced back to the kommandant, but the door clicked shut. She was alone with the SS. There was no chair for her.

Werner spoke calmly, pausing between sentences to sip his coffee. The soldier, a blond, serious young man with round glasses, nodded and listened sometimes cocking his head like a dog, listening.

Agna, of course, understood much of what Werner said, but she was not going to let him know that.

'He wants to know if you think we are stupid?' the boy said in perfect Norwegian.

'Hauptsturmführer Werner has an intolerance to wheat. Another officer due to dine was busy with administration duties and did not join for dinner until dessert, by which time all the bread had been either consumed or cleared away.

'Hauptsturmführer Werner and this officer were the only men who were not poisoned prior to the Aktion.

'He has some questions:

'First, why are your papers not complete? There is no record of your father's heritage. It says "unknown". He wants to know if your father was a Jew or a gypsy. He thinks perhaps you are Untermensch of some kind. That, for your information is those races that are sub-human. Russian slavics, Jews, negroes and so forth.'

I know what it means, Agna thought.

'Secondly, he asks what kind of poison you used, which made many of his men very ill?

'Last, he asks if others making the bread were complicit in this act. We will question the workers and discover the truth in any case, so it will be better for you if you answer honestly.'

Agna opened her mouth to speak, not knowing what she might say. No words came. Her mouth was dust-dry, her insides boneless-weak. Her heart pumped in her head. She closed her mouth for fear she might throw up and teetered, dizzy on her feet.

Werner spoke and again, the boy translated.

'He asks why you are so pale. Are you going to fall down? He asks, did you also eat the bread?'

Werner leaned over, his hands clasped together on the desk.

'Speak, please,' he said in Norwegian.

'I... I...'

'You... you... what?'

'I... I... I... did.' She put a hand to the wall to steady herself. 'It's St Antony's fire!'

Words arrived. They flowed. They appeared in her, as they did for a shaman she once saw, delirious, dancing around a fire shaking a rattle. Now it was she who was a voice for unknown spirits.

Werner looked at the soldier, who shrugged.

'Yes, that's the truth. A fungus in the grain. It can poison bread, it can make people mad. In old times, people thought they were visited by demons when they ate it. Whole villages would fall ill, some people would go insane and see visions! I shouldn't have stolen that roll, but I was hungry. I've been ill all night!'

Werner called out, 'Meier!' The kommandant entered.

She watched and between her well-acted moans, took in their tone, their expressions, how the kommandant stood, how Werner scrutinised him. They spoke about her life, though they might have been discussing the weather the way they were talking. She recalled the exchange and stored it in her head in as much detail as she could. She thought it could save her life.

'She says the wheat or rye from which the bread was made was contaminated with a fungus. It's happened before apparently. It sounds quite the fairy tale. Does this make any sense?'

'Actually, yes,' the kommandant replied. 'She was exceptionally quiet on the way here, which is unusual for her, and in my view had no clue why she was being taken. I could not tell her, as I also did not know. My mother's family are from the Tyrol, a region not unlike this part of Norway in some ways. There's some history of it. The fungus is ergot. Rye grain is checked thoroughly and regularly. If the fungus is found, it can contaminate a whole barn of grain. If it is not found and goes into the mill it will cause the bread to be poisoned. It is not common, but it happens, especially if the air is moist when the grain is harvested. It's known as St Antony's fire. It can cause cramps, burning, convulsions, delirium and visions. Even death if consumed in large doses. I once treated a farmer and his family, who had been less than careful. Their daughter, who was only twelve years old, was convinced ghosts were clawing her skin.

'To reassure you, as long as your men are rested, well-hydrated and given aspirin to relieve the cramps, they will be fine.'

'No Norwegians are ill, that we know of, other than this girl. It seems convenient for the Milorg, don't you think? That my men are poisoned an hour before an Aktion,' responded Werner.

'Yes, it does. But it's not implausible. We are in the town hall, if there is a history of this kind of thing in the region, we can find it in records.'

'How did they not check the grain, if it is customary?'

'A good question. Even if they do check the grain, a lot of the men of the village who might help with the harvest escaped before we arrived. Women do the work now. It's possible they didn't know.'

'Why are you protecting her?' Werner cut in. 'Because of the mother? Yes, we know about that.'

'I'm not protecting anyone. She may be lying and if she is she will face consequences. Or she may be telling the truth. Reason tells me that if she did this, she would have run away rather than gone home to bed to wait to be arrested.'

'Not if she believed we would not work it out. Not if she thought we might believe it to be simply rotten food. But for luck we might have assumed the poison came from any number of sources. I think she did it. Someone gave her poison and instructed her. Milorg. Don't worry, I'll get the truth from her and even if I don't...' He shrugged.

Agna almost fell then. In that moment her sickness, her dizziness, were no act.

'With respect,' the kommandant continued, 'if the SS take a girl like this and shoot her, if they make yet another "example", then my life with these people will become more difficult than it already is.'

Werner sat back, finished his coffee, and thought a while.

Agna took the opportunity to rub her tummy and groan. Not too much. This had to look convincing.

Werner watched her performance with a critical gaze before speaking to the young soldier.

'He says we will get to the matter,' the soldier said. 'He says we will go for a tour this bright and beautiful morning. Please take us to the farm where the grain is stored.'

The farmer was surprised by the arrival of an armoured car, a small van and a truck full of soldiers.

He took one look at Agna as she climbed out of the back of the car, with her head bowed, and held his hands high in surrender.

'No Milorg here,' he gabbled 'You can search everywhere. I'm not hiding anyone or anything. I don't care what this girl told you. She's lying.'

'You are not in any trouble, farmer,' the soldier reassured him. 'We only wish to examine your grain. You did not hear of the events of the night in Rullesteinsvik?'

'No. What events? There is a boy from there who fulfils orders, but he hasn't turned up. What did you say? You want to examine my *grain*?'

'Calm yourself. We are not looking for contraband. We believe there is ergot in the grain, does this mean anything to you?'

'What?' The farmer lowered his hands and put them on his hips, his mask of fear slowly changing into dumbfounded confusion. 'Ergot? Really? The season was not too dry, but it is very unlikely. I only heard of it twice in this area, and I am forty-seven. It was not from this farm, let me assure you.

'The women check each batch for rat droppings, moisture, stones, all sorts – before it goes to be milled.'

Agna kept her eyes on the ground. As meek and poorly a creature as she could be.

She had to convince them of the presence of the ergot, even if they could not find it.

The farmer led them to the three barns where the different grains were stored. Inside the largest was a mountain of rye.

Werner leaned down and picked up a handful, letting it fall slowly through his fingers.

'Where is ergot?' he said to Agna.

'I don't know.' She turned to the young soldier. 'Tell him I never worked on a farm, tell him I don't even know what it looks like.'

'I will personally examine every batch before it leaves the barn,' said the farmer.

This was translated. Werner spoke and his words were translated back.

'Thank you, farmer. That will not be necessary. We cannot afford that risk.'

Werner left and they followed.

Soldiers poured from the back of the truck. Three of them carried equipment Agna had never seen before.

Tanks on their backs, connected with pipes to huge cannon-like guns with stout barrels. Only when the soldiers reached the three barns, mirroring each other's stance, pointing the barrels of these strange guns at the walls; only then did she realise.

'No. No. Please,' she shouted. 'Our village, the camp. We'll starve!'

The guns roared flames like dragons.

The planks of the barn walls were brittle and dry. They caught easily. But to be sure, the soldiers walked along and around each of them, setting new fires in each wall.

The fire was hungry. It ate the walls, and found the grain.

The column of smoke was so solid and reached so high, it was seen in Dallansby and Kysten and, I expect, by the Russian prisoners on Fjernøy.

They handcuffed Agna's hands behind her back and she did not – could not – object. Then they marched her to the back of the small van.

Now she knew why it was there. For her. Her whole life had been a tide taking her to this shore. For all her naughtiness in Miss Bridget's class, all the times she ignored her mor. All the times she... Did. Not. Listen.

A soldier walked towards her. He was carrying a hessian sack.

'What's that f—' She flinched as he forced it over her head. The last thing she saw was the blazing barn, black smoke billowing into the sky. The last thing she heard was the farmer's cries.

Then the van door opened and the soldier guided her up a step, and shoved her in. She fell, painfully, to the floor. The bolt shut. The engine grunted into life.

Agna waited a while before calling out, 'Hey?' to see if a soldier – or anyone – was in there with her. There was no reply. She could barely hear herself above the engine. She was deaf now, as well as blind. She sat up, shuffled to the side of the truck and leaned against it. Every time the van hit a pothole, the engine strained. For a second she smelled fumes, and wondered with sick urgency if they were feeding the exhaust into the truck. She'd heard rumours of such things. But the smell faded, and she sat, breathing rapidly, and told herself to be brave.

After a time, the bumpy farm track gave way to smooth road.

Time passed. More than an hour. They were not taking her to Dallansby, then. But where?

She leaned forward, and shook and shook her shoulders and head until the bag fell off.

The inside of the van was coal black, but in the roof was a crack and she could see the precious blue sky.

And thought of me. *Oh, Liva, what have we done? What have we done?*

Eventually, the truck slowed and turned a corner. Once, twice, a third time. The engine cut, the van stopped and Agna's heart beat loudly in the sudden silence. A dog barked close by. She was shaking. What now? The door opened and the silhouette of a soldier filled the light. He shouted at her, waving his hand, beckoning her out. She stepped down. He grabbed the sack and forced it back over her head.

But for a second, she had glimpsed the German shepherd straining on a leash, barking madly. High stone walls topped with barbed wire, barred windows. Banners. Swastikas.

Burly hands forced her on. A door creaked open, then there was the thunder of boots and guttural German voices. She was taken along unseen passageways and down steps.

The clunk of bolts drawn, the handcuffs unlocked, they pushed her in. The door closed. The clatter of boots receded.

Agna pulled the sack off. First there was only darkness. Then, she noticed a small shaft of daylight and cold air whistling through a high broken window. Bars on the window cast shadows on the cell wall. The bars were unnecessary, she thought. A five-year-old couldn't squeeze through that space.

Her eyes adjusted. She was in a cell, with scarred chipped walls. A single wooden bunk filled most of the floor space. There was no mattress, no pillow, no blanket. Apart from the bunk, there were two small pails on the ground, one containing water and a metal ladle, the other empty. In the door were two hatches, one at eye level, the other at the base. The lower hatch was slightly taller and wider than the pails.

Slowly, her heart calmed and she stopped shaking. They had not taken her to the woods and shot her, which she knew the SS sometimes did. They had not taken her to a camp either. This was a prison, or like so many buildings, had been made into one.

She began to shake again from cold as much as fear. She watched the little warmth she held inside, escape in every cloud of breath.

The day passed. Hours of uncertainty. Listening. Alert to every sound. But there was not much to hear; occasionally distant doors slamming and muffled German voices.

At dusk she hoped for food. But no one came. Agna was both hopeful and afraid of someone coming. But there was only the night. Darkness joined the cold as her new enemy. She could not sleep, only sit, then move about blowing into her hands or putting frozen fingers under her armpits, or rubbing them together like sticks to make a fire. She thought of Sergei. Is this how he and the other prisoners lived each day? Freezing. Hungry. Not knowing if the next dawn was to be their last?

And if she lasted till morning. What then?

She told herself not to cry. And not for the first time, her body disobeyed her.

The moon reached a place in the sky where it shone, like a torch beam, through the window – on to the wall.

There were scratches, made by someone, which had been mostly covered with tarry paint. She ran her fingers over them and realised they were distinct shapes. Letters. Carefully, she began to pick at the paint. It came away in flakes, like the crust of an old wound. It was slow work. But with much picking, the letters were revealed.

They were carved deep.

-- MORD- --T W---P

What did it say? Who was this message for?

She thought of different combinations of letters to fill the gaps. And of Mor – because that word was clear – her own mor standing on the porch looking into the night. She would know of this, of course. The kommandant would have told her.

Mor, Mor. Then the words appeared like magic.

Oh, Mor, do not weep.

That was what it spelled. Agna repeated the words, over and over, like a prayer, as she rubbed her hands together and put them under her armpits, and stamped her feet.

Oh, Mor, do not weep.

She waited. For dawn. For her execution? She told herself no. They could have done that already. Was she being punished for what happened then? Was this the start of a long sentence?

She slumbered against the wall. And dreamed of the island before the invaders. Of summer. Of the thin tops of pine trees in a whispering breeze, of dark moss beneath the branches and the soft carpet of fallen pine needles, the cool and peace of the heart of the copse. And she woke with a start.

When will I see you again, Fjernøy?
When shall I see you again, Fjernøy?
When shall I see you again?
Will I...
She cried.
She knew she might die in this place.

As the old saying went, *Winter has long fingers, with nails that grow sharp; that claw, first in the stomach, then the mind.*

'I'm so... so young.' She cried more, and let it all out, and told herself that was okay. To get it out.

Dawn arrived. She heard the sound of doors opening and closing.

'Zielt!' An order shouted, some distance away. Followed by a loud bang, echoing in the cold air. The bang made her start. Gunshot?

She waited for them to come. But they did not. Flakes of snow filtered through the window and floated to the floor of the cell.

Hours filled with nothing. They don't need to shoot me, she thought, they'll let me freeze to death, and say it was an accident.

Eventually, it was night again.

Mother, do not weep.

Mother, do not weep.

Mother, do not weep.

Agna whispered and rocked. Longing for food, for warmth, for summer days, fishing with me and the others. Picking blueberries on the islands, multeberries in the mountains. Laughter. Swimming. Fires in the dusk. Not hearing 'time for bed'. Sergei, and his warm embrace.

She woke when the top hatch opened. An eye watched her. The hatch shut, then the one at the base of the door opened.

'The buckets,' a voice croaked.

'Where am I?' she whispered.

'The buckets! Now, or not at all!'

She fetched them and was about to push them through the hatch, into the world that existed beyond the cell, but paused.

'What is going to happen?'

'The buckets!' the voice said again, then whispered, 'Give them what they want. A name in the Milorg. They believe you acted on your own, but under instruction.'

It was a male voice. No hint of a German accent and – she guessed – belonging to someone not much older than herself.

He replaced the toilet bucket. Then the other pail, filled with fresh water.

'I'm freezing, and starving!' she said. 'When will I eat? Can I have a blanket?'

'Do you have money?'

'No. But—'

The hatch shut.

So, they were not going to kill her. At least, not if she gave them what they wanted. But she had no Milorg name. Only her own. Or mine.

She woke.

How long had she slept? What was that sound?

Something scuffled in the dark. Had to be a rat. Agna sat up, pulling her feet in tight.

Moonlight set a yellow, blurred square on the floor, and, as though walking on to a stage, a brown mouse came into the light, a tiny fur bag of bones, with huge ears, round eyes and a thin worm of a tail. It stood on its hind legs and looked around.

'Hello, mouse,' said Agna. It looked into the dark, saw her and pelted to the door and under the tiny gap.

How had she slept in this cold? Exhaustion, no doubt. Although the cell was still very cold, she was not shaking and she could move her fingers more freely. No biting wind blew through the window. And the light from the moon was oddly distorted; fuzzy and wide.

She pulled the bunk to the wall with the window, stretched and grabbed the ledge. She knew instantly, before she tried to pull herself up, that she did not have the strength. So, she stood on tiptoe to see as much as she could.

There was a wall of snow behind the bars, totally blocking the window. Had the snow drifted, then frozen? No. The snow was packed and uneven. Someone had made this, to keep the cold breath of winter away.

Someone had helped her.

At dawn Werner came with an SS soldier she recognised, from the dinner. Another not-much-more-than-a-boy with round glasses. Similar to the one at the town hall. Did they make these boys all the same, like toys in a workshop?

She sat up, though the effort of lifting her head made her dizzy. Werner scanned the cell.

He spoke and the soldier translated.

'He wants the name.'

Agna had expected this. She had rehearsed her answer. But the words had to be dragged from her mind, and pushed through her mouth; as though speaking itself was something new. Or something forgotten.

'Accident... fungus... grain.'

She braced. For questions, for blows. But they turned and left.

She fell back on the bunk.

At some time, the hatch opened.

'Hey,' the voice whispered.

'What?'

'Look.'

A steaming bowl was pushed into the cell. A wooden spoon rested on the top of what might be porridge, along with a blob of what might be jam.

Agna had strength then. She fell off the bunk and crawled to the bowl of porridge. It was not so hot it would burn, but enough to warm her belly. She ate quickly and licked the inside of the bowl clean.

'Th... thank you,' she said. 'More. Please?'

'I can't. And don't say anything. Now return the bowl and spoon. Quickly. I have a blanket for you.'

She returned the empty bowl and the boy exchanged it for a warm blanket.

'I will come before dawn,' he said. 'And then you must return the blanket, do you understand? They mustn't see, or know.'

'Who are you? Why are you doing this?' Agna asked. Again, there was no reply.

In the night she woke and there was the mouse in the moonlight, clawing at a lump of something on the ground. She had wolfed the porridge so messily; some had fallen to the ground.

Agna thought of getting up, of taking the tiny lump herself. But fought the urge and instead, whispered, 'Hello again.' This time it did not run, but watched her. So as not to scare it – Agna stayed stock still.

To you, she thought, *I am a giant.*

The mouse alternated between picking at the lump of porridge, and checking on the giant.

Agna smiled and whispered, 'Hello, Litenmus.'

After some wearisome mouse work, it prised what was left of the nugget of porridge from the floor and ran off with its treasure. It returned a few minutes later, searching the floor with quivering nose and whiskers.

'Optimist, eh?' said Agna.

As promised, next day the boy knocked on the door before dawn, and Agna handed him the blanket.

Not much later, the cell filled with winter light, Werner and his translator arrived.

They stood in the open doorway, not *doing* anything, not *saying* anything. Werner stared at her, an animal in the zoo. Not one he was especially fascinated by. In fact, he looked bored.

'Give us the name,' the translator said.

'Can I have some food?' Agna asked in a mouse-meek voice. 'Please?'

'A name.'

'Name of what?' she replied. 'Who?'

Werner smiled, turned on his heel and walked away.

'The name of the Milorg who gave you the order,' the translator said.

'I told you. The fungus in the grain. It was an accident.'

'He doesn't believe you. You are lucky. He could give you to the people who run this place. He is an honourable man, he won't allow them to do what they would. And your mother is a good Norwegian citizen. Once you give the name there will be no further punishment.

'We are only visiting today. We'll be back in two days on camp business. Perhaps three. Or four. We will see you then. He has given instructions. So, think. When you decide to give the name, let the guards know. They will give you food and then you will go home.

'You know, with fluids and heat, a body can survive as many as forty days without food. But in winter the body uses calories to maintain warmth.

'Be assured that with the cold and no food, you will survive only a few days. Before you die you will tell us anything we ask. I have seen this.

'Let me tell you a story. I have seen a Russian prisoner pick up a lump of ice that was once soup, that his friend had dropped, before he passed out. I told him not to eat this ice, because the other prisoner had scarlet fever. This is why he had collapsed. But this prisoner *did* pick it up, and he thawed it and drank the soup. He got ill. He did not last. It was inevitable. But so was his decision to eat the soup. Do you see?'

There was not much food in the next days, but there was some. Porridge. Stale bread. A soup with potato and broth made, Agna was sure, from stewed bones.

It was like the meagre rations they gave the Russians.

And now how she understood Sergei, his hiding, his lying, his secrets. How he might do anything. To keep himself alive. His comrades too.

The war was everywhere. It made you do strange things.

The war was here. In her belly. In the nights. In her dreams.

It took all Agna's will power to save the tiniest lump of potato, or scrap of peel, or crumb of crust and leave it on the floor at the foot of the bunk.

Once dark came, she would lie, waiting for her tiny friend.

Perhaps, Agna thought, *Litenmus, this giant is not so bad after all?*

It came and went, and Agna teased out morsels, so that Litenmus would spend time searching, or standing on its hind legs looking at her.

'Sorry, Litenmus,' she told it. 'I ate the last bit. I couldn't help it.'

The mouse's nose twitched, it squeaked, and Agna smiled.

Once, at the bottom of the bowl she found a bone. She kept it, and gnawed on it. It was a comfort.

Werner did not come after two days, or three, or four. And now she thought, this was a game. To fool her, to convince her she was not important enough.

And part of this game was to make her think. What were her options after all? That is what they wanted her to think about.

Starve. Freeze. Or give them a name.

When would they run out of patience? When would they hand her over to whoever ran this place?

Questions, questions. With no answers. There was only the world she now lived in.

Too exhausted to stay awake.

Too hungry to sleep.

Waking dreams.

Sergei, holding her warm and tight, kissing tears from her cheeks.

His eyes searching the work hall. For her.

'I'm here,' she says, but he does not see her, he does not hear.

Mor, standing on the porch, looking at the sky.

Fjernøy.

'Oh... Mor... do... not... weep...'

But Mor cannot see or hear her.

She was woken by banging and clanking.

The fierce barking of dogs. Boots and doors. Doors and boots. Close now.

Agna rose, quickly rolled the blanket and shoved it under the bunk. Then lay back down, listening.

She heard scuffles and clunks through the wall, which meant the cell next to hers was occupied. By the sound of it so were many others.

The tide of noise subsided. Voices – male and female – cried out.

'Stay brave, comrades!'

'Long live the king!'

'Damn Quisling!'

Then, 'VERBOTEN!!' Truncheons hammering on doors, rattling across bars.

'SILENCE!'

'Go to hell,' a brave voice shouted, followed by muffled cries of pain.

After that, the night was silent.

Agna was the mouse now, ears and eyes alert to the night, hardly daring to make a sound or even breathe.

She lifted a trembling hand and tapped on the wall.

Thud, thud, thud.

Thud, thud, thud came straight back.

Agna raced off the bunk and lay on the floor, with her head as close to the door as possible. The floor was freezing. She tried the hatch, though she had tried it a hundred times, every which way, and it was always locked and only ever rattled slightly.

'Hey,' Agna whispered. 'Who are you?'

'Strikers. Who are you, where are you from?'

'Agna. I am from Rullesteinsvik.'

'Ah, we are teachers. One of us is from Kysten. Possibly you know her.'

'Miss Bridget?'

'Yes. She is in the cell opposite me, one down. I saw them throw her in there. Wait...

'*Bridget.*' Then, louder, '*Bridget!*'

'Verboten!' a guard's voice snarled. But the voice was not followed by the *thunk* of boots, and after a few minutes, Agna heard a whisper of a whisper:

'Hallo? Brina, did you call me?'

'Someone who knows you is here.'

'Miss Bridget, it's me, Agna!'

'Agna... the feral child?'

Agna smiled at her old nickname.

'Yes, Miss Bridget. The feral child. Why have they arrested you?'

'We refuse to teach their nonsense. Never mind me. How are you? Everyone knows you poisoned their food.'

'It was an accident.'

'No matter. Some of those they came to arrest got away in the commotion. To some you are a hero.'

'Some?'

'There are many stories about what happened. Some blame you because now there is no grain.'

'How is my mor?'

'She is doing all she can to get you released. She is doing okay. Better than some.'

'Oh.' Agna did not need to ask why.

'What of the village? The camp?'

'The SS run Fjernøy now. No Norwegians work there, not even police. Life is tough in the villages. There is a black market, but prices are more than most can afford.'

Agna was hungry for more. But none of this was good. None of it.

It was she who was cursed by her own hand. Not the kommandant, not the policeman, not Werner. Her. Agna. Her hunger died. But there was a question she had to ask.

'How is Liva?'

'Not so good. Haakon has run off. The mother is so ill. There are only the two girls to care for her.'

Agna thought on this.

Agna the feral, the troublemaker. *She* had led them to the island, *she* had spun my mind with tales of poisonous, nightmare-inducing mushrooms, *she* had told the tale of the poisoning that made Werner burn the grain. Now folk were starving.

And what of Sergei? No food would get to the island. There would be more boat trips to the mainland in the dead of night.

'Sergei, I am so sorry. Liva, I am so sorry.'

'What?' Miss Bridget said.

'Nothing... If you get out, will you give Liva a message?'

'Of course.'

'Tell her... to be as strong as the trees, she will know what that means... This is all my fault. You always said I was a troublemaker, well, here is trouble.'

'It was an accident. You said. Look, Agna, let us pretend for a moment that you did it. Would it be so bad? You stood up to them. You fought back. Can't you see what they are doing? Resistance is punished with reprisals. They want us to blame ourselves or each other for what *they* do. But I know you are smarter than that.'

'At least I am no longer by myself. It has been awful here.'

A sigh was followed by a pause. 'I'm sorry, Agna. They are taking us tomorrow. To camps.'

Agna's heart sank into an endless well. A black pit inside her, where she dwelled like a lost spirit, banished from the earth, in one of Miss Bridget's stories. Every time she thought she'd reached the bottom of this well, something happened to send her further down.

She swallowed tears. These too were endless, it seemed.

'Where?'

'I don't know. The latest news sheet said there are hundreds of these camps.'

'Somewhere abroad, then?'

'No. Hundreds only in Norway. Thousands in all the countries, wherever they stamp their boots. And some, in the east... there are stories, Agna, and they are hard to believe... They are making an example of us. But it's not easy for them, because we organised through the news sheets. Many teachers are striking. Those that aren't Nazis, I mean.

'They are doing the same thing with you, Agna. An example to intimidate others. Eventually they will have to let you go.'

'But, Miss Bridget, you are many, I am one.'

'I know, Agna, I know. I wish I had more words of comfort.'

'You could tell me a story?' Agna laughed quietly.

'I thought you were too old for fairy tales? You said that many times before you left school.'

'I didn't mean it.'

'Do you remember when I taught you about the Spartans?' asked Miss Bridget.

'No... wait, were they the really fierce Greeks? Who lived such simple lives, and had great warrior crafts?'

'That's it, those are the very words.
'Once upon a time...

*'The warlord, King Philip of Macedonia,
threatened to invade Sparta.*

"Shall I come as friend or foe?" Philip asked.

The Spartans' reply was simple, "Neither."

*Losing patience, Philip sent another message:
"Then I will come as foe and I will fight. And
if I win, I will turn you from your homes, I will
enslave your people, I will break your temples
into rubble. Nothing will be left."*

The Spartans replied again, with a single word.

"If."'

In the morning, the guards came, shouting, 'Schnell!'
over and over, threatening beatings if the strikers did
not vacate their cells and run down the corridor.

There was no time for goodbyes.

Agna was alone again.

But later, in the dark, she found the memory of the
voices, of the sound of their whispered breaths, a comfort.

There was no food that day, nor the day after that.

On the day following, the kommandant came to see
Agna.

She didn't hear him enter. She woke in the morning
light, to see his face, impassive and serious.

'Mor?' Agna said. She looked past him, through the open door.

'No. Only I. She is in home... your home...'

Agna steeled herself to speak but she could not. A bloom of tiny jellyfish swam in front of her eyes. The world of the cell blurred and shifted like the sea.

'Please,' she whispered. 'I want my mor.'

'You can go home...' the kommandant said.

Agna searched his face. He was not lying. But he continued, 'You only need give them a name.'

'Them?'

'Tell them, or...' He struggled to find the words. 'Or... they will kill you.'

Agna tried to say, 'It was an accident.' But it came out as, 'Itwajaxshideeeeent.'

'I know. For what it is worth, I believe you.'

He took a lighter and a packet of cigarettes and lit one. He sat on the end of the bunk and rubbed his eyes with the heel of his palms. He looked so tired. 'Werner will wait till you give a name, or you die. He will not care if name is Milorg true or not. It is enough you *think* the name is Milorg.'

Agna said nothing, showed nothing. She just stared at him.

'I tell you,' he said. 'They will kill you.'

'They? You are all the same.'

'Are we?' The kommandant threw his cigarette to the floor.

'The war is soon over, but even if Germany lose, the Reich will keep Norway and also Denmark. What you do has no mark on this. You make no difference. Give them the name. And after war, I promise there will be no punishment for him. It is all I can do.'

The dreams still came. Stronger and more vivid.

Dreams of summer. All the golden, green colours and blue shining sea and silver fish.

There were other dreams. Nightmares.

They came again and again. The shadows of the cell, where the moonlight did not reach, formed into something inhuman. She saw it when she was awake. And when she slept. Only in her dreams it came close. She would wake with a frightened start. The shadow was there in the cell. And it seemed real. As she fell asleep, it was closer still. She told herself it was only a shadow. Then slept and it came closer.

The shadow was on her then, there was no light at all. She did not know if she was awake or dreaming. But if she was awake, she could not move. And if she was asleep, she could not wake.

It spoke with Werner's voice.

'There is no escaping us, Agna. There is no way to defeat us. Do you see, do you understand?

'*You think you are brave, but everything you do makes matters worse. For yourself, your mother, your village. For Norway.*

'*Fight, if you like, but then we shall end you too.*

'*You will not simply cease to exist; you will cease to have ever existed.*'

In Agna's delirium, she whispered, '*If.*'

The door opened at dawn, when they liked doing business.

Werner was there and the translator and the kommandant, with someone she had not seen before, a boy, perhaps seventeen or eighteen, in a big jumper and wool hat.

The translator peered into the latrine bucket, then kicked it.

'How long since this needed to be emptied?'

'Days,' the Norwegian boy replied. She knew his voice. He had given her food. He had delivered the blanket after dark and taken it before dawn.

'Sit up, girl,' said Werner. 'Look at me.'

When she did not, he put a finger under her chin and lifted her head. No sooner had her eyes met his, than a blow across her face knocked her head sideways and pain exploded in her brain. He grabbed her chin and made her look at him. She felt blood in her mouth. The blow had knocked her teeth.

'Who poisoned my men?' he said in Norwegian. 'Do NOT look away.'

Agna opened her mouth to speak, to breathe, and could not do either.

'Litenmus. Not me. It was...' She stopped her mouth. But the words had run out, shocked into being by the pain.

'Who is Litenmus?'

Agna gathered herself. Breathe, just breathe. And stop more words, before they come!

'I won't ask again,' said Werner.

'Hauptsturmführer, please!' the kommandant said in German. 'It means little mouse. She's delirious, can't you see?'

'Good. Hold her.'

Hands grabbed her and turned her body round, forcing her face down on the bunk. Her hair was pulled, so she was made to look up at the end of the bunk, where Werner squatted. He spoke, the boy soldier translated.

'He says your papers are not entirely in order. Who was your father, girl? Are you a Jew?'

'This is not—' the kommandant started. But Werner spat back, 'If she is Untermensch, she is mine.'

The translator said, 'What are you, girl? Jew, Roma, Sami?'

'Nor... Norwegian,' Agna gasped.

'Who gave the order?'

The iron taste of blood filled Agna's mouth. It ran down her chin. She looked at Werner. The shadow was not dark any more. It had searching eyes. A thin mouth. She held Werner's gaze, even though she talked through the translator.

'There was no order,' she said.

'Are you Milorg?'

'No.'

Werner put his face close to Agna's. His breath stank of coffee and cigarettes.

'You want to eat? You want go home?' said the translator. 'Name?'

'I am Agna.'

'You did this?' said the translator.

'I didn't know the bread was poisoned. If there had been more, I would have eaten more of it myself.'

Werner looked at the translator and nodded. The soldier released her and her head fell forward, still reeling from the blow. Drops of blood dripped to the floor.

'Hmmm. Well, Kommandant. She is telling the truth,' said Werner.

Agna waited, listening for the clunk of the door, the familiar screech of the bolt sliding into place.

When that did not happen, she lifted her head. The Norwegian boy stood in the open door.

'Don't move,' he said. 'I will fetch some bread; I will warm some soup. After a day or so, they will take you to a women's camp.'

Winter, early 1945

Liva

I stared out of the window into the night.

'Close the curtains, we'll be warmer,' said Tove, standing by the stove, stirring broth. 'There is nothing to see.'

I looked anyway. There was no book of fairy tales to read. No Haakon, or even Agna, to annoy. Only Tove. And she was dull as bone broth without dumplings, and was, anyway, worn out looking after Mor and doing housework and gathering and chopping larch wood.

In the evening, I lived in my own world, in the dark beyond the window.

Life under the invaders is full of secrets and hidden things, I thought.

I had a lot of them. And no one to share them with.

The island (before that secret had been discovered).

Haakon and his news sheets.

Smuggling food to Sergei and the prisoners.

Poisoning soldiers.

Secrets with consequences.

Agna. The camp. The villagers. There was scarcely any food. People were beginning to starve.

'Oh, Agna, I am sorry,' I said to the night. And I was. But whenever I thought of going to Agna's house and telling the kommandant it was me, not Agna, who poisoned the bread, a barrel of quivering eels wriggled in my stomach, my mouth dried and I felt sick.

'I thought you were fetching wood?' said Tove.

'I will. There's not much left.'

'I'll chop more tomorrow. We can't let Mor get cold.'

Mor was in bed asleep. It was a great worry, how she did not get better, but spent her days sleeping, or sitting in the chair by the stove coughing.

'Go *on,* Liva.'

'I will, I'm just…'

'Day dreaming! As always, only it is night. Is night dreaming different?'

I pulled the curtains wide, scanning the ground in front of the house.

'Why do you look?' said Tove. 'Before you go out. *Every* time.'

I shrugged.

'If they were going to arrest you, they would have done it, silly,' said Tove. 'And *you* haven't done anything. You are not guilty simply by association.'

'What does that mean?'

'It means you have nothing to worry about.'

'Tove, what do you think they are doing with Agna?'

'We discussed this. Keeping her in the camp. She sows trouble that one, and now she reaps.'

'Haaky could be in a prison now, if it wasn't for Agna.'

'We have been through this too,' said Tove with a hefty sigh, pointing the ladle at me. 'He panicked. They weren't after him. They were after Milorg. The rumour is that they guided those bombers in. Truth is, if it were not for Agna, Haaky would be here with us now. That feral! I'm glad she's in prison.'

'Tove. *She* is brave. *She* is fighting the invaders.'

'What are you trying to say... exactly?'

'Girls, please,' Mor's voice croaked from the bedroom.

Tove came from the stove and I came from the window, and we stood, hands on hips, nose to nose, to whisper our argument. I got my blow in first:

'Go on, say it! A quiet life is what we need now. Keep our heads down, wait for the war to be over. Because the Germans will lose, but keep Norway. Then what? Pray Haaky and Pappa will be delivered back to us? You think they will go unpunished? We have to fight. Then *maybe* Norway will be free.'

'That's a big maybe, sister. Grand words. You are so naïve. There are more German soldiers arriving all the time. They will lose France and Russia, but make peace and maybe keep Poland and Czechoslovakia, and for sure, Denmark and Norway. Churchill and Stalin won't help us. The sooner it's over the better.'

'You're a coward!'

I watched my words hurt Tove, sure as a wasp sting. Her bottom lip quivered.

'Who makes broth? Mor? She is too ill. Who brings in the money now you can't work at the camp? It isn't you serving Germans in the hotel in Dallansby, or making the beds of visiting officers. You think I like that? *I* should not be working. Pappa should provide, Haaky too, but what good are they to us? Pappa is with the Brits. He may never see home again! Who chops the wood? Haakon? He is in hills. Who holds your hand when you cry at night, and soothes you before you wake? Yes! And you don't even know it. Who will run this house now and get more medicine from the kommandant? You?'

Now it was my lip trembling. Me who was stung, and so sharply, because Tove spoke the truth, though I knew better than to admit it.

'Oh, yes, you are *so* brave to do these things,' I said. 'Well, *I* have done brave things.'

'What? Playing truant, using Mor as an excuse? Don't make me laugh.'

'No, really brave things, to help with the war. You are not brave!'

'Not brave, no, I do what I have to because I have no choice. You think I wouldn't rather be dancing to records, sneaking aquavit with my friends. Visiting Oslo like girls my age used to, to buy a dress? Being chatted up by young men. But there aren't any, are there?'

'Oh, there's plenty of handsome young Germans. I've seen you smile at one.'

The slap came from nowhere. It stung more than any words. I rubbed my cheek.

It had been years since we'd had an actual fight and I knew if it was not for Mor in the next room, we would now. But we were older and tougher and this would hurt more. We stood like rutting reindeer, ready to lock antlers and I thought, *Tove, you will now suffer.* I opened my mouth to explain the many ways, but the words caught in my throat. Tove looked to the broth. It was bubbling and would need to be stirred and moved to the edge of the stovetop. And the stove needed more wood.

'I...' I started.

'What?'

'The brave thing. I did it.' My words came from nowhere.

'Did what?'

'Nothing.'

'*Liva?*'

'Nothing.'

'Liva. I know that face. What?'

'I put the poison in the bread. Not Agna. It was the poison mushroom powder, the dried fly agaric the elders used to keep flies away when they made jam.'

'No, you didn't. Why would you say that?' Tove almost laughed.

'Because I did. Now you know.'

Tove's jaw dropped. She glared at me, and I nodded.

The anger on Tove's face vanished, replaced with round-eyed horror.

'*Why?*'

'Because I thought they might come for Haaky! I think he was more involved than he ever let on. And they had their list. And now... now...' Tears quickly followed my confession. 'Agna is in the dark and all alone, I feel it, I see it in the night. No fire. No warm bed. Or bowl of broth. And there's so little bread, and it's so expensive and that's my fault too. And all the village heirlooms used to buy food for the prisoners. And now the prisoners and the villagers suffer. It's my fault. And I should tell.'

Tove grabbed my arms, whispering fiercely.

'You wouldn't help *anyone* doing that.' She held me tight. And I nestled firmly in the crook between her neck and shoulder, sobbing and sobbing.

'What's going on?' Mor's ghostly voice sang from the bedroom. 'Is everything all right?'

'*Yes, Mor,*' we sang back.

'There's nothing you can do,' Tove whispered into my ear. 'And you must not... You must not tell *anyone* what you did.'

I wept and snuffled, trying to contain my tears, till Tove held my shoulders tight and forced me to look her in the eyes.

'Yes?' she said. She spat in her hand and held it out. And held it there, in the silence, till I did the same and shook her hand.

'I won't,' I said. 'Not till all this is over, anyway.'

'Good,' said Tove. 'Now go and fetch wood. There's nothing more you can do.'

Those words. *There's nothing more you can do.*

I went and fetched more wood, then sat at the window, and asked, into the darkness: *Agna, what would you want me to do?*

The darkness answered. And what it said, made me afraid.

Someone always rose before dawn to put logs in the stove and brave the cold to visit the outhouse. If Mor or Tove heard me, they would just go back to sleep.

But when to get up?

I told myself to try to sleep. But knowing what I had to do, I found it hard.

Eventually, when sleep itself seemed a dream, I decided to get up.

The bed was warm, and the dark full of soft, warm sounds: Mor's breath, Tove's snuffles. I wished for nothing more than the whole house to be filled with snores, even Pappa and Haakon's troll grunts.

I sneaked out of the bedroom.

I put two logs in the hot ashes in the stove, shut them in tight so the heat would build, and made sure the vent was open, so they would catch and burn.

I scribbled a note on a brown paper bag.

Dear Tove,
    I have gone to make amends.
    Don't worry, I am not doing anything dangerous.
    Tell Mor I've gone to Dallansby to collect rations.

I paused, putting a hand to my cheek, where Tove had slapped me. It still smarted.

    Sorry about what I said. You are brave.
    Liva X
    P.S. Burn this note.

In my mind, I added:

    P.P.S. About it not being dangerous, I'm lying.

The rucksack, clothes and skis were where I'd left them the night before in the wood store. I got ready in the dark. I wore an old jumper of Haakon's he used when orienteering. He always said never trust a jumper with no holes in. If it's that old, it's a good one.

I had never skied at dawn and often wondered why Haakon bothered. Now, today, I knew. My nightmares had been full of that terrible swastika, its mechanical spider legs black as night, its white the snow of Norway, the red that surrounded it, a sea of blood.

This world was not a nightmare, but a living dream: the fresh snow, branches of trees that shone with green fire. The crisp blue of the empty sky. Distant mountains, giants watching me.

I didn't want the journey to end. As I approached Dallansby, it got harder and harder to put the sticks in the snow and urge myself forward.

There was only one sentry at the checkpoint.

I showed him my papers and the ration book. He signed for me to remove my rucksack, which he looked through while I stood in my skis, panting, hoping he'd think it was from effort not fear.

'There is no bread in our village,' I said as though this might explain it. He looked at the ration book, and at me. He didn't seem to understand Norwegian.

He handed the rucksack back and waved me through.

The baker's door had a 'Closed' sign in the window, and it was so frosted up I couldn't see in. But the door had a letter box, so I opened that and peered in. A wonderful smell hit me, a wave of joy. My knees buckled. I allowed

myself a few seconds enjoying the doughy, baking won-
der-scent, before knocking.

'Hallo!'

The baker came. Through the letterbox, I could see his
pinny and bulging tummy.

'We are not open yet!'

'I've come from Rullesteinsvik.'

'You could have come from Trondheim, it would
make no difference. There are more orders than bread
to fill them. The authorities take priority. And the cost is
high now. If you leave ration coupons, I may be able to do
a small order the day after tomorrow. And don't tell me
a sob story about your starving family, because I hear it
a dozen times a day.'

I didn't know the baker, only what Haakon had told
me. I knew he was a good man. But clearly he'd been
toughened by war, like weather ages dead wood.

'I have money,' I said. 'Please let me in.'

'I don't take money, only coupons. Off with you, or I'll
call the police and say you tried to bribe me!'

'I'm Haakon's sister, Liva.'

The door opened, the baker surveyed the empty street,
stroking his beard, then ushered me in.

He fired a lot of questions at me about Haakon and our
family. Things only a sister would know.

Then he took me to the bakery behind the shop. There
was a great basket of rolls, already made. I had to swallow
so as not to drool.

'Here.' He gave me a roll.

'It's all accounted for, Liva. I can give you some small amount because you are Haakon's sister. But they check the orders and stock every day. The grain has to travel a long way and the price is steep. Bending rules is dangerous and getting more so.'

'Like delivering news sheets?' I mumbled through a mouth of bread.

'Oh, you know!'

'Haaky never said, I guessed. And he was involved in more than that, as I am sure you know.'

The baker folded his arms and scowled in such a way that I instantly regretted telling him.

'No comment. Who else knows about him?'

I thought of Agna, in a cell or hut or camp, being questioned by the black caps.

'Who else?' he asked again.

'Er, no one… as far as I know.'

'How many coupons do you have?'

I put the ration book on the table. 'I need to return with bread, for appearance. That's not why I'm here, though.'

I reached into my trousers and pulled out the small bag I had hidden. I took from it two silver coins. 'Haakon left this in the house. But there's more. I need to speak with the Milorg.'

The baker eyed the coins suspiciously.

'That's a lot of bread.'

'The Milorg.'

'You can't just make an appointment. They don't know you.'

'Haaky is one of them now, they could send him?' I said, my voice suddenly high.

'It doesn't work like that. I don't know where he is but it's nowhere close. He's too recognisable and he's on their lists.'

'Oh.' I deflated like a birthday party balloon. So, he had been right to flee. 'One of the others, then?'

'There's a market for goods, if you have... this.' He nodded at the coins. 'You don't need Milorg for that.'

'It's something else.'

'What?'

'I'm not allowed to say,' I said, congratulating myself on this pretence.

'Hmm. Well, there are different branches of Milorg, as I am sure you know.'

'The communists. Those are who I need to talk to.'

'Liva, I don't know how much Haakon told you, but these men are... ruthless. They fight like dogs. They sacrifice their own for their cause, without thinking. They take risks. They murder collaborators. They are on our side, but that doesn't make them good.'

'I know. But it's them I need to speak with.'

It was a tense time, waiting for the delivery boy to arrive. He was then sent by the baker to fetch the Milorg operative.

The man who came was short, dark-skinned and unshaven, with fierce blue eyes. A northerner, I guessed, maybe part-Sami. He wore a threadbare cap and hole-ridden coat. There was an odd calmness about him that made me nervous.

I was left with him, while the baker and the boy went in the shop.

The man took a roll and tore off a chunk with his teeth, staring at me while he chewed. He was waiting for me to speak first. I gave him the coins.

'Funds for our war chest?' He weighed them in his hand.

'I want to see Haakon,' I said.

'Of course you do.'

'Where is he? Is he well?'

'He's alive. If I knew where he was, I wouldn't tell you.'

'I'm his sister.'

'If the fascists believed the sister of our comrade knew his whereabouts, you'd be in a cell. You would have told them already.' He placed the coins on the table. 'You put me in danger for this? You want to buy your brother?' He smiled. It wasn't friendly.

'No. I need to buy food.'

'There's a market. You don't need us for that.'

'It's for the Russian prisoners on Fjernøy.'

'Do you know how many camps there are? How many prisoners? Our effort is now best served in sabotage and assassinations.'

'You can stop your comrades from starving.'

'We can't get to them. If we could we would get them food. We have done it before. Now? The SS control the camps.'

'Yes... I...' I stumbled over my words. The idea had seemed so good in the dark. In my dreams.

The man smiled again, without much sympathy. 'I should take the coins anyway. Leave you a receipt, received with much thanks, comrade!'

'Can... I...? Please give me the coins.' My voice was too high, my heart was beating fast. Why, I wondered, do people rarely behave like you imagine they will, or should?

The man stopped laughing. 'Here.' He passed the coins back to me. 'Spend the money on food, you are going to need it, believe me. I will get a message to your brother telling him you are well. Goodbye, sister of our comrade.'

'Wait!' I said. 'I know a way to reach the Russians. A way not guarded by Germans. You can get supplies to them. They'll starve if you don't.'

He paused, his finger on the door handle. 'Why do you care?'

'I worked on the island; I know some of the prisoners. And I hate the SS. It was me who poisoned them, me who sabotaged their Aktion. Don't tell Haakon that, I'm trusting you.'

The man let go of the door handle, and there was no denying it, he was weighing me up, as if suddenly I was as important as the silver. There was no hiding what was in those eyes. Curiosity, and perhaps respect.

'You?'

'Yes. We had poisoned mushroom powder on the island, from before the invasion. I know the island very well, that's how I know the route in. You can get to the fence on the west side, it's up a cliff so steep it isn't guarded and the perimeter will be easy to get through. You can even put the supplies over the fence when they're foresting.'

'You think we can go in and out and the SS won't notice? You are brave; in fact, I am sure we can use you. But not for this.' He turned again.

'Wait! There's more, much more.'

'More what?'

'Of this.' I held up the coins. 'It's buried on the island.'

Now he really laughed.

'Buried treasure. Is this a fairy tale? Is it guarded by nisse?'

'Yes, you could say that, and under the Germans' noses. One of our boys took all our valuables the day of the invasion; gold, jewellery, diamonds. He took it and buried it. We think it cost him his life.'

'How much more?'

'A fortune. You need that money, don't you? The end of the war is coming and whatever happens in Norway, whether we are free or not, you will need money, won't you? I mean... the Milorg will need money.'

He shrugged, pulling down the corners of his lips and scratching his chin. 'It's always useful.'

'I can draw you a map,' I said.

'I have to speak with people.' He came back and reached down, to take the coins. I was relieved that he took only one. 'There is no need for a map. If we run this mission, you will show us yourself. We'll call when we need you. And if this is a trap, we will kill you. Do you understand?'

Tove

I was chopping larch logs. Liva was filling the basket and piling it in the wood store.

'This is a good way to get warm, eh?' said Liva.

'Sure,' I said, swinging the axe.

I *was* warm. But my shoulders ached and my stomach rumbled.

We had more than some, with my work in the town, but cooking, bartering, cutting, lifting and carrying wood, took its toll. Life got less bearable every day. I was exhausted and with summer coming, I'd have to dig a new latrine pit.

The cold never let up. I was hungry as a lost winter wolf and the fire was a baby dragon, with an appetite for logs.

I put the axe down and leaned on the handle, looking down the path towards the village.

'Are you resting?' Liva asked me, after a time.

'No, look.'

A hooded figure was walking along the path to our house, a figure stooped and stumbling low. Possibly an old woman. This person walked like Mor did on the rare occasions she made it out of the house.

This was not an old woman, though.

'Miss Bridget!' Liva cried. She ran to the teacher and hugged her.

I walked down to greet her too.

'They let you go!' I said.

Miss Bridget nodded. 'Almost all of us. They had to, the camps are so full of Russians and Milorg they don't have room for us, and a lot of communities kicked a fuss up about us. With everything else the Nazis have going on we are one headache too much, so they released us.'

'Come in,' said Liva. 'We have some tea that we were saving.'

'No. I cannot stay.'

There was a crack in her voice. She seemed to hide under the hood, but we could see her face. It was too thin, too pale.

'They didn't feed you, did they?' Liva said. 'We have food. Fish. I caught some off the rocks, even though they don't come inshore much this time of year.'

'No. I have two messages for you. First this, but read it later.' Miss Bridget slipped a folded note into Liva's pocket. 'What have you got mixed up in, Liva?'

'I don't know what you mean.'

'I think you do.'

'Miss Bridget, what is this? Please, you are weak, come in.'

This was the ghost of the woman we knew.

'Don't worry about me.' Miss Bridget forced a smile. 'I can find work teaching Norwegian to soldiers. No matter what's going on in Europe, they seem sure they will be staying here. I can earn money. I can pay for food.' Her voice shook with a fierce pride. 'Anyway, as I say, I came to deliver another message. From Agna.'

'You saw her?' A dread pit opened in my gut. I wanted to hear more, but feared it too.

'No, we only spoke. Her cell was near mine in the prison, before I was moved. She was the moved to a camp also. Not mine. She asked me to tell you, "Be as strong as the trees." She seemed in good spirits under the circumstances,' Miss Bridget said, and I could not tell if this was true or not.

I tried to get the note off Liva, I tried to get her to tell me what it said. But Liva ran off.

Liva

In the latrine, I read the note. I knew Miss Bridget's handwriting. This was not written by her. The words put ice in my stomach.

Tonight. Midnight. Coast path. Half a kilometre south of village, by shore.

I tore it up and dropped it into the pit.

Part of me spoke to myself, in no uncertain terms: *I should not have gone to Dallansby. They can find the island and the path without me.*

But another part said: *Look at Miss Bridget, look at the villagers, at our diet of fish-bone stew, old potatoes and old dried mushrooms, even tree bark.*

How long will winter last? What will the Nazis do now? They have their back against the wall. And Norway is that wall. The future is not a certain thing. Things are bad, but how much worse will they get?

And if it is this bad here, what is happening on Fjernøy?

Questions sang in my mind, dancing to the tune of dizzy hunger.

Don't do this!
You must do this.
I can't.
I must.

Which of the voices was mine, or was I only the girl listening to them torment me?

Then I thought of the man; his cruel laugh, his veiled threats. A man who could do terrible things.

Was that a good thing?

I wrote a note for Tove.

> *There is something I have to do. Don't know when I'll be back. It's not dangerous, don't worry.*
> *Liva x*

Tove

Liva came home the following evening.

It was no small relief when she finally trudged up the path.

I waited on the balcony, wrapped in coat, hat, scarf and mittens.

Oh, the look she gave me! *Oh, hell*, she must have thought, *I'm for it now.* But I greeted her with hugs and kisses and tears and pulled her inside, sat her by the fire, and gave her tea and a hunk of bread to chew. We spoke quietly so as not to wake Mor, sleeping in the bedroom.

'I heard you rise,' I said. 'I told Mor you went to Dallansby to interview at the hotel where I work, and that if you were successful, you'd work immediately. I've had to make up such lies to cover for you, you imp!'

'But you didn't stop me?!' said Liva. 'I swear I didn't know I'd be gone this long.'

'I thought you'd gone out for a pee, and when you didn't come back, I looked for you, then I saw your note. I came out but had no idea which way you'd gone. And besides, I didn't want Mor disturbed.'

'What's that on your face?'

I fetched the hand mirror. Liva's face was streaked with grime. Her eyes were wide and wild.

'Now you look like one of the Milorg!' I said.

'It's ash and mud and boot polish. So as not to be seen.'

'And were you?' I said, now more than a bit afraid. 'Seen?'

'No. Well, that's not quite true. We were seen. But mostly the thing was a success.'

'*Mostly?* We? What happened? Tell me! If you have put us in danger the least you can do is tell.'

'No. I'm not allowed.'

Those words. Like bombs falling.

'Not you as well now, sister. Not you. It's too much. Will I lose you too? I don't want to be here alone with Mor, I don't!'

The silence then was deep as the sea. I had a million questions I knew I could not ask. If only to protect Mor. Knowledge can be dangerous. I wiped Liva's face with a damp cloth. And she thanked me. For respecting the rules. For not scolding her.

'There are only so many secrets a girl can keep,' she said at last. 'Listen up. And never tell anyone *obviously*.' Liva spat in her hand. I did the same and we shook.

'It was a hell of an adventure, Tove. I know I can exaggerate, but every word of this is the truth, I swear.

'Good things happened, but something terrible too and I will need your help. The most important thing I suppose, and what I must tell you first, is that I saw Haaky.'

I dropped the cloth I was using to clean Liva's face. I am sure my jaw dropped too.

'He's safe and well. He'll be back in the hills now. He was so brave.'

As I finished washing the dirt of the night from Liva's face, she told me her tale.

Liva

My heart calmed a bit once I was away from the village, but I tell you, when you are just by yourself like that, it's awful. I had no torch, there was no moon, there were no silhouettes of islands, or distant mountains to help me navigate. A good night for a mission and that is why they chose it, I suppose, but I had only the snow on the ground to see by.

I got to where the path drops by the shore and a boat could get in. Half a kilometre, I think, but how would I know?

'Hallo?' I whispered. There was nothing but shadows there and I waited and waited and reckoned I had the wrong place. Then the shadows became the shapes of men, coming out of the thicket. They wore fishermen's coats and jumpers and caps. And they had rifles or machine guns.

There were four. The one in charge said, 'We had to wait, see you weren't being followed.' No one was introduced, of course, only then one stepped forward and said *my* name.

Well, I almost exploded with joy! I hugged Haaky *so* tight.

Then the man who had spoken first, the one in charge, made this clicking sound. Three times. There was a reply from out at sea and I heard oars in the water.

A boat had been there the *entire* time, only a few metres away. It was the kind with a small mast but that you can row too, with long oars.

There were two men in this boat and they brought it to the shore and we filed in.

I was told to sit at the back and guide them, but first they put the camouflage all over my face.

In the boat were crates and a bag. I thought it was food for the Russians. But the bag was bulky and then I was sure it was guns.

'We are not going to fight, are we?' I said.

'We are going to bury or hide these,' the man said, and that was the only explanation I got.

I whispered to the rower where and when to turn. And I saw why they needed me. I was map and compass. But it was so dark I was not sure I could navigate. Haakon helped. This trip is in our bones. As we got closer my eyes were like an owl's and I could see the shape and size of the islands. I realised I knew the way, even in the dark.

All was deep night and silence, apart from some bird's cry, now and then. I didn't *want* to see or hear anything.

All I could think about was floodlights and engines, gunfire and dying at sea. This was war and I was in it, with Haaky and the Milorg. I rubbed my pendant that Agna gave me, and I prayed.

Keep us safe, keep us safe, and crossed myself. But now, you know, I think I was not praying to God, but to the night and the sea.

We saw the lights from the camp and then came the hardest part, rowing out and around, exposed, because there was no shoreline to cling to. The Milorg had their guns ready the whole time, Haaky too. It was as if a battle might start any second.

Round we went and I took us in, and whether by luck or not, I got us to a tiny inlet, a shelf of rock Agna had shown me. Haakon would never have found it.

I thought they'd leave me in the boat, but the man said I was to show them the perimeter and also that everyone was to take turns working as lookout once we were up.

They pulled the boat up and leaned it against the cliff, so it couldn't be seen from the top. Then up we went, one after another, through the forest, and soon saw the perimeter where they had cleared the trees, and there were posts and barbed wire.

We made a kind of den there, and while some of them kept their rifles trained on the camp, the others buried the guns.

Three of them made their way to the perimeter with the crates of food. I thought they would be in and out, that they would make their way to the huts, but the man told me they had to get inside and hide and wait till dawn, then, when the prisoners went into the woods on work duty, make contact with them and arrange a way to make exchanges, or for the prisoners to find the food and guns.

It was the longest night and longest day I ever lived. We could do nothing, only lie still and wait and whisper, and hope we didn't see any soldiers. We saw prisoners in the distance. They were felling trees near the perimeter, cutting off the branches and dragging the logs off with great chains. They were ordered around by kapos. Bosses, the Milorg told me, who are prisoners, not black caps. I even saw two of them beat a man who was too weak to work. It was awful. The Milorg boss said there would be a 'reckoning' for these kapos, after the war.

Then the terrible thing happened, and... it was sort of my fault.

Time went on and I was bursting for a pee. It's fine for the men, they just went against a tree. I was allowed to sneak back the way we had come.

So, I did, and found a small clearing. When I stood to do up my trousers, there was a black cap, staring at me. A young one.

He was so shocked, he didn't even raise his rifle at first. We just stared at each other. As I stood there, not knowing what to do, he *did* raise his rifle. To have a rifle pointed at you, and a boy with his finger on the trigger.

It's not a feeling I could ever describe. Only that it is cold then, in your heart. Very, very cold. And everything around you is in very, very sharp focus.

He opened his mouth to shout for help, but before he could two Milorg appeared, rifles pointed at the black cap. I have never been so pleased to see anything in my life. Then another came from the side and he had a huge hunting knife which he put to the black cap's throat. He looked to his boss then, and I tell you, he was for sure looking for permission to slit the black cap's throat.

A nod, and he would have done it in a second. Like Pappa putting a shot rabbit out of its misery. But the boss shook his head. The black cap knew if he shot his gun or shouted it would be the last thing he ever did. He lowered his rifle and they were on him like dogs, knocking him to the ground, tying his hands behind his back and stuffing a cloth in his mouth.

One of the Milorg spoke German and he questioned the black cap, who answered with nods or shakes of his head, though at times they had to take the cloth out of his mouth, to let him speak.

It seems he had only just joined the SS and arrived from Germany. He wasn't on patrol or guarding or anything, he was walking about the west of the island because he was quite bored and he thinks Norway is very pretty and was thinking of doing some sketching. He even had a notebook and pencils with him.

It was very tense. The boss did the questioning and the other man and Haaky had their rifles trained on the perimeter. What if the SS came looking for this boy? What if they discovered our men hiding in the perimeter?

The boy kept looking at me, pleading with his eyes. As if I was the only person who could help him, because – though no one said it – they were probably going to kill him. I tried not to look at him when he looked at me, but I couldn't help it.

Eventually they put the cloth back in his mouth, and we waited. And waited. It was awful. The silence was tangible with this awful feeling that there could be guns and blood and death. That this quiet world of snow and trees and grey skies could explode or vanish in a second.

After another lifetime of waiting, we saw our men by the perimeter. They signalled, and I think the plan would have been to wait till dark for them to come to us. But the boss waved frantically for them to come over, so they did. Of course, there were tracks, but it had started to snow and when the coast was clear, one of the men went into the open and brushed the prints with a branch as much as possible. That was the scariest bit. Had it not been for the snow we would have left sooner, I think.

Anyway, the men who had been on the perimeter had a large bag, no doubt with our village's valuables in it, and were grinning when they returned. The smiles vanished when they saw the black cap!

Then followed fierce whispered talk about what to do. Kill him and bury him there and then? No, because the dogs would find him. Throw him over the cliff, because it might look like he had slipped and fallen? The tide might wash him away or it might wash him in. Use him as hostage? The boss said the SS would not bargain, that they would simply demand his return, and murder more prisoners or Norwegians, to show what happens when you kidnap a black cap. In the end they decided to take him down the cliff to the boat and, once we were off and on the sea, throw him overboard. He'd freeze to death before he could reach the shore, and if they did find his body, they would think it was an accident.

And then I was truly afraid, because we were at war, weren't we? People must fight and people would die, we knew it. But we also did *not* want to know it. Knowing it is one thing, seeing a boy pushed in the water, watching him flail and gasp and try to swim, but freeze and drown is another. When it came to it, of course they had to untie him and take the cloth out of his mouth. I was crying at this point and I had already said, 'Must you?' but the boss man told me to shut up and I am ashamed, because I did shut up.

I tried to remember the terrible things the Nazis had done. To turn my heart to stone. To tell myself he deserved it.

But he looked at the boss and said, surprisingly, in Norwegian, 'Please don't,' and to me, 'Don't let them.' As if *I* had the power to decide...

Anyway, as you might guess from how I am telling this with such enthusiasm, they didn't kill him.

We spent a while hiding by the boat and waited for dark. There was some talk about how the boy might have useful information about the camp. And a lot of disagreement between the men. One said he was a prisoner, and something about a Geneva Convention, and that they'd have to turn him over to the British, who'd come over from Shetland with supplies. Another said, the SS didn't recognise the Milorg, so he couldn't actually surrender to them, and it was best all round to kill him. 'No one will shed a tear,' he said to the boy.

When it was dark, off we went home. Haaky and the others headed to the hills I think, with the prisoner, where there are caves and huts and the Germans rarely go.

I don't know what will happen now. I made Haaky promise he wouldn't let them kill him. The old way, spit and shake. He said it would be justice. But would it? What good could it do?

Besides. All this will be over soon, won't it?

Dawn

News sheet spring 1945

NORWAY, HOLD STRONG!
VICTORY IS CLOSE.

British and American armies advance into Germany from the west, the Russians from the east. Defeat of the Reich is inevitable.

The Nazi High Command talk of Total War. Yet, other actors within the Reich push for negotiated surrender; to retain the lands of all German-speaking people, and of Denmark and Norway. There is talk of making Norway their last stronghold. Thanks to our spies, we know this is no rumour.

Many in Norway are aware of this and are fearful.

However, our king and government in exile have assurances from British and American powers.

There will be no settlement!

This war will be prosecuted to its end. The only outcome acceptable is surrender without condition by Germany and its allies. Hitler, his henchmen, Quisling and all Norwegian traitors will face justice.

The Russians and Fins are fighting the Nazis in the north of Norway. Across our nation, in mountains, forests, ports and villages, our fighters appear without sign or warning. They blow up railways, steal supplies, attack barracks and liberate prisoners. They vanish as quickly. Our country, our mountains, forests, islands and fjords – these are our allies and protectors.

We can also report that the Germans have attempted to develop new and devastating weapons in Norway. Weapons that can destroy cities that could have won the war for them. Thanks to the operations of Norwegian heroes these plans have been thwarted.

Norway, it is darkest before dawn. We must keep strong. We must hamper the enemy, we must not in the hour of our victory abandon our cause, no matter what actions the Nazis take. No matter the cost.

There are many among you, in your communities, in families, who have performed heroic deeds, in total secrecy and under constant threat.

Your efforts will blossom and flower in this new spring.

Support the Milorg. The time has come. Freedom is at hand.

Long live the king.

God save Norway.

Late spring 1945

Tove

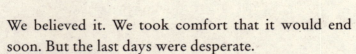

We believed it. We took comfort that it would end soon. But the last days were desperate.

We knew what was coming, the Nazis knew too. But did they throw down their arms and wait for the end? No. Just as we, at the beginning, believed the impossible, that we would in the end be free. Now in the last days, they believed in their own impossible dream, that they would keep Norway, that the Reich would survive. And even if they knew in their hearts that this was a lie, they knew only blind obedience. It made them even more dangerous. You see, each soldier, from fanatics like Werner, to profiteers like Hans, to professional men like the kommandant, to boys in ill-fitted black-cap uniforms, each and every one of them had made an oath.

'I will be loyal and brave. I pledge obedience unto death.'

This oath was not to Germany, not to the Reich, not even to the army. It was to Hitler.

As long as he lived, the oath stood.

But then Hitler ended it, with a bullet to his own head.

Liva

I told Tove later that my dreams were full of trolls, groaning and moaning. Gnarled, snaggle-toothed, wart-ridden monsters, with eyes like swamp pools. The creatures that always haunted me. But these were not trolls who hid in shadows under bridges, or in caves, but gigantic beings filling the sky, looking down on the villages, fishing ports, forests, valleys and mountains.

The trolls looked down and laughed, and talked with each other in a rough guttural tongue I could not understand. It surprised me greatly that, for once, I was not afraid of them.

It turned out the trolls' grunts were the sound of trucks. Tove heard it all. But did not wake me.

When the rolling thunder of engines vanished in the night, she pushed me gently back on to the bed. We sisters and Mor slept soundly until after dawn.

I woke to the smell of fresh coffee, which Tove served us in bed along with toast made from stale bread, refreshed with water. Each slice carried a scraping of blueberry jam.

'What's *this*?' I said.

'I've been saving it,' she replied, as though this would explain it. 'Mor, after breakfast, I want to take Liva to see something. Something rather special. We will not be gone long.'

'See what?' I said, suspicious of Tove's smile.

'Don't go out,' Mor said. 'It's not safe. Mrs Skogvold told me of SS in Kysten, who have been shooting people.'

'No, Mor,' Tove said, holding Mor's hand and rubbing it. 'No one will shoot us. I heard in the night. It is safe, I promise. Liva, you heard too. It gave you nightmares, I think.'

'Heard what?'

'You'll see. After breakfast.'

I stuffed my toast in my mouth and burned my tongue with coffee. 'Breakfassht dun. Show me.'

The sun was up and harsh. Steam and wisps of mist rose from the lingering patches of ice and snow.

Tove took me by the hand, pulling roughly, trying to get me to run.

'But... soldiers,' I said.

'What soldiers?' Tove laughed.

We ran and ran and ran the short distance to the centre of the village.

On the common stood a tall makeshift pole; a rough, thin sapling with its branches shorn. From the top of this pole a home-sewn Norwegian flag shifted softly in the breeze.

I stopped dead. A girl turned to stone in a fairy tale.

'Well?' Tove beamed.

'I... I...'

I had lived this moment a hundred times. Dreamed it, seen it, breathed it. I had imagined songs, and dancing and cheering, and hats flung in the air.

But there was just Tove and me, staring at the flag on the pole.

'Where is everyone?' I said. Two women stood on the dock by the shore, looking out to sea. Other than that, no one was about.

'Off to Dallansby.'

'Oh,' I said. My first thought was that we should dance. There was no music, only the breeze in the treetops, and the whistle of the wind from the sea, chilling my cheeks. And, I realised, in spite of what I'd imagined a hundred times, I didn't want to dance. Not at all.

'Is it over?' I asked.

'That's what some say. Others say not. It is *here* anyway. Maybe everywhere else too. It *must* be... almost. No one would put a flag up else, would they? Perhaps the Germans have gone to fight in the north. Maybe to surrender. This is why folk have gone to Dallansby. Everyone is desperate to know. There's a plan to get hold of a radio.'

'Oh,' I said again. 'I see.' I looked at the flag and at Tove, then at the flag again.

'Look,' Tove said, putting a hand on my shoulder. 'If it is *not* over, it can't be long now.'

'Yes. If you say so.'

'Are you okay? You are shaking. You're very pale.'

'I feel I am dreaming,' I whispered, gazing into her eyes. 'Am I?'

'No. You know what this means don't you?'

I tried to get words out, but it was difficult. I swallowed, and took a deep breath, 'It means... it... Will... will...?'

Tove nodded, her eyes glistening with tears.

'Pappa come home? And Haakon?' She smiled. 'Yes, I really believe they will.'

I fell to the ground then, to my knees, covered my face with my hands and began to sob.

Tove

People emerged from their houses, like animals from their winter lairs; assured, finally, that it was safe.

There were rumours of gunfire and explosions in the night. But no one knew for sure. The wind had been from the west. Had the sounds come from fighting inland or out to sea? There was a lot of mist; if there were lights and flashes from guns, no one saw them.

The soldiers left as quietly as they could. The only thing anyone knew for sure was that if the camp had been evacuated, it must have happened by sea. Only the SS had left from the land.

There was rumour of 'liquidation', but no way of finding out. No one had a boat. And no one, it seemed, was keen to find one and go to look.

Apart, of course, from Agna.

She'd been kept in the internment camp till the end. It turned out she had an okay time of it. Compared with others at least. Thanks, I am sure, to the kommandant.

She appeared at our porch in the morning, hungry for news. She didn't stay long, just enough for us to learn Dallansby and the nearby villages were free too. We wanted to know everything, but all she was interested in was the island.

'Rumours of gunfire in the night,' she said.

'Where are you going?' I shouted after her.

'To get a boat!'

'There aren't any!'

'I'll find one.'

'I want to come, there's things I have to tell you,' Liva said.

'Wait on the dock, then!' And she was gone.

'You are not going anywhere, Liva!' Mor and I both said.

'Try to stop me!' she replied.

Liva

The morning sun burned off the mist. I watched the distant black smoke from the fires on Fjernøy spinning and curling into the sky. And waited. Two hours. Maybe three. Tove came to find me, with a basket of rolls and fish cake and coffee.

'Mor says again you can't go to the island,' Tove reported. 'It's too dangerous. Haakon would say that if he was here. Pappa too.'

'They are not, though, not yet. Agna isn't going alone,' I said, folding my arms, keeping my eyes fixed on the sea.

'Aren't you scared?'

'Yes, I am.'

'Agna won't be back any time soon. She won't find a boat.'

'She will.' I believed this, but also reckoned, in my heart, that Agna would most likely go straight there, as soon as she could. I decided to wait anyway.

Agna came from the south, rowing a small, paint-flaking, tar-and-cloth plugged boat. It seemed a miracle the thing was even floating.

Her strokes were deep and fast but when she reached me, she fell back, wheezing and gasping.

'The... the camp. It has made me weak, Litenmus. Will you row?'

'Of course,' I said. Agna forced herself to sit up, and offered me a hand as I boarded.

'What do you think we'll find?' I said.

'I am not hopeful. But I must know.'

I took the rowing seat and Agna huddled in the stern, trying to catch her breath.

There was none of the joy that Tove felt in Agna, nor of the villagers who came back from Dallansby. *Dear Agna,* I thought. *It's not over for you, is it?*

'They had guns, Agna. Hidden.'

Agna sat up and forward, her face a mask of shock. 'What?'

'And food. They may have used the guns if they had to. It's possible it was those guns that were heard in the night.'

'That's impossible.'

'No, it isn't.'

I told Agna my tale then, the same as I had told Tove. But more quietly this time, with simple stated facts.

Agna listened, silently guiding the boat with arm signals.

When I finished, I waited, but she didn't answer at first; she looked at the islands and the sea, deep in thought.

'Well? What do you think happened?' I said.

Agna shrugged. 'After they lost a soldier? God knows what they might have done.'

If it was possible, she looked even more tired; drawn with sadness.

'But they might have fought, Agna. Sergei might be... okay,' I offered.

'I know. I have hope, Litenmus... but I am even more afraid.'

'Did I do the right thing?' I said. 'With the food and the Milorg. I didn't know they would bring guns, I swear.'

'I guess we'll see.' Agna's voice held no anger. She even smiled. But the words were a punch in my heart. I had been bold with strength since the moment I saw the flag flying in the breeze, but now felt helpless, as we got closer and closer to Fjernøy.

I imagined blood and bodies. I tried to see a different picture, Russian prisoners, alive and triumphant. But I could not. As we neared, the island grew large and – in spite of the sun – seemed not like an island at all but a vast, dark green shadow.

The makeshift pier stood, the deck of the floating dock creaked and bobbed in the swell.

The smoke had all but died away, though wisps of it still drifted into the sky.

We approached, alert as deer when the hunter is near.

'Do you think we should have brought a gun or something?' I whispered.

Agna shook her head. 'Too late for that. Besides, they've gone. There's no one here. No one alive anyway.'

'How can you tell?'

'I've got a sense for these things now,' Agna said with certainty. 'Come on. Let's go and see. Whatever there is to see.'

We came ashore and, step by careful step, made our way along the track, through the corridor of trees.

The entire camp had been burned down. There was nothing but a circle of ash and charred, smouldering timber, where posts had been. It was hard even to see the shape of what had been, other than the strings of barbed wire and the bit of the perimeter fence where the flames had not reached. The towers, where soldiers with machine guns had overseen the entire camp, were gone too. Gone up in flames and smoke.

I led Agna to the far side, to where the Milorg had hidden the guns and food. The wire had been cut there.

'Look!' I pointed to the trunk of a tree, where there were tell-tale pepperings of small, perfectly round bullet holes. Other trees told the same tale.

We searched the brush and thicket, near where the guns had been hidden. And found only one thing, one small part of what had happened.

Agna picked the rifle up. 'This isn't German.' A nearby bush had rust-coloured stains on its leaves. Blood.

'They fought,' Agna said. 'At least that. At least.'

We went back to the dock and sat dangling our legs.

'Well?' I said.

'Well, what?'

'What do you think?'

'I think I came for answers and didn't find many, Litenmus.'

Not for the first time that day, I had to think carefully before asking the question burning in my mind.

'What I mean, Agna, is... do you think he's alive?'

Agna looked at the sky and the islands. She took a breath and opened her mouth, but then bowed her head.

'What? What were you going to say?' I asked.

'Nothing. I don't know if he's...' Now it was Agna's turn to struggle to find words. 'How can I?'

'You have a sense for these things, you said.'

'All right, Litenmus.' She reached out and held my hand. 'Yes. If anyone can survive such terrible things, it's Sergei. My nisse. I do believe he's alive.'

Being a little better, Mor took to sitting on the porch until sunset most days.

'The light and warmth are medicine,' she said. It was true enough. But the real reason, we knew, was to look for Haakon's return.

One day Agna and I walked to Dallansby to get rations, and as we arrived, we heard accordions, drums, trumpets. A chorus of singing. The old songs. The sky was full of music.

We ran to streets alive with cheers and dancing and flags, so many flags! Folk had hidden some, and of course, been busy making them.

We joined in. Even Agna, who had not smiled or laughed much since she came home... and then, looking into a cafe window, I recognised the Milorg man.

The cafe was empty, other than two men at a table, drinking coffee and smoking, watching the reeling, chattering crowd through the open window.

One man wore the same dark cap and coat as he had on our mission to the island.

'Hey,' I said. 'It's me, Liva!'

The man nodded and raised his cap.

'A wonderful day, yes?' I said.

'The day we defeat the fascists is a *very* good day.'

'Do you know where Haakon is?'

The man looked at his companion.

'Come on,' I said. 'It's over.'

The second man nodded.

'He is in the hills, guarding the prisoner.'

'Does Haakon even *know*?'

'This?' The man nodded to the street. 'No. We'll get a messenger up there tomorrow. It's a day's walk, too late today.'

'I'll go,' I said. 'Now. I'm fast.'

It was only then I noticed; the men both wore armbands: the hammer and sickle insignia. Communists.

'Why shouldn't I?' I said. 'He's my brother! What can it matter now if I know where your hideout is? You owe me.'

'I told you, it's too late today. And besides, we need to take food and clothes for the men, and take care of other business. And the path is gruelling.'

'Business? Are you not celebrating?' I said.

'Sure, but while people dance and drink, *our* work is just beginning.'

'What work?'

'Finding out what happened to comrades at Fjernøy, for a start. And there are hundreds of thousands of German soldiers in Norway. We are working out what to do with them all. It's a headache, I can tell you.'

'Do with them? I have an idea or two.' I hadn't noticed the short, dark-haired woman behind the bar. She came over, a bottle in one hand and tiny glasses in the other.

'You are Milorg, aren't you? Let's toast. On the house.' By the way she swayed and the sing-song of her voice, I thought this was not her first drink of the day.

'To Norway, and the return of the king!' Agna and I took a glass each to be polite. The men did not move.

'Not our king, comrade,' the man said. 'We didn't defeat one fascist ruler to welcome another.'

The woman laughed and shook her head. 'Try telling *them*.' She nodded to the street. 'To Norway, then. Skol!'

'Skol!' everyone said.

'We want to go to the hills now,' said Agna. The words were simple, and politely spoken. But the room was suddenly quiet.

'Come on, it's okay, Agna,' I said, pulling on her arm. 'Haaky will know tomorrow and be home the day after.' But Agna was a rock, stuck to the floor, staring at the man.

'Agna?' the man said. 'You are from Haakon's village, no? You are *the* Agna?'

'Yes.'

'You, I will toast.' He pointed at his empty glass, and the woman duly poured.

'You owe me nothing,' Agna said. 'But—'

'Wrong, girl. You saved the lives of fellow operatives. She played her part,' he nodded at me, and I admit, I blushed with pride.

'Then at least let us deliver this news to her brother,' said Agna.

'You boys must be hungry,' the woman said. 'I was about to warm some rolls and serve gravadlax and excellent sausage. A few other treats. The Nazis left in *such* a hurry. Come on, our Milorg heroes. It's the girl's brother after all.'

'Would you get a message to our mors in Rullesteinsvik?' I said, and then, to the men, 'We can reach them before nightfall, the days are so much longer now.'

The second man looked at us all in turn, before sighing, and shrugging. 'Well, it is one less thing to do. But you deliver a message, clear? Tell our man there *he* needs to take care of the business.'

'Now.' He clapped his hands and rubbed them together. 'Some food would be most welcome. Oh, and we will need a good map, for our young comrades.'

'He wasn't wrong about the path, was he?' I panted, as we came out of a copse of pine into a clearing, facing a steep climb of streams and rock and brush.

We scrambled and walked and helped each other. The path was easy to lose and difficult to find. The passes were high and often we trod only on crumbling loose rock, hugging a cliff on one side, and a try-not-to-look-down, stomach-churning drop on the other.

We carried food and a bag of change of clothes, which we held high, wading through rivers of fast-flowing melted snow. It was hard, especially for Agna, who was still weak. But the news we carried, and the need to arrive before dark, was fuel and fire in our hearts and kept us going.

It was too much of an effort to chat properly, though I did manage to complain, often and loudly, while Agna remained silent:

'Hill. I am sure he said, *up in the hills*. When does a hill become a mountain, exactly?'

The only other talk was of what 'business' the man had referred to. I kept going on about it, and Agna replied, 'Who knows?' Or, 'Could be anything,' or, 'Doesn't matter.' But I wouldn't let it go, until eventually Agna – who was ahead – turned around, and panted, 'The prisoner, Liva. The black cap. Taking care of *him*.'

I remembered the way the boy had been all the way back on the boat trip. How scared. And now I was scared too.

That was the end of any talk, until we came out of a final patch of woods into a grass covered clearing, high and open to the sky, lit in fire – orange by the falling western sun.

On the far side of this clearing stood a cabin, next to a coppice of short pines, nestled in the bottom of a sheer rock face. A hunter's hut. Its windows were dark. No smoke rose from its chimney. The only way to approach was across the grass.

As we neared, a man emerged from the coppice with a rifle raised.

'Halt! What are you doing here?'

'I am Haakon's sister, Liva.'

'Haakon!' the man shouted. My brother's face appeared at the window, then he burst through the door, looking first surprised, then worried.

'What are you doing up here? Is Mor okay? Tove?'

'They are both fine. Mor is much better.'

'What, then?'

'It's over, Haaky.'

Haakon took a few steps forward before stopping still, with his jaw falling open. The man dropped his rifle on the ground.

'Over?' said Haakon He took a few more steps, but faltered again, held his arms open with a huge grin and said, 'Wait. Who won?' Then he laughed madly, clapped his hands together and lifted me up and spun me round and round.

'Haaky! I cannot breathe!'

'Not dancing?' Haakon said, trying to grab Agna's hand.

'Where's the black cap?' said Agna, putting her hands in her pockets.

'Inside.'

'What did he tell you?'

'Nothing very useful. He'd only just arrived from Germany before we got him, but speaks Norwegian. Information about the camp. Most of it, we knew. I think he tried to lie about how bad it was.'

'Did he say what the plans for the camp were, at the end?'

'No. Said they weren't told. Maybe they only planned on winning.'

Agna marched straight into the hut, and I followed.

He sat with his back against the wall, in the shadows. His hands were bound tight, his upper right cheek was bruised. Crusts of dried blood decorated his uniform. His boots and socks had been taken. His eyes were alive; crystal-bright with fear.

'You really are just a boy.' Agna stood over him. 'How come you speak Norwegian?'

She stepped forward and kicked the sole of the boy's bare foot. Viciously.

'Ow! Why you do that?'

'How come you speak Norwegian? And don't lie. Wir können Deutsch sprechen, if you prefer.'

'In my town they take boys from Hitler Youth. Every boy fourteen years or more is conscript now for home guard and older ones like me it was here or east. I learned some Norwegian, I told not true that I speak more, so they send me here. Understand?'

'Why?'

'I think it will be more comfort here?'

'Is it?'

'No, not for me.'

'Hitler is dead. Germany has surrendered. Everywhere, unconditionally.' Agna paused, watching this sink in. 'Aren't you sad?'

'Will I go home now?'

'The men who sent us, if they had come you would be dead now. You want to go home? You want to live? Answer my questions. Understand?'

The boy nodded.

'What would they have done, once they knew you were missing?'

'I told the boy, Haakon, already.'

'Tell me. I want to know about the camp.'

'Why? What does it matter now?'

'It matters. I worked there for a time, before the SS took over.'

'Ah, like the girl who poison our soldiers.'

'That was me. I tried to kill them all. Didn't use enough poison. My mistake. I'll know better next time. Who knows what else I might do. You're lucky I'm in a good mood. So, tell me... what will they have done, once you were missing?'

The boy sighed. 'I do not know for sure, but there would a punishment. If they think I fell off a cliff, no, but kidnap, yes.'

'There was a prisoner. Sergei. The trickster. You know him?'

'I heard of him. I never saw him.'

'Was he...' Agna breathed rapidly. 'When they got you, was he still there, was he still alive?'

'I don't know. He was strong. Probably, yes. I would have hear if he dies, but then...'

'What?' She kicked the sole of his foot again. 'What?'

'Many was die.'

'You want to go home?'

'Very much.'

'Good. Continue. What was the plan, for the camp?'

'For us to stay. But if we must, move north, burn it, evacuate.'

Agna took a deep breath and clenched her fists.

'And the prisoners?'

The boy looked at the floor then. Agna waited, until he looked up again.

'Kill the weak and ill, move others to bigger camp in the north.'

'That's the truth?'

'I swear.'

Haakon and the Milorg man stood in the doorway, watching.

'What do we do with him?' said Haakon.

'Do you have a message at all from our comrades?' said the man.

Agna opened her mouth to speak, but I blurted, 'Only to come down the mountain with the prisoner.'

The Milorg man said, 'Really? Somehow, I don't believe you. Haakon and I will stay longer. We will bring the prisoner. He will slow you down and you want to return to your families, yes?'

The boy stiffened. They were wolves, he was nothing more than a cornered rabbit.

I put my hand on Haakon's arm. 'You're my brother, Haaky. And it's over. Over I tell you.'

'Do you think he would be the first?' said Haakon. I recoiled. This young man looked and sounded like Haakon. But I did not recognise him.

'Leave him to me,' said the man. 'That is an order. You will be in a hurry to get home, Haakon, I can bring him down. It'll take longer with him being tied.'

'No,' I said, firm as I could. 'We will all leave together.'

'Oh,' the man said. '*You* are Milorg now? You make decisions and give orders?' He was joking, but there was menace in his words.

'I earned my place.'

The man took off his cap and scratched his head. 'Well, yes, but you are not a captain.'

'Actually,' said Agna, 'it was she, not I, who poisoned the black caps.'

He just sighed and said, 'You will leave him with me, Haakon. That is an order.'

'War's over,' said Liva, 'You can't give Haakon orders, he isn't in the Milorg any more.'

'Aren't I?' said Haakon.

'No, you are to return to your previous position as annoying, stubborn, bossy older brother. You were very good at it!' We Norwegians laughed, even the Milorg man.

'Very well,' the man said loudly. 'We'll all go down first thing. Even the black cap.'

I looked at the black cap. He was crying.

The hut was small, and only had two bunks. Agna and I took them, and we slept like the dead. The man and Haakon took turns watching the black cap.

At dawn we had rolls, strips of dried reindeer meat, cans of boiled potatoes and black coffee. Most of what was in the hut they left. But Haakon made sure to find the book of fairy tales and give it to me.

'You can read it every night,' said Haakon. 'I won't complain.'

'Actually, it belongs in school.'

Both the man and Haakon carried rifles. Agna and the boy were the last to leave the hut.

She spoke to the boy, in words she knew he nor any of us understood, and which she hoped she could remember. It took a lot of nagging from me to get her to tell me what she said:

'Be gone, spirit, leave this home, pack your shadows, your dark cold shadows, and leave. Let the golden light of dawn banish you, as mist. Let this house be a place of joy and love once more.'

I listened keenly to Agna's voice. It was louder, with a strange music in it too. It didn't sound like her.

'What language was that?' the man said, as Agna and the boy came out into the cold dawn air. 'Sami?'

Agna did not answer.

The journey home was easier, being mostly downhill and because we knew the way exactly.

Near Dallansby, the path forked and the man said he was leaving the prisoner with us.

'What will we do with him?' I said.

'Whatever you like.' He shook Haakon's hand, and they made an arrangement to meet in the following days.

'Here, change into these.' Haakon threw a sack containing the clothes he had worn for weeks, at the boy's feet, then stepped forward, took his knife and cut the ropes binding the boy's hands. The boy stared at the marks on his wrists; dark bracelets of welt and bruise.

'The path to town is there, once over the second bridge, go left,' said Haakon, pointing. 'Walk into Dallansby, find Milorg, or better, police, and give yourself in. Say you got separated from your unit.'

'What about these clothes? What do I say?'

'Say your uniform got soaked when you fell in a river, and someone gave them to you. Say you stole them. Say anything. Just don't tell them you are SS.'

The boy nodded, Agna and I looked the other way, and he got busy changing.

'Then what?' he said.

'You'll go to Germany, after a time.'

'There is no Germany, only ruins. People were starving there too, when I left. There is only rust and piles of stones.'

When he was ready, the boy stood stiff upright and held out his hand to Haakon.

'I know if had not you and your sister made action, they will have kill me. Thank you.'

Haakon glanced at the hand, into the man-boy's eyes, then picked his rifle off the ground, slung it over his shoulder, and without another word, turned and walked down the path that led to the road, that led to our village.

'Go home,' said Agna. She and I also turned away from the boy and followed Haakon.

Summer, now

Georgy

Tante Liva and Bestemor Tove sit back. Their story is almost done. It's hours past midnight. As we are so far north, the sun will soon rise.

Their eyes glint in the light. I am surprised to see Liva crying.

'We got home late. The next day the celebrations continued in the village.

'A great deal of supplies had been "liberated", and a radio too. It should have been such a happy day.'

'Wasn't it?' I said.

'No, Georgy. Not for me.'

Liva

Haaky, Tove and I helped Mor walk the path to the common.

I had imagined – somehow – that we would all gather at Mose and Agna's house. Like before the war. But everyone was on the opposite side of the common, gathered at Mrs Skogvold's house.

Inside they must have been packed like blueberries in a jam pot. The rickety porch had too many people on it. Others swarmed outside like bees.

Snippets from the radio were shouted out and spread around. Later, there would be dancing and song. For now, there was being together and listening.

As we drew near, I left Mor with Haaky and Tove and walked to Agna's house.

No flags flew there. Both of the front windows were smashed. Shards of glass littered the porch.

'Where is Agna?' I asked an old woman, making her way to Mrs Skogvold's house.

'Her mor is being held for questioning. Collaborator, they say, but I think it's for her own safety. Some have thrown stones at her. In Kysten they have been cutting the hair of such women. The girl has gone to wait for Mose's release. She left an hour ago, before all this started, I saw her.'

'Did she say when she will be back?'

'Back? She was pushing a cart. Looks to me like she was going away. The cart was full. It's probably for the best.'

I ran and ran and caught up with Agna, halfway along the track to town.

'Agna! Agna!' I shouted, as soon as I saw her.

'Hi there, Litenmus,' she said. She did not stop pushing the cart.

'Where are you going?'

'To get my mor.'

'But what is all this?' I said, gesturing at the cart.

'We are leaving. For now, at least.'

I went and stood in front of the cart, so Agna could push it no further.

'What? You never said anything,' I almost shouted in disbelief. I held up my hands and shrugged. 'Nothing!'

'They arrested her last night. I got up early, went for a swim. When I got back, the windows were smashed. Many of our things had been taken.'

'Who did that? Who?'

'Oh, no one knows that, Litenmus,' said Agna, her voice laced with bitterness. 'Believe me, I asked. There is no point in trying to stop me. Soon as they release Mor, we are going. We might come back, or maybe we'll sell the house. For now, we just need to go.'

'Who is questioning Mose? The Milorg?'

'The police.'

'The police! Five minutes ago most of them were working with the Germans.'

'Well, some of them have been arrested by those who weren't such friends of the Reich, or who only collaborated a bit, and there are those who worked with the Germans but were secretly helping the Milorg... I don't know, it's complicated and it's stupid.'

'I guess some of them were just doing what they were told.'

'Well, isn't that the problem? Do you always do what you are told? Do I? Sometimes, but not when what you are asked to do is wrong. Miss Bridget taught us that.'

'Did she? When?'

'Every day.'

Agna pushed the cart then, and I had no choice but to stand aside. I walked alongside a few steps before taking a corner of the cart and helping push.

'Were you not going to say goodbye?' I tried to hide the wobble in my voice.

Agna stopped pushing and turned to me.

I had never seen her cry before. Not like this. Never.

'If I had come to say goodbye to you, Litenmus, I would never have the strength to leave. Do you understand?'

We both cried then, and held each other a while before continuing to push the cart.

'Where will you go?' I said.

'North.'

'Isn't it still dangerous there? There's been so much fighting. Bombing.'

'We know people, relatives of my father. And I will look for Sergei.'

'Relatives? Sami. You know, Agna, I worked something out a long time ago. The book, at the start of the war. The church records. The book you destroyed and made it look like an accident. You weren't in those records, were you?'

'No.'

'You wanted, always, for them not to know who you are. What is the truth? You are part-Sami. And maybe also part-gypsy or Jewish also?'

Agna let out a sigh that was almost a laugh, and stopped pushing and put her hands on her hips. 'Tell me, Liva, why do you want to know?'

'I guess I just want to know who you are?'

'No. You want to know what I am. And so did they. It's how they decide what you are worth. A human or an Untermensch. If you live or die. They were only ever interested in what you are, not who.'

'Oh. I'm sorry. Well, then, to me you are truly the huldra. A hidden creature, whose true identity is a secret, and who can make curses on the invaders, and—'

'Litenmus. You know who I am. You know better than anyone. And that is what matters. Now help me get this cart to town.'

And I did. That was the last I saw of her for many years. She didn't ever find Sergei. After the war, that famous iron curtain drew tight around Europe and the border between Norway and Russia became a wall, and no news passed from one side to the other.

After that? Well, a blur, but I do remember when we went back to school...

Miss Bridget sat on the desk at the front of the class, swinging her legs, looking, I thought, more like a naughty child than a teacher.

Next to her, was a wooden crate.

'Is... is it b... b... books, Miss Bridget?' said Lars, who was not so little any more, being ten years old, and growing faster than a spruce tree.

'No. There will be books. The library will be full once again. This is something else. From a far-off land, with blue skies and endless sun.'

Miss Bridget reached into the top of the crate and took from it an orange ball, which she held in the air.

It looked like a small sun.

'Wh... what is it?' said Lars.

'You probably had one when you were younger. At Christmas. Don't you remember?'

Lars shook his head.

'Orange,' I said.

'I can see what colour it is,' said Lars.

'That's its name,' I explained. 'Orange, or appelsin. Go ahead, Lars, eat it.'

Lars went and took it off Miss Bridget, put the fruit to his mouth, and bit, and immediately spat it out. Some of the others laughed.

'They are teasing,' said Miss Bridget. 'You have to peel it. Come on, children, the government has decided we all need some vitamin C.'

The younger children got out of their chairs and gathered round Lars and Miss Bridget, with hands outstretched. They were like baby birds, clamouring with their beaks open to be fed.

'There's more than enough!' Miss Bridget said, handing oranges to eager hands as quickly as she could.

The children returned to their seats. The youngers looked to us olders to see the best way to get inside the strange fruit. With nails, it seemed, and teeth, or – for some of us olders – a knife.

All the chatter died down. There was a great deal of frowning and concentrating and some grimacing too, at the shock of tasting the vitamin C crammed fruit. The air filled with the oranges' fizzing scent. There were a lot of sticky faces and fingers.

There was no lesson as such after that, only chat about the end of the war, and the return of the king and men who had been away.

Some of the children were silent.

'What shall we do with the Nazi books?' said Henrik.

'Burn them!' someone shouted. There were some cheers, but they were silenced by a firm, 'No!' from Miss Bridget. 'Never. Do you understand, children? Have I taught you nothing?'

'But, Miss Bridget,' I said. 'They are no good to us. No one will want them now. What can we possibly do with them?'

Miss Bridget looked at the children, and for a second, I thought later, it was as though our roles were reversed, and *we* had asked a question to which the teacher had no answer.

Yet Miss Bridget, being Miss Bridget, pondered a while.

'I will talk to the Milorg, we will take them to where the German soldiers and the traitors are being held. We will give them back, and they can do what they like with them.'

'Yeah,' Lars shouted out. 'They'll n... need t... toilet paper!'

'Lars!' Miss Bridget snapped 'I will not toler—' But we were laughing so loud we could not hear her.

Home time came, and we went to put on our coats and collect our satchels. Some took the peel of their oranges, to show to their families. When everyone had left, I came to the front of the class, with my satchel.

'Hallo, Liva,' said Miss Bridget.

'Hallo, Miss Bridget. I've got something for you. Haakon kept it safe for us.'

The book of fairy tales, which was very old and worn even before it had gone on its adventure, was falling apart. Its spine was exposed where strips of the cover had fallen away. Many of the pages were crinkled where they had got damp and had turned yellow, brown and brittle.

'The pages are fragile,' I said.

'Fragile? Yes,' Miss Bridget said, taking the book in her hands. 'Well, we had better look after it, then, had we not?'

When I turned to go, Miss Bridget said, 'Wait, Liva.' She reached inside the crate. 'There is one left. Please take it.'

'No, thank you. You keep it, you did not have one.'

'Oh, it's not for you, Liva,' Miss Bridget smiled. 'It's for Haakon.'

Georgy

Liva falls back in the driftwood chair, sighing heavily, as though she has just returned from a mountain hike.

'That was the end of it. My memories after are mostly a fog, though I remember the day Pappa came home clearly. A day of joy, of course. But in truth he barely recognised me, he could not believe I was now this young woman. He had missed so much. He asked where his little mouse had gone, and I could only say that she grew up.

'Mor died a few months later. I think it was only hope that had kept her alive, and once everyone was home, only then could she give in to the sickness.

'I remember too the day of Haakon and Bridget's wedding. Quite a scandal, because she was a few years older than him. Indeed, she had even taught him, when he was only ten and she nineteen!

'Do you know what is strange, Georgy? We did not talk much of such things after the war. The years and seasons changed, but our lives were uneventful and hard. We only wanted to rebuild our lives. And we did. Then the oil money came at the end of the 1960s. And we changed. The whole country changed. Is that it Georgy, are we done?'

'Yes. Thank you. You've told me so much. Only... one more thing. Did Agna never find out what happened to Sergei?'

'No. We knew there had been a gun fight, that some had escaped and others not. I did not even find *that* out until years later, when she returned for a short time. I had been living in Oslo a while then. I rarely came back myself.'

'That must have been emotional,' I say. 'To be reunited.'

Liva sighs and shakes her head. 'We had changed. The past was the past. We talked, she of life in the north, me of Oslo. But these were different worlds. The things that bound us together no longer existed. We made promises to keep in touch, to write. But we never did. So much hung in the air. How Agna and Mose left. What she had done for me. Unspoken things. There have been summers here and I have heard of her, and her eccentric ways. But I haven't been to see her, nor has she come here. Not for many years.

'Anyhow. Me telling you this has taken hours; it is so late. What will you do with this, our memories?'

'I don't know exactly. But I am pleased. Important to get those stories, before... too much time goes by.'

Tove laughs. 'Before Liva and I die, you mean? Yes. It's only one family's story, of course. Every family who lives through a war has many. Many sadder stories are written every day. I sometimes wonder if there's any hope. I don't look at the news any more.'

'Will you come, tomorrow?' I ask.

'Where?'

'Fjernøy.'

Liva frowns with concentration, then shrugs. 'If I had not told you these things, I would say no. But you have dug up memories. How will we get there?'

'I'll figure that out.'

I rise early, and take Bax into the woods, to find the strange old woman.

Liva and I head down to the shore, in the early afternoon.

I have Bax on a lead. I don't want him to scare Agna again. She is there, waiting, just as we arranged. An old woman dressed in fisherman's jumper, boots and oilskin. She eyes Bax with suspicion.

'Oh! Hei, Agna,' Liva says.

'Hei, Liva, hva handler dette om?'

'We have to speak English, Agna. For the girl.'

CHRIS VICK

'My English is poor. You want to know why I am here? This girl says she want see Fjernøy. She says me she does not know where, so she ask I show. I say I meet here and give her... er... veibeskrivelse... kart. I do not know English.'

'Directions. A map.'

'Ja.'

'Hmm, she said the same to me.' Liva folds her arms and raises an eyebrow, waiting for me to give her an explanation.

'I... I want to see, to hear more. From both of you. About the island,' I say.

Agna looks at Liva.

'She is our family,' Liva says. 'She is interested in the war for a school project. I told her about it. The island. The camp.'

'You want to know about the war?' Agna says. 'There are museums in Oslo. And this... internet.'

'But I am interested in your war.'

Agna shrugs. 'So, the di-rex-shuns.' She speaks to Liva, gazing at the sea, pointing, counting with her fingers.

'Please,' I interrupt. 'Will you show us? Will you come?'

'Why?'

'It... would be good to hear your memories, Agna. And you know the way.'

The old woman eyes me keenly. 'Liva can tell.' And with that, Agna walks past us, back into the woods.

'Wait!' I say, running after her. She turns and stands with raised eyebrows, fierce eyes, folded arms. I glimpse the girl in Tove and Liva's story, hiding in this old woman's body.

'I say you,' she barks. 'There are museum.'

'I can't persuade you?'

'I don't know this word, *purse-wade.*'

She turns, but I put a hand on her arm.

'Is this how you looked at them?' I say. 'How you spoke to them?'

'Who?'

'Werner. The kommandant.'

She opens her mouth, shakes her head, and laughs, in spite of herself.

'Agna, Fjernøy is the museum. You and Liva are my guides.'

Her eyes examine me. Then she stares out to sea. 'I have many memory there,' she says with a slight tremble in her voice.

'I know,' I say. My hand is still on her arm. 'Liva told me all about it.'

I row the old wooden boat. Up the small calm fjord, to the open sea, across blue, green, white choppy water. A breeze ruffles my hair and my cheeks smart. I stop rowing, to pull my jacket tight. Bax stands on the prow, paws expertly placed. I pull on the oars, the weight of us and the wind make the going a slog. I sweat and groan, but I won't admit it's hard, or even slow down. By the time the island is in view I'm exhausted.

The water in the approach to the natural harbour is calmer.

Agna insists she rows now. And although she is so old, she does.

Liva raises her arm and uses it as a compass to guide us to the shore.

We land on the beach at mid-tide. The small bay is as I imagined: the curve of rounded rocks, the shingle crashing and rolling on the shore. The wall of dense trees ahead. It's exactly as Liva described it.

'The tide is rising,' Liva says. 'We must return before low or we'll be stranded.'

We get off the boat on to ground that is reassuringly still, after the windblown sea.

There is no path now, only great pines, crowding close together, their branches entwined. Fingers threaded and hands held. Silent sentinels of whatever lies here.

We walk inland. The world darkens, softens. I look back to the sea shining between the bars of tree trunks and the wind gentles to a whisper.

'This way,' Liva says, marching on, ducking under branches, stepping over roots. Somehow, I'm reluctant to lose sight of the shore. But on we go. It feels like the forest will go on for ever; it sucks us in, like Hansel and Gretel. But we haven't left any breadcrumbs.

Deeper in, the trees thin, and thin again, until we enter a large clearing. Here there are only a few trees and uneven ground of bare rock, marshy dark ponds, clear pools and patches of long grass.

In the middle of the clearing are three wild cherry trees, rich with leaves and heavy with crimson fruit. Some have fallen on the ground. I pick up a couple.

'Don't eat those,' Liva says.

'This is where the prison camp was?' I ask.

'Yes, but our camp was here before the Nazis built theirs,' Liva says, her words hard and flung like stones. 'Remember that.'

I nod, and don't know what to say.

There is no sign of any camp at all, no sign of the island's former life.

Liva and Agna walk forward, slowly, looking about. Agna kneels by a clear pool and cups handfuls of water into her mouth. Then she walks around, scouring the ground till she stops by a group of large bare rocks. 'We can make a picnic here.'

'Shall we make a fire too?' I say. 'It's chilly for summer.'

I head back to the boat with Bax at my heels, to fetch the basket and rucksack with our provisions.

I want to ask all sorts of questions, but it seems wrong somehow. I even have ideas of looking for the heirlooms; the treasure, if any of it is left. But that seems wrong too. Here it's very... I can't find words to capture it. It is dark and silent and heavy, sort of haunted. But only sort of.

Peaceful? Yes. That's the word. It reminds me of the churchyard where Grandpa is buried. A gothic and broken place, in the shadow of yew trees. But it's a beautiful place and restful too. The island is like that, but it's not a... graveyard.

Then I remember that, of course, it is.

Bax and I come back to the clearing and I prepare the picnic. Brown goat's cheese, honey, a big chunk of smoked salmon.

Liva and Agna are on the far edge of the clearing. I can just about hear their Norwegian chat. They point here and there as they wander about, pausing in some places. Then they stop and laugh, almost bowing over, holding on to each other like sailors in a storm.

Later, they are crying and, I notice, holding hands.

I see only the clearing, and the dense trees that encircle it. They see other things.

They return and we eat. I'm desperate to ask what they talked about, but I don't. It would be an intrusion.

As we eat, the wind picks up, shaking the tops of the trees. We are sheltered from it, but clouds slowly hide the sun and the air grows colder. So, we stoke the fire and feed it with dry, fallen logs.

A full squall comes, disturbing the trees, making the fire flames dance and spark.

Liva goes to the shore and returns to tell us it's too windy to go back to the mainland.

My phone doesn't catch a signal, but Bestemor Tove knows where we are. I wonder if she can get a boat big and sturdy enough to rescue us. But Liva says the squall is not forecast, so it can only be local and won't last.

As the day draws on, it doesn't abate. We use coats and the picnic blanket to cover ourselves.

I walk all round the island, till I get a signal and send a message to Tove. She replies, saying we can call the coastguard, but when I return to our camp and suggest it, Agna and Liva just laugh.

'It's not so cold with the fire,' Liva says.

'It is not rain!' Agna says. 'We need not the help.'

'We can live in nature! We have aquavit.'

'The Norwegian way,' I say, shaking my head. I've heard conversations like this a thousand times.

'Tsk!' Liva says, and snuggles down with her arms folded. We build makeshift beds of pine branches, we gather wood, fill our water bottles and settle in.

Eventually curiosity gets the better of me. I ask if Liva and Agna have been talking about Sergei.

'Ja,' Agna says.

'Maybe he made it back to Russia, with the army?'

'Yes. I want I... håp, uh... Liva?'

'Hope.'

'Yes. I hope. And I hope too he take our treasure with him. That with it, they pay for life. Many life. You understand?'

'Yes. I hope so too,' I say. 'There is the internet. You could try to find out? I could help? Difficult, though. The Russians and the west are not friends.'

'Countries are friends or enemies?' Liva says. 'Ha! Before the war, Russia was bad, then in the war allies. After, enemies, ready to drop nuclear bombs on us all. Then friends after communism. Now they are enemies? Don't make me laugh. There are no countries. Only people. Bits of wood on the sea.'

I am not sure I get what Liva means by that.

We talk then, about lots of things. But not war.

Evening comes, the clouds have gone. The wind is still blowing, but we're okay, here, in our camp.

Night arrives. I look at the silhouette of the trees. And think of the prisoners and then of the bit of Liva's story where she and Agna row to the island at the start of the war, and the tale of the song.

I remind Agna of it.

'Liva told me. The boy visits the huldra in the forest, and each time he stays longer, and leaves sprout from his fingers and his skin hardens like a tree bark. One day he doesn't return. The villagers search for him, but the huldra has turned him into a tree, so he might stay in the forest for ever.'

I tell Agna how Liva told me of her and Agna singing as they rowed to the island.

And now they sing again, and I know the words, even though the song is in Norwegian.

> *'The tree grew strong and fast.*
> *Strong and fast, strong and fast.*
> *And he was never seen again,*
> *Never seen again.*
> *Never seen again.*
> *Never seen again.'*

They hold hands and talk about Sergei, till they grow tired.

Agna and Liva sleep peacefully, snoring gently. I decide I'm going to look for Sergei, I'll make contacts, search records. I'll try to find out what happened to him. If that's what Agna wants.

I don't think I'm going to sleep. I gaze at the trees and stars, cuddling Bax, using him as a blanket, and listen to the wind in the branches, the distant rush and rattle of pebbles on the shore.

When the fire gets low, I feed it a log or two.

The night is cold and dark. But it does not last.

Author's Note

As with other books of mine, in places, I have changed the facts to suit my story. However, much is taken from real events, from my family's history and that of Norway under occupation.

Agna was inspired by my grandma's sister, Esther. When my great-grandfather died, my great-grandmother took in lodgers to make ends meet. She had a fling with one of them, a Jewish sea captain. Esther was the result of their brief affair. It was quite a scandal at the time. Like Agna, Esther grew up an outsider and a rebel. Crucially, her father's details (including his religion), were not in the official records. She lived the entire war right under the Nazis' noses. If discovered, she would have been classified as 'Mischling of the first degree' (a mix-ling) and legally Jewish. Anything could have happened to her, including the worst imaginable.

Just like Haakon, my Uncle Sverra delivered resistance news sheets inside loaves of bread. Radios were banned and all media heavily controlled and filled with Nazi propaganda.

The sheets were a vital source of information, truth and – above all – hope.

And like the villagers of Rullesteinsvik, our family buried their heirlooms for the duration of the war, but unlike my story, they recovered them afterwards.

Pappa's story is based on my mum's uncle who fought with the army, then escaped to England with the king and government. He stayed after the war. Mum came to visit him in 1961, and met my dad. The rest, as they say, is history.

Over the years, I dug deeper and deeper into Mum's stories. The spark for *Shadow Creatures* was her first memory, from the end of the war, when she and other children took food parcels to the gates of a prison camp. In writing the book, I asked her lots of questions, and got lots of advice. For Mum, it has been like opening a box of lost treasures. She read an early draft of opening chapters. I asked for her thoughts, and she said, 'It just feels real to me.'

Norway's war...

In 1942, 14,000 teachers went on strike, refusing to teach the nazified curriculum. 1,400 of them were arrested. There were many Miss Bridgets and, of course, many Miss Hildurs too.

Norway had a small population in WW2, fewer than three million citizens. They caused so much trouble that Hitler sent 400,000 soldiers to keep them under control, draining the Nazi war machine of precious soldiers and resources. The German/Norwegian administration governed over 600 concentration and prison camps. To be clear, that is just in Norway. There were many thousands of camps throughout Europe, some dedicated purely to the business of mass murder. Rebellious Norwegians were interned, but many, many more Russian prisoners of war, who were treated appallingly. Like Sergei, they made boxes and toys as thank yous, and for trade. Some have been collected and displayed at the Perspectivet Museum in Norway.

For the last year or so of the war, the camps in Norway were run exclusively by the SS. In WW2 across Europe, about six million Russian soldiers were taken prisoner. Half of them did not survive.

The line 'Mother, do not weep' is taken from the Polish composer Gorecki's 'Symphony of Sorrowful Songs'. The line was written on a cell wall in Poland by a young resistance fighter and used as a lyric by Gorecki.

Finally, the Nazis banned some 18,000 books across Europe, including many fairy-tale books, which were seen as 'corrupting'.

I don't expect this tale of rebellious sprites and spirited rebellion has corrupted you, reader.

But if it has, that may not be a bad thing.

Acknowledgments

Much of writing is a solo affair – just you the writer, your imaginary friends and a notebook/laptop. However, books 'happen' with more input, advice and support than you might think.

Heartfelt thanks, as ever, to my wonderful agent, Catherine Clarke.

To my writing chums: Steve, Fin, Clare, Lu, Mel, Dave, Helenka and Lucy. Your support meant a lot when I was 'lost in the woods'. And to the Rogue Critters too, for their 'write this one' advice.

To Mum, for our stories and history. This may not be a conventional way of capturing the memories, but I hope I've done them justice.

To Sarah and Lamorna, as ever, for love and support.

Lastly, to Fiona Kennedy, Megan, and the team at Zephyr. The role of editor is probably a mystery to anyone outside the writing 'business'. You see the finished statue, the editor sees the lump of clay you start with, the stained overalls, the blood, sweat and tears. They see too the beating heart that will bring the statue to life, even when the writer cannot always see it themselves. It's a critical role, and I am hugely grateful to have one of the very best as ally and mentor.

Chris Vick
Bath
March 2024